PRAISE FOR *Blessed:*

"[A] wild and ultimately fascinating, if at times grisly, alternate universe." ***Kirkus Reviews***

"A hearty meal for the thinking vampire reader." ***Horn Book***

"Sure, the vampires, werewolves, and angels provide the lure, but Smith's obvious affection for her characters makes this more than the typical cynical genre exercise." ***Booklist***

"Smith's writing style is sometimes dramatic, often humorous, and always energetic… A satisfying blend of excitement and intrigue." ***VOYA***

"Readers will particularly enjoy the relief from the scary omnipotence of Brad during the action at Sanguini's, chock-full of foodie treats and in-jokes for vampire and literature fans…" ***Austin-American Statesman***

"As in the previous installments of this smart, sexy trilogy, Cynthia Leitich Smith doses every page with winking pop-culture references and groan-worthy one-liners. In this final volume, her homage to Stoker's classic novel is most app

BookPage

"A good rea
with all the

Library Journal

ALSO BY CYNTHIA LEITICH SMITH
Eternal:

"I can't wait for the next installment. Listen up America, if you want to fall in love with a teen series – pick this one." ***Once Upon a Romance.net***

"Suspenseful, entertaining, and enthusiastically gruesome, Smith's latest will be lapped up by vampire fans." ***The Horn Book***

"A true page-turner, I can't imagine any fan of gothic suspense/romance not thoroughly enjoying this – and not just young adult readers either." ***Dallas Morning News***

"Smith has built on centuries of vampire lore to create a spooky, snarky, supernatural world all her own." ***BookPage***

"Fanpires will not be disappointed with the newest addition to the genre." ***VOYA***

"Readers should be hooked by this fully formed world, up through the action-packed finale." ***Publishers' Weekly***

"At once glamorous and gruesome... Let the fingers fly through this flowing fantasy." ***San Antonio Express-News***

"[A] witty, dark love story of death and redemption." ***Booklist***

blessed

CYNTHIA LEITICH SMITH

WALKER
BOOKS

First published in Great Britain 2011 by Walker Books Ltd
87 Vauxhall Walk, London SE11 5HJ

2 4 6 8 10 9 7 5 3 1

Text © 2011 Cynthia Leitich Smith
Cover illustration © 2011 Angelo Rinaldi

This book has been typeset in Galliard

Printed and bound in Great Briatin by Clays Ltd, St Ives plc

British Library Cataloguing in Publication Data:
a catalogue record for this book is
available from the British Library

ISBN 978-1-4063-2787-8

www.walker.co.uk

For Rita

The dying man spoke, "Now God be thanked that all has not been in vain! See! The snow is not more stainless than her forehead! The curse has passed away!"

—Mina Harker's journal, quoting Quincey P. Morris, in *Dracula* by Bram Stoker (1897)

CONTENTS

antipasto

primo

⮞ *secondo* ⮜

✂ *dolce* ✂

⋇ contorno ⋇

antipasto

GOOD-BYE

Have you damned me? I wondered, staring over my shoulder at the lanky devil in dark formal-wear. The one with honey cream sauce on his collar and blood on his tie, the one who'd so newly remade me into the same kind of monster he was.

It was past 2 A.M. in the dining room of my family's Italian restaurant, and moments earlier, I'd agreed to a fool's bargain. To drink deeply from the throat of the boy lying beneath me, the boy I loved, on the condition that if I could wrench myself away before taking his life, the seductive fiend known as Bradley Sanguini would concede defeat, leave us in peace, and abandon Austin, Texas, forever.

Brad understood the thirst, the intoxication, far better than I did, and he'd acted like I had no shot at it.

Lost in the salty red mist, the sweet satisfaction, for a few moments, I'd feared he was right. But somehow I'd torn myself from the blood, the bliss. And won.

Now Bradley gaped at me, slack-jawed in amazement, before recovering enough to offer a saucy wink. "Baby," he said in a rumbling voice, "I underestimated you."

His full lip curled, and the vampire chef turned away to slip through the crimson velvet drapes separating the dining room from the foyer. Seconds later, I heard the front door open and gently shut.

Good riddance. In that moment, I didn't give a damn whether the monster kept his word, whether that was the last I'd see of him. It was enough that he was gone for now.

Then Kieren's whispers drew my attention. Kieren Morales, my best friend and true love—it sounded like he was praying. And why shouldn't he have been? He gleamed with sweat. His hands and neck had been savaged. It was a miracle that I hadn't killed him.

"Hey," I whispered, "let's get you cleaned up."

"You'll have to move off me first." Offering a wry smile, he added, "But only if you really want to."

Kieren never teased me that way, never dared to flirt—another sign of a surreal night. Or maybe he was just too wrung out to self-censor what he was really thinking.

I blushed, suddenly hyperaware of my position, half straddled across him on the bench of a black leather booth.

Bracing myself with one hand on the table, I pushed off and then helped Kieren sit up. Most of his shirt seams had burst, the material falling from his shoulders in tattered wet ribbons. The top button of his jeans had come undone.

How much blood had he lost? A lot. Too much? I couldn't take him to the ER, and not only because a medical exam would out him as a human-werewolf hybrid.

Kieren was a prime suspect in a murder investigation, the result of a simple but effective frame job by Bradley that had drawn on human prejudices against shape-shifters.

What's more, I couldn't call in Kieren's Wolf mama, even though she'd trained as a healer. As far as the Moraleses knew, their eldest had already ditched town en route to a Wolf pack that was supposed to protect him. Kieren wanted them to go on thinking just that.

"Brad's obsessed with you," he began. "We can't expect him to just—"

"Give up?" I suppressed a sigh. Even if Brad didn't leave us alone, he still couldn't force me to love him. "Maybe not. Okay, probably not. But I have supernatural power of my own now, and, Kieren, you can't watch over me forever." Brave words, especially since I wanted nothing more than for him to go on doing just that.

The front door opened, and we froze. The pastry team wouldn't arrive for hours, and besides, they used the kitchen entrance. I darted to the nearest wait station and snagged a steak knife.

"It's all right, Quince," Kieren assured me. "I recognize the scent—"

His pal Clyde stumbled in, flailing to extract himself from the heavy drapes. Clyde was a little guy, a sophomore with salt-and-pepper hair. He was also a were-opossum, from a long line somehow related to a giant Ice Age marsupial.

Put mildly, he had issues with my newly undead status.

Brandishing a battle-axe nearly half his size, Clyde took in Kieren's bleeding neck, bleeding hands, and ragged clothing before turning toward me. "Back, you demonic hussy! Step away from the Wolf!"

I blinked at that. It was endearing, Clyde coming to Kieren's defense. Usually when confronted with danger, the Opossum played dead.

I took a step forward. "Easy now . . ."

Baring tiny, sharp teeth, Clyde swung the blade my way, almost losing his balance. "Back, you unholy—"

"Enough!" Kieren said. "Can it, Clyde. It's Quince, got it? She's *still* Quincie."

Clyde's glare disputed him, even as it lingered on the bustline of my T-shirt. "Oh, yeah? Was she 'still Quincie' when she was sucking your blood like a Slurpee?"

"I *let* her bite me." With a grimace, Kieren stood, shaky in his black cowboy boots. "We had our reasons. The rest of the damage, I did to myself." He raised his square jaw. "I thought you'd be halfway to Matamoros by now."

"I, uh . . ." Clyde broke eye contact. "Your mom's van is parked out back."

Kieren took a deep breath. "Fine, you can wait for me there."

Clyde set the axe on a nearby table. "You've got three minutes," he said. "Then I'm calling your mom to drag your hairy ass out of here. I mean it, Morales."

A moment later, Kieren and I were alone again. Returning the steak knife to the wait station, I fought to wrap my mind around what was happening. Did Clyde say three minutes? Only three minutes?

After a lifetime of friendship, tonight Kieren and I had finally admitted our deeper feelings for each other. And now we had to say good-bye.

He touched his fingertips to his sticky neck. "Towels?"

"Right," I agreed. The trip to the kitchen and back took only seconds.

I cleaned off the blood with one towel and then ripped the other to wrap his hands. Fortunately, the wounds had already begun to heal—a benefit of his Wolf DNA. "Do you want something for the pain?"

Kieren didn't answer. His arm circled my waist, and we moved to reclaim the small dance floor of my family restaurant. I relaxed into his embrace, his body warm and damp against mine. I knew what Kieren was thinking. If we had only three—two?—minutes, we wanted to make the most of them.

Then he shook his head and took an uncertain step backward, and I tightened my hold. He could hardly stand. "We don't have to do this," I told him. "You should—"

"Hush," he said, running a fingertip from my temple to my chin. "Can I lean on you?" A huge question coming from Kieren, who'd always thought of himself as the strong one.

I welcomed his weight, and we danced in that swaying way where all that matters is the touching. I didn't beg him to stay. I didn't tell him how I remembered holding his hand on our first day of kindergarten and not holding it during our tour of NASA on his ninth birthday. I didn't tell him how at thirteen I'd chickened out under the mistletoe or how lately I'd let the girls at high school assume we were more than friends. I didn't admit that my lips still buzzed from tasting him, and so did every slick, secret part of my body. Most of all, I didn't apologize for having let Bradley manipulate me. Or say how sorry I was about not being alive anymore.

And I didn't admit to Kieren how alone I'd be without him or that I could never again watch a sunset without thinking of the moonrise, too. I had to be brave. I *had* to. I didn't want him to remember me as a weepy, clingy mess.

Each second neared our last.

We danced.

"Kieren . . ."

"Shhh . . ."

We danced.

"I'll be okay." Was that me lying? Or him?

We danced.

"Close your eyes," he whispered, brushing his lips against mine. "Know that I'm missing you already and that you'll always be in my prayers."

PREDATOR OR PREY?

*W*hen I opened my eyes, I stood alone in the middle of the dance floor.

The restaurant was all I had left.

Only three nights earlier, on Friday the 13th, Fat Lorenzo's—my family's Italian bistro—had been re-launched with a vampire theme and renamed Sanguini's. The preternatural angle was supposed to have been make-believe, all in fun.

The new joint had proven itself a sensation. Five stars from *Tejano Food Life*. A rave from *The Statesman*. A nod from *USA Today*. We'd made not only every Austin TV news program but also the twenty-four-hour cable news networks.

It wasn't just our food that the reviewers raved about. It was the faux-castle décor, the staff's creature-of-the-night regalia, the gothic fantasy made real.

Wickedly delicious and deliciously wicked.

"Hell's Kitchen Serves Up Culinary Heaven," according to the *Capital City News*.

Then two nights ago, Bradley and my uncle Davidson—who'd managed the place and who had been my legal guardian—had revealed themselves to me as *real* vampires. Homicidal vampires who'd been trying to frame Kieren for their crimes. They'd been working with my high school's vice principal, likewise undead, to distance me from my human life so I'd be more open to taking my supposedly destined place among them.

I'd been caught by surprise, and not just because I'd known them (especially my uncle) so well. According to popular belief, vampires were extraordinarily rare, possibly extinct. Beyond that, I hadn't been at my best, even before my transformation.

For weeks, Brad had flattered me with his attentions, delivered with glass after glass of red wine, dosed—I'd found out later—with his own unholy blood. The combination of alcohol and dark magic had intoxicated me, made me emotionally unstable, more susceptible to his suggestions, and generally an idiot. Not to mention what it had done to my humanity and fashion sense.

Taking the axe that Kieren and Clyde had left behind, I shuffled out of the lonely dining room and down the lonelier back hall. Ducking into a restroom marked PRED-ATOR, I leaned the long handle of the weapon against the counter and then splashed my face.

No mirror hung above the sink—another thematic touch, playing on the popular misconception that the undead can't cast a reflection.

Hardly anyone knew much about vampirism—except that it was demonic in origin. By the mid-1700s, though, leaders of most major religions and various heads of state had acknowledged its existence, and according to a show I'd seen on the History Channel, the undead may have played a key role in the French Revolution, the sinking of the *Titanic,* and the JFK assassination.

Still, that didn't give me a lot to go on. What the hell had I become?

I tore the sign that read PREDATOR off my restroom door and the PREY sign off its companion. The unisex approach might've been cutting-edge, but it was also a lawsuit waiting to happen, and I was calling the shots now.

I left the cross hanging where it was, on what had been the Prey door.

* * *

I needed to work. I was Mama's daughter that way. The restaurant had always been more like home than my actual house was. I needed to cleanse it, reclaim it, if I ever hoped to feel safe and whole again. If that was even possible.

I dug through the storage closet—filled with artifacts from Fat Lorenzo's—until I found the *M* and *W*. Then I grabbed the toolbox and nailed the letters back on their respective restroom doors.

Afterward, I returned to the closet for white cardboard and black markers. In the break room, I made two signs that read CLOSED FOR FAMILY EMERGENCY, one for the front door and one for the back.

I probably didn't need to haul the battle-axe around, but it made me feel better, having a weapon close.

On the employee bulletin board, someone had posted a newspaper clipping.

OBITUARIES

AUSTIN—Travis Reid, age 16, was called home by our Heavenly Father on September 13.

Reid was a sophomore at Waterloo High School, where he belonged to the Environmental Club and the Spanish Club.

He was preceded in death by his grandmother Christina Acosta. Survivors include his parents, Isabel and David Reid; his sister, Sierra;

his grandparents Barbara and Clarence "Dutch" Reid; his grandfather Karl Richards; and numerous aunts, uncles, and cousins.

Visitation will be at 7 P.M. today at Lane Family Funeral Home Chapel. The service will be at 10 A.M. Tuesday at Bouldin Creek United Methodist Church. Burial will follow immediately at Magnolia Shade Cemetery.

The family has requested that memorial donations be sent in Reid's name to the Austin Zoo and Rescue Sanctuary.

I hadn't known Travis well, but he'd been shy, kind, and awkward, a pal of Kieren and Clyde's, who'd briefly worked at Sanguini's as a dishwasher. Beyond that, Travis may have been the only werearmadillo I'd ever met. His people were distant cousins to the Ice Age glyptodont, which had rivaled the VW Beetle in size.

He'd been murdered by Ruby, the same werecat who'd staked my vampire uncle earlier tonight before running off, hopefully forever. Not everybody with a tail or a heartbeat was a good person. It wasn't as simple as that.

In the manager's office, the digital clock read 3:38 A.M. I stashed the axe in the safe, changed the combo, and grabbed my leather-bound planner book, nicknamed Frank. A gift from Kieren.

Kieren. I flipped to a tasking page, determined to concentrate.

Sanguini's would have to remain closed until I found a chef to replace Bradley. Talk about lousy timing! The place was booked solid for I-didn't-know-how-long, and the customers would have hissy fits. But I had a much more serious problem than that.

Bradley had infused our signature dessert—the chilled baby squirrels, simmered in orange brandy, bathed in honey cream sauce—with his own blood. He'd hoped that those most predisposed toward viciousness, most likely to relish a vampiric existence, would order the horrific-sounding dish, ingest his blood, and thereby eventually join him—us—among the demonic.

According to Ruby, his intention had been to create an undead army to help him take over the underworld of Texas, whatever that meant. God only knew how he'd hoped to control the newly risen, but anyway, I didn't find out about the plan until it was too late.

Before he left, Bradley had told me to consider the soon-to-rise neophytes a "parting gift," but I didn't for a minute believe that, after all of his scheming, he had any intention of actually abandoning them. Or, for that matter, me.

Regardless, Brad had been serving up death at *my* restaurant. What had been Mama's and, before her, Gramma and Grampa Crimi's restaurant. That made his victims my responsibility.

Frank in hand, I sprinted to the reservations book on the hostess stand in the foyer. Sanguini's wasn't big. We could serve fifty at a time, and we'd done only one seating for Friday's party and two on both Saturday and Monday nights.

So, we'd served some 250 guests—plus those in the bar area. I figured upward of 325 total, give or take. I couldn't know for sure how many had tasted the tainted dish, though, especially since people often split dessert orders.

I remembered chatting with guests from as far away as El Paso, Oklahoma City, and New Orleans. Not to mention the foreign exchange students from Ethiopia, the family on vacation from London, and the Middle Eastern studies professor on her way to Iraq. And then there were the innocents they would eventually kill or contaminate in turn.

I didn't have to be a math whiz to realize that, in no time, the world could be faced with a full-scale preternatural crisis. But it wasn't just about numbers.

Members of my staff—including my hostess, Yanira; my expeditor, Sergio; and my waitress pal, Mercedes— were among the infected, and they were practically family.

I turned to the calendar in my planner book. It took about a month after ingesting demonic blood for the transformation to occur. The first wave of Bradley's victims would rise undead sometime after October 11, more with each passing sunset.

Happy Halloween to me.

QUOTH THE RAVEN

*A*nticipating my arrival, Bradley had apparently excused the kitchen staff from cleanup. So, after posting the closed signs outside, I cranked Stevie Ray Vaughan on the sound system and attacked the job like I'd been tipped off to a health-inspector visit. I sprayed, wiped, and scrubbed. I spared no chemical cleanser, taking refuge in the mindless, familiar work. It felt surreal, like sleepwalking, but right then I couldn't obsess over Kieren leaving or my own undeath or what my uncle and Bradley and the vice principal had done. Overwhelmed, I'd shut down inside. So I sprayed, wiped, and scrubbed some more.

Once the stainless-steel countertops gleamed, I threw Brad's copy of *A Taste of Transylvania* and his prized collection of black-cherry cooking utensils into one of the trash bags and then hauled it outside to the Dumpster.

Cutting through the parking lot, I noticed Kieren's mama's van in the back row. The side read *Endless Love Bridal Planning*. Hours earlier, he had ripped the driver's side door from its hinges so he could get to me. It made sense that Kieren had chosen to leave the damaged, easy-to-ID vehicle behind, but then what? Did he take Uncle D's convertible or Clyde's car? And where was Kieren *going*, anyway? The Wolf pack's location was a secret that, until recently, even he hadn't known.

It was just after 5 A.M., the sun wouldn't be up for another couple of hours, and I'd run out of to-dos to distract myself. The shock of all that had happened had begun to dissipate, and my throat ached. I felt my knees buckle from the losses, and nearly fell to the asphalt. It seemed like the right thing to do. Dead things had no place walking around.

Then the headlight beam of a motorcycle zooming north on Congress Avenue glinted against metal lying in the beaten brown grass of the empty lot next door. I jogged over to discover Kieren's turquoise-and-silver crucifix. He'd torn it off last night before we'd gone inside to confront Brad. I'd flinched at the sight of it, but had my reaction been psychological or supernatural?

Contrary to popular opinion, the effect of religious symbols varied, depending on the symbol, depending on the vampire, but I'd always thought of myself as a believer. If I touched the crucifix now, would my fingertips burst into flames?

I crouched in the hard-packed, dirt-and-weed lot, feeling watched, even though the normally bustling restaurant-shopping-entertainment district was empty and quiet. Was Brad watching me from the shadows? From around a corner or some nearby rooftop? Had he left for good or just gone into hiding, biding his time?

I hesitated as a black bird landed a few feet away and began pecking and scratching at the ground. Another joined it. Another, another, another . . . until I was surrounded by swooping, prancing, cawing. I'd never seen so many crows. Ravens? Hundreds? Thousands?

They blanketed the empty lot and lined the arch of the streetlight, the roof lines, the phone and power lines, the branches of nearby trees, the restaurant itself. They chattered and danced and then, as if on command, went eerily silent. Eerily still.

Someone else might've viewed the birds as a bad omen, but I'd always thought crows were magnificent and proud and, really, what could be scarier than me?

Besides, they were creatures of God, like human beings and the shape-shifters who straddled the human and animal worlds. I was the unnatural one.

A train whistle blew in the distance, and I snatched the necklace from the ground before one of the birds could beat me to it. Kieren had broken the chain, so I fastened the latch to a link. His neck was thicker than mine, and the cross fell against the V between my breasts. I braced for the burn, but the metal against my skin felt blessedly neutral.

Tension leaked from my knotted muscles, and, startling the crows, I spread my arms wide. As they rose, screaming, flowing in black waves into the dying night, I closed my eyes and raised my grateful, tear-stained face to heaven.

THE ARCHANGEL MICHAEL
The Sword of Heaven
The Bringer of Souls

To: Zachary
From: Michael
Date: Tuesday, September 17

You are hereby directed to assume guardianship of the vampire Quincie P. Morris until such time that either: (a) she agrees to end her existence or (b) her soul is utterly extinguished. This assignment should last approximately one year or less.

Approach the subject with calculation and caution. Do *not* become personally invested this time. Though her soul may be temporarily salvageable, she is still demonic. Should she become an immediate threat to the living, do not hesitate to destroy her.

Make every effort to appear human. Avoid showing your wings. Be discreet when using your holy sword. Employ the power of heaven's light only as a last resort.

Complete and file D-1a forms on the subject every seventy-two hours.

See attached Yahoo! map.

REST IN PEACE

*I*n the break room, I watched a News 8 cycle, making sure Kieren hadn't been arrested, until dozing off on the faded floral sofa.

"I'm here," he said. *"You're not alone, never alone."*

I found myself back on Sanguini's dance floor. "Kieren?"

"You can't forget me," he answered, leading me in a waltz. *"We're one blood."*

"Who?"

"I know you," he replied. *"You'll try to fight it. But you'll only be fighting your true self. It's done. It's destined. In*

time, you'll come to accept it." He pulled back his sleeve to reveal two dress watches. "In time, you'll come to me."

"Bradley."

Sure enough, Kieren's legs and torso lengthened, his chest narrowed, and his goatee disappeared. His brown eyes shone hazel, his complexion lightened, and his dark hair slipped away like a shadow to reveal a blond widow's peak.

I fought to free myself from his embrace, but Brad was strong. Stronger than I'd realized. Stronger than he used to be?

"Relax, baby." He threw back his head, flashing his neck. "Have a drink!"

I awoke on the sofa, alone and trembling.

I'd slept so long that, on foot and careful to proceed at a casual, natural speed, I couldn't hope to make it to Travis's burial service until noon. I'd considered skipping the whole thing, but regardless of all that had happened, it felt important to pay my respects. Travis had been one of Kieren's best friends, after all, and a Sanguini's employee.

Dealing with the cursed baby-squirrel eaters would have to wait.

And of course at some point, I'd have to face the macabre mess waiting back at my house. Uncle D. Or what was left of him. I wasn't ready for that, either.

I felt weaker outside in the sunshine. Not like I was sick, but more like a human being. Movie myths aside, daylight couldn't destroy me. I'd seen Brad and my uncle out and about often enough, and Austin was famed for its sunshine.

I'd always taken long strolls in the old neighborhood— listening to the wind chimes and clucking chickens, checking out the new construction, nodding to the statuary of saints. My walks had usually grounded me, given me a leisurely chance to think, away from the bustle of work and high school.

Today felt different. I was agitated. Wary. Every once in a while I'd feel a tingle at the back of my neck and— to no avail—scan the landscape for Brad. I might exist like this for centuries. How long would it be before I stopped looking over my shoulder?

No, it was worse than that. Brad could travel short distances as mist, dust—unseen. I shuddered despite the sunshine. If I started obsessing, I'd be useless.

Along the way, I passed a pink cottage and noticed piñata remains littering the side yard beneath an oak tree. Children lived there. Vulnerable children.

Kieren's blood had made for a filling meal, but how much control did I have? How long might it be before I prowled this neighborhood on the hunt?

Magnolia Shade was a cozy, slightly overgrown cemetery kept up by the historical society. I hoisted one leg after the other, like scissors, over the white wooden border fence. The Reids must have had a family plot here for generations.

By the time I spotted the grave site, the crowd had begun to break up. I estimated over a couple hundred mourners. From a distance, I recognized most of the sophomore class, plus a handful of Sanguini's employees.

In my Fat Lorenzo's T and running pants, I wasn't dressed for the occasion, and I had no desire to make small talk. So, I hung back, behind a pecan tree, and watched.

A crow settled on a nearby branch as snippets of conversation floated my way.

". . . so young."

". . . closed casket."

". . . grab some barbecue?"

A handsome woman in a tailored black dress strode in my general direction and, a beat later, I recognized her as Kieren's mother, Meara Morales. She looked pensive, preoccupied, at least until I stepped from my hiding place.

"Quincie!" Miz Morales rushed to hug me like I was her own cub. "Are you —?"

"Fine," I said. "I'm fine. It's just been . . . an intense few days."

Her generous eyebrows drew together. "You smell of Kieren and blood."

* * *

Rolling down the gravel road in the Moraleses' Chevy, I launched into an edited version of last night's events. I emphasized that Kieren had delayed leaving only because he'd discovered that I might be in danger and that his injuries were on the mend. I made a point of mentioning Miz Morales's van, still parked in the restaurant lot. But I didn't say word one about Uncle Davidson or my own undeath.

"So," she interrupted, "Sanguini's 'vampire' chef *was* a real vampire."

"You knew?" I had no idea how much Kieren had told his parents.

She turned at the cemetery gate. "Mrs. Levy told me."

"Our English teacher?"

Navigating through the neighborhood, Miz Morales explained that Mrs. Levy had stopped by the house to say that she'd helped Kieren slay Vice Principal Harding yesterday at school. "She knows about us. She swore, though, not to reveal our secret to anyone."

Miz Morales was talking about her Wolf heritage and, by extension, that of Kieren and his baby sister, Meghan.

The existence of shifters had been widely dismissed as legend until the mid-1800s, when a Maine senator shifted into a werebear at President James Buchanan's inaugural ball. The poor Bear was promptly shot dead, setting the standard for the majority of human-shifter interactions that followed. Consequently, many werepeople, as they preferred to be called (regardless of the fact that the term "man-people" didn't make literal sense), and hybrids chose to pass as human beings.

Miz Morales braked at Congress and Academy. "By now, the medical examiner has confirmed that the vice principal was undead. And certainly an attack by a vampire in wolf form could explain Mr. Bianchi's murder every bit as well as—if not better than—an attack by a werewolf."

Vaggio Bianchi had been our original chef, the world's biggest Sinatra fan, a hit with the older ladies, and my honorary grandparent. It was his murder that Bradley and friends had timed to occur in Sanguini's kitchen right before Kieren had arrived at the scene. The facts against Kieren were circumstantial, but if the cops ran his DNA and found Wolf, the truth wouldn't matter. Equal rights, equal justice . . . those concepts weren't generally applied to werepeople, not in the human-controlled world, anyway.

Even before the murder, the Moraleses had already decided that Kieren would leave home to join a Wolf pack at age eighteen. But the investigation had moved up that timeline. Though the police had only questioned him, it had quickly become clear that Kieren's lingering in Austin wasn't worth risking his being arrested and outed as a hybrid.

I glanced over at Miz Morales. "If the cops are thinking vampire . . ."

She parallel parked on my dead-end street. "It helps, of course, but Vaggio wasn't simply drained. Vampires typically kill to drink, and APD hasn't been able to pinpoint a motive for such an elaborate setup or anything to link the vice principal to—"

"What about me?" I asked. "I go to Waterloo High, Vice Principal Harding worked there, and I own Sanguini's."

"I'm sure the police have already considered that." Miz Morales ran a hand through her thick hair. "As have I."

Something in the way she said it hinted that Meara suspected me of she-wasn't-sure-what. Or at least that she hadn't ruled out she-wasn't-sure-what.

I couldn't blame her. She had been best friends with Mama since before I was born, had always treated me like family. But nobody—however unwittingly—had been in thicker with the evil vampires than me.

Shifters might be immune to demonic infection, but humans certainly weren't.

As I gazed out the passenger-side window at my cheerful-looking green-and-purple house, my jaw clenched at the memory of last night's events. I'd walked in on Ruby in Uncle D's second-floor bedroom only moments after she'd staked him through the back.

The werecat was some kind of spy or assassin or both, working undercover against the undead. She'd been pretending to be my uncle's girlfriend.

Ruby had taken one look at my newly red eyes and extended fangs and sprang at me — claws out. I'd had no choice but to shoot her in self-defense.

Fortunately, it had looked like only a flesh wound, and as a shifter, she'd heal quickly. Wherever she'd gone.

Gone. Ruby was gone. But Uncle D's body was still upstairs.

Suddenly, it clicked. "I know the motive in Vaggio's murder," I announced, "and I can prove a direct connection between him and at least one confirmable vampire." Opening the car door, I added, "I can clear Kieren's name!"

*M*y God!" Miz Morales made the sign of the cross. "That's your uncle!"

I winced at the sight of Uncle Davidson—the medically verifiable vampire who'd managed the restaurant where Chef Vaggio Bianchi had been murdered—sprawled facedown and naked on his bed, his bottom half mostly covered by brown-and-gold linens.

His neck had been broken and bloodied. His heart had been staked.

"They killed Vaggio," I explained, "to bolster Sanguini's mystique, to frame Kieren, and most of all, so Brad could take Vaggio's place as Sanguini's chef."

"But why Kieren?" Miz Morales asked. "Why did he matter to them?"

I'd been afraid she'd ask. "Brad viewed him as a rival. For . . . my affections."

While Miz Morales punched 911 into her cell, I retreated from the bloody scene, taking refuge in my own bedroom. It felt familiar, but not. Like everything else today.

I glanced at the long-stem red calla lilies in the crystal vase on my dresser—a gift from Brad—and then bent to pluck the gauzy, white sleeveless nightgown from my Oriental rug. This was what he had dressed me in on the night I'd died.

Without thinking, I ripped it in two and then ripped it again.

By the time Meara had finished her call, I'd thrown the scraps away.

Minutes later, Detectives Zaleski and Wertheimer arrived.

Zaleski towered—at six foot five, six foot six?—and was built like Sasquatch. At one in the afternoon, he already had a five-o'clock shadow. Wertheimer was slight, with an upturned nose, and he stood an inch shorter than me. I'd have bet money that Zaleski was a Bear and

Wertheimer some kind of omnivore shifter (maybe a Possum, like Clyde). I suspected they already knew that Kieren was both innocent and a Wolf.

All I had to do was fill in the blanks, leaving out a few minor details (like the fact that the bad guys had killed me). Over Meara's protest, I admitted to having shot Ruby on the theory that the police would've figured it out anyway.

Zaleski said he believed that I was acting in self-defense, though Wertheimer did confiscate my grandfather's gun and take a sample of Ruby's blood from Uncle D's room.

I wasn't worried about being charged with anything. Even if they thought it had been attempted murder, there was no recorded history of anyone ever being convicted for a crime against a wereperson, and we all knew it.

I also mentioned that Ruby and my uncle had bragged last night about killing the officers who'd been originally assigned to investigate Vaggio's murder.

I'm not sure it was all by the book (possibly, as shifters, the detectives had their own way of working within a system that sometimes discriminated against people like them). Their demeanor did become more formal after the small army of uniformed officers showed up. But in any case, everything had changed. Kieren had not only escaped being officially charged in Vaggio's murder; now he was cleared of suspicion for good.

*   *   *

As a TV news van turned onto my street, Miz Morales put the sedan into gear.

"Did you call Kieren?" I asked from the seat beside her. Meara had stepped outside with her cell phone while I'd been talking to the police. "Do you know when he'll be back?"

"Quincie," she began, "I'm sorry, but no."

"But—"

"Regardless of the investigation, Kieren agreed to leave for the Wolf pack."

"I know, but—"

"He can't manage his shift, so he can't live in the human world—period."

In my excitement, I'd almost forgotten. Full Wolves like Miz Morales could shift at will to Wolf form and back. No drama, no trauma, no carnage.

From what I understood, it was harder for them *not* to shift when the moon was full, but moonlight was by no means required.

Meara's half-human son, Kieren, on the other hand, couldn't even make it halfway or control himself—his teeth and claws—once a shift began. He was a danger to himself, to everyone. As much as he'd wanted to, Kieren had never mastered his inner beast.

"But now he doesn't have to go right away. He could

wait until he turns eighteen, like you'd planned. Or until after graduation."

"Quincie, it's done." Her voice left no room for argument.

I argued anyway. "What if the Wolf pack helps him? If he can finally fully—"

"Don't get your hopes up," Miz Morales warned, hitting her turn signal. "Hybrids . . ." She pursed her lips. "They're rare for a reason. Most werepeople are too responsible to bring bi-species kids into the world."

Whatever that was about. I turned my face away from Miz Morales's watchful gaze. If I got too upset, my eyes might turn red. My fangs might come down. I couldn't chance revealing myself. Undead or not, I had lives to save, a restaurant to run.

"How long will it be before I can go back home?" I asked, changing the subject.

"What do you mean, go back home? You're only seventeen."

I wasn't sure what Miz Morales was getting at. I didn't have any parents or grandparents. Uncle Davidson had been Daddy's only sibling, and Mama had been an only child. "If you think I'm going into foster care—"

"Of course not!" Miz Morales exclaimed. "While you were packing, I called Roberto, and he called our lawyer. From now on, you're going to live with us."

PARENT TRAP

*A*s Miz Morales and I hauled my luggage through the back door of the white stone and stucco McMansion, her husband, Dr. Roberto Morales, was stirring a tall pot of potato soup in the kitchen. He put down the long wooden spoon, wiped his hands on his checked apron, and gave me a hug. "Meara told me about your uncle. You know—"

"Yeah, I know." I stood, awkward a moment, before disengaging myself.

It wasn't that I didn't like Roberto. He was one of those king-of-the-grill dads, the kind with season tickets to University of Texas football games, but also geek chic with his neatly trimmed mustache and engineering faculty gig. Plus, he was a hell of a lot less intimidating than his wife. But I'd talked myself out with the cops and was still pissed at Miz Morales, at the world, about Kieren's leaving.

I made a show of setting my bag down and rubbing my shoulder, even though the weight had felt like nothing. I'd have to be vigilant about keeping up my charade. It was ironic—a vampire pretending to be human for a mixed-species family, a mixed-species family pretending to be all human for the human world.

"You should hydrate," Miz Morales said, sliding her cell out of her purse. "Roberto, how about you grab Quincie a bottle of water and help her upstairs with her luggage? I need to check messages, and then we can all sit down and discuss plans for Davidson's memorial. Unless, Quincie, you want to wait a—"

"No," I replied, louder and harsher than I'd intended. "I mean, no, he's not worth it. You don't have to go to any trouble."

The Moraleses exchanged a look, and then Meara put an arm around me. "Of course you feel betrayed. You're entitled to your anger. But listen, love, you need to understand something."

It was all I could do to not shrug her off.

"Vampirism . . . It's a kind of evil and unearthly insanity. It corrupts the victim until they're no longer the same person. Your uncle died when he became a vampire. He lost the last vestiges of himself once his soul rotted away. Don't mistake the fiend he became for the man he was. Both of you deserve better than that."

"The real Davidson Morris loved you," Dr. Morales added.

I understood what they were saying about Uncle D, and that helped. The idea that the real him never would've played matchmaker between me and Brad.

On the other hand, it's not like I hadn't heard of the concept (vampires equal scary badness—got it), but I hadn't dared to think the whole thing through in such a matter-of-fact way. At the risk of being self-absorbed, what about *my* soul? If I was damned, who was I to save anybody? And how long could I trust myself? I never wanted Kieren's family to feel about me the way that I felt about Uncle D.

"Where's Meghan?" I asked. A four-year-old sounded more manageable at the moment, and I owed the cub an apology.

"Stomachache, she says," replied Dr. Morales from the stove. "Yesterday, it was a cold. I let her stay home from preschool, but she's just upset about Kieren leaving."

"And Brazos," I said. As if killing people weren't enough, Bradley and friends had also poisoned the Morales family's dog.

Dr. Morales ladled a bowl of potato soup for me to deliver to his young daughter.

I'd claimed I wasn't hungry and passed on a bowl for myself. I'd found out early that being undead meant it was nearly impossible for me to keep down solid food, though I could get by on animal blood. God, this whole thing was a nightmare. How on earth was I supposed to handle the logistics of eating (or not) in front of the Moraleses? But I couldn't think of a way out. I had no one else, and they knew it.

I paused, halfway up the stairs, listening. I heard Meara mention the word *suspicious* and then Roberto, more reassuring, say something about shock.

The Moraleses cared about me. Maybe more so now that Kieren was gone, because of how close we'd always been. Because I was orphaned again, and they'd just said good-bye to their only son. It wasn't enough to give Miz Morales a blind spot. She was too much the Wolf to let down her guard completely, but deep down, she wanted to believe the best of me.

I kept climbing the stairs, more slowly than I had the thousands of times before. This time, Kieren wouldn't be waiting. Not today, not ever again.

Upstairs, the air felt thick and soggy. In her white wicker bedroom, Meghan napped, snuggling with her stuffed toy rabbit, Otto. I bent to click off her humidifier, which had run out of water, and set the steaming bowl of soup on her nightstand.

Meghan startled awake, and I glimpsed the animal in her eyes. "Quincie?"

Yesterday evening I'd stopped by, looking for Kieren, only to find myself overcome by blood lust when Meghan had opened the door. It could have gone much worse. From what I understood, the initial thirst upon first rising was the most intense. But I could still be a danger to this sweet little girl.

Tugging at her waffle-weave blanket, she said, "You yelled at me."

I had. I'd raged at her to shut the door, to shut me out for her own safety. "Sorry, kiddo. I wasn't myself."

I left it at that. It wasn't like I could explain, not really. The whole situation was too terrible, and she was too young to understand. I longed for her absolution, though. I adored the cub, thought of her as almost my own baby sister. Kieren would want me to look out for her. She was the closest person to him that I had left.

Meghan hugged Otto tighter. She wasn't stupid, but she was only four. At four, the word *sorry* carried more magic. Her nostrils flared, and her gaze flicked to the nightstand. "Is that soup for me?"

At my nod, Meghan grabbed the spoon and, after wolfing it down, stuck her finger in the bowl to catch the last few drops. Finally, she banged the bowl on the nightstand and practically snarled, "I don't know about you."

I didn't know if Meghan meant that she didn't know if I was still human or if she meant that she didn't know if I was still a nice person. So I just picked up her dish and spoon and hoped that, whichever it was, Meghan would forgive me soon, and that, in the meantime, she wouldn't tell her parents.

Defending Camelot

As long as nobody shish-kebab-ed my heart or chopped off my head or lit me on fire or dunked me in holy water, I'd live forever. Supposedly.

As I stood in the doorway to Kieren's messy bedroom, forever sounded like a long time. More than once I'd called the room a Wolf studies hot zone. Modern and historic texts in various languages crowded the shelves, and more dotted the white Berber carpeting. Not to mention the maps—yellowed and new—all dwarfed by the colorfully pushpin-marked one of the Western Hemisphere that nearly covered one wall.

Kieren had explained once that pack membership was earned through brains or muscle. Because of his human heritage, he wasn't as physically strong as a full Wolf, so Miz Morales had insisted that he devote much of his time to scholarly pursuits.

I wandered to Kieren's desk, glancing at the JFK quote on the calendar: "In a time of turbulence and change, it is more true than ever that knowledge is power."

With luck, Kieren's library might tell me what I needed to know—about what I'd become, whether it might be possible to save the baby-squirrel eaters, and, if so, how. But first I had Sanguini's employees to think about, Mama's restaurant.

I didn't just feel responsible for what Bradley had done to who-knew-how-many among the staff. They needed their jobs to support themselves, their families, to pay tuition or pay back student loans or buy frozen burritos and instant noodle soup.

Besides, I had to keep a close eye on the infected among them. The transformation process made people unstable, emotionally erratic. Worse, if they somehow died before the month was up, they'd turn into monsters immediately.

I plugged in my cell charger and pulled my laptop from my backpack, grateful that the house was wireless.

TO: Sanguini's Staff
FROM: Quincie P. Morris
RE: Temporary Closing
DATE: September 17

I'm sorry to report that Sanguini's manager, Davidson Morris, died today. No memorial plans have been made at this time.

In addition, Chef Henry Johnson/"Bradley Sanguini" is no longer employed by the restaurant. (If you see Brad, do not approach him, and please immediately contact Detectives Wertheimer and/or Zaleski of the Austin Police Department).

Consequently, we are temporarily closed.

Initial interviews for a new manager and chef will be September 23, and Sanguini's will reopen at sunset on September 27. We also need to hire two bouncers and two dishwashers.

Please help spread the word.

Paychecks will be calculated based on a standard work week and direct deposited that same day. My apologies for the inconvenience. Thank you for your understanding.

I stared at the screen for a long moment before pushing SEND. The e-mail wasn't enough. Not informative enough or sensitive enough. It wouldn't begin to reassure the employees who'd watched me grow up. And they'd all be deeply suspicious of Brad, which wasn't necessarily a bad thing. But I didn't know what else to say.

I sprawled across Kieren's water bed, logged on to a food-service-industry job website, and posted help wanted ads for the chef and manager positions. Then I surfed to the *Cap City News* and did the same. Just in case we ran into trouble, I ordered the announcements to run through the end of the month.

Satisfied, I pulled a black leather-bound volume of incantations off a shelf and flipped randomly to a chapter labeled "Human Sacrifice."

Miz Morales strolled in and set a tray of food on the nightstand. Under her predator's gaze, I stirred the steaming potato soup, noting the accompanying iceberg wedge salad topped with sliced radishes, scallions, and a diced hard-boiled egg.

The white dishes with green trim matched the folded napkin, the green tumbler filled with Dr Pepper, and the thin green-and-white-striped straw sticking out of it.

I hadn't managed to fully hide the spell book beneath the pillow beside me, and a corner of it peeked into view.

I hadn't managed to fully hide that I was still mad at Miz Morales for not summoning Kieren back, either.

"Try the soup," Meara said. "It might make you feel better."

I sipped from the straw. "I should head over to the restaurant. My—"

"Why don't you take a few days?"

I shook my head, trying to sound reasonable. "Sanguini's has only been open for two nights. Three, if you count the launch party. If I could reopen today at sunset, I would, but it'll take time to—"

"Quincie, I know how much the place means to you, how much it meant to your mother." Miz Morales pulled the desk chair to the bed and took a seat. "Think about it, though. As your new guardians, Roberto and I are responsible for the restaurant."

"Only until my twenty-first birthday," I reminded her—not that as a wedding planner and an engineering professor they had a clue about running the place.

Besides, I couldn't risk them poking into my business, especially at a time when I was worried that, say, the bar staff might sprout fangs.

"Why don't you take it easy for a while?" Miz Morales tried again, and I could hear her much-faded Irish accent thicken. "Give yourself some time. Heal. Think about regular teenage-girl things. Have you sent in your application to U.T.?"

That's when it fully hit me. I had honest-to-God parents again. Not just a devilish, devil-may-care uncle-guardian. Roberto was a professional academic, and he and his perfectly coiffed werewolf wife had raised a supernatural studies scholar, one who'd also been at the top of our high-school graduating class. Now that their priorities dictated (to some degree) my priorities, school had just become a hell of a lot less optional.

It meant so much to me that the Moraleses cared. But it was also going to be a major pain in the butt if I didn't get on top of the situation. And fast.

I pushed my advantage as a grief-stricken waif. "I get what you're saying. I do. Thing is, with losing my uncle and Kieren, working at Sanguini's is the only thing I have left that seems normal. I mean, I hugely appreciate you and Dr. Morales taking me in."

"But that's a big change, too," Miz Morales said, glancing around the bookish, boyish room. "Besides which, we've just plopped you in the middle of Kieren central."

I took a chance on the broth. "I'd be thinking about him all the time anyway."

She scratched behind her ear. "Me, too."

SLEEPING SOLO

*P*ity I'd never learned to read German, Latin, or any of the other languages in over half of the leather-bound books. I dismissed a handful of the rest as fiction, including a paperback copy of the novel *Dracula* by Bram Stoker. The spine wasn't creased, and the first few pages were still stuck together at the top corners.

After hours of squinting at tiny print, I came across a red spiral notebook and, flipping it open, recognized Kieren's handwriting. Jackpot.

* * *

Vampirism:
- Demonic infection that turns humans into the undead and rots the soul

Vampires:
- Exist indefinitely by drinking blood
- May travel in the company of werescavengers for victim-disposal purposes

Origin:
- Unknown; possibly created by Wolf sorcery to cull the human threat

Cinematic/Literary Myths:
- Don't reflect/cast a shadow at all; must sleep on unhallowed earth; require invite to enter private homes; possess power over the weather and to enthrall others
- Carpathians: Count Dracula and his spawn

Powers:
- Neophyte: heightened strength, speed, reflexes, hearing (?), healing (?), climbing ability
- Young: ability to take wolflike form
- Age 50+: ability to turn into mist or dust
- Old Blood: ability to take batlike form

Vulnerabilities:
- Religious symbols (effect varies), holy water and wafers, sunlight (weakens), garlic, wild roses, being deprived of blood (may trigger blood lust)

Methods of Destruction:
- Fire, beheading, holy water, impaling (any stake/ knife, not just wooden), or removal of the heart

Opposition:
- Wolves, Bears, Cats, interfaith coalitions, freelance hunters

Spiritual Status:
- Damned. Some theorize that neophytes can be saved if beheaded, their mouths filled with garlic, and their hearts staked; considered a controversial theory

Again with the eternal damnation.

My gaze flicked back up to *possibly created by Wolf sorcery to cull the human threat.*

Kieren had *never* said anything about that. I wondered how long he'd known, what he'd felt about it. My Wolf man had been vocal about his hatred of vampires, but he'd softened his stance on the demonic infection after it had happened to me. Well, maybe not on the demonic part, but on the blaming of the infected themselves.

I slipped the paper into my backpack and resolved not to think more about it until tomorrow. My body could've kept going, but my brain needed rest, and as for my heart . . .

I still had the Moraleses and my "family" at Sanguini's.

But last night I'd had Kieren, too, and tonight our time together was a memory.

I pulled the spell book I'd hidden from Miz Morales out from beneath the pillow beside me, and a three-by-five photograph came with it. A photo of me, taken in August at the wedding of one of Meara's bridezilla clients. Kieren and I had tagged along to help manage the event, but I'd quietly imagined that the night was ours.

I could hardly believe it. Kieren—studious, serious, at times maddeningly distant—had slept with a picture of me under—on?—the pillow beside him.

Crawling beneath the denim comforter, I rested my cheek on the cotton pillowcase where his cheek had rested, curled my body between the sheets that his body had warmed. Imagined him by my side. It almost didn't seem possible. But Kieren might've loved me as much as I loved him.

In the dream, I'd gone back to the day Kieren had first mentioned getting a water bed, maybe a month after my parents had died. We were seated across from each other at a two-top at Fat Lorenzo's, splitting an order of fried mozzarella sticks with dipping marinara. Some sauce had spilled onto the checked plastic tablecloth, and I wiped it up with a napkin.

"What if you start to Wolf out in your sleep?" I asked, keeping my voice low. "The claws go wild. The mattress leaks all over the place. You know how your mama is about her Berber carpeting."

"The most important part of being a *Canis dirus sapiens*," he replied, gesturing with a cheese stick, "is controlling the Wolf, regardless of circumstances. The water bed is a night-by-night test."

Kieren had always been ungodly hard on himself.

"Besides," he added, sipping his Coke, "what if I don't always sleep alone?"

It had been the first time either of us had come close to hinting about sex.

The memory dimmed, replaced by his body pressed tight against mine on a thin twin mattress. It felt wrong, suffocating.

I smelled peppermint, blood, and Chianti. I heard the creak of the bedsprings and the clicking hearts of mice. "Kieren?"

A voice chuckled. "You're the bee's knees."

Brad. He'd drugged me, entombed me in his basement. Just like the night I'd died.

I yanked at the thick ropes binding me to the rusted iron headboard. I remembered suspecting Kieren of Vaggio's murder. I remembered Brad promising to never leave. How empowering it had felt, the way he'd thirsted for me.

Were those his lips nibbling beneath my breast? Didn't they feel divine?

KINDRED SOULS

*C*ome morning at Sanguini's, Miz Morales's Endless Love van had already been towed for repairs. But The Banana—a yellow 1970 Cutlass convertible that had belonged to Uncle D—was now parked behind the Dumpsters and covered with a tarp. It hadn't been there yesterday morning.

Bradley? God, I hoped not. So far as I knew, he really had left town. Detective Zaleski had swung by the Moraleses' last night to report that APD had searched

Brad's house and it had looked like he'd packed up and shipped out for good.

The werecat Ruby? Possibly. It would've been nothing for her to snatch Uncle D's keys. Zaleski had also mentioned that her DNA in Uncle D's bedroom had been a match to that at Travis's murder scene and on one of two sets of partial remains—identified as missing police officers—that had been found behind the bushes in my backyard. The medical examiner had determined that scavengers had gotten to the bodies.

Partial remains—where my little-girl sandbox had once been. It was all too gross and depressing to think about.

Just then, I heard a car engine and, running to the alley, spied the back end of a gleaming SUV with Illinois plates, turning west into the neighborhood. Black, not beige like Brad's Ford Expedition, and much, much bigger.

I heard a footfall behind me and, fisting my hand, spun to face—

"Mornin', Miss Quincie. Morning light. Lighter. Sure is bright, awful bright outside. Aren't you awfully bright?"

Mitch. He was a dear pal and an Austin celebrity who, at sixty-plus, served as an unofficial ambassador for the local homeless community. He was also an early victim of one of Bradley's "experimental" dishes and a full-blown vampire—one of many if I didn't do something about it. And soon.

This morning I noticed that Mitch had traded in his famed flannel pj bottoms for camouflage cargo pants and that his latest cardboard sign read:

UPBEAT UNDEAD
HIPPIE WORKAHOLIC
SEEKS HEMOGLOBIN

"That's a very rectangular sign," I said. "And your handwriting's improving."

Color me new to supernatural small talk.

"Yep, yep," he replied. "Mitch wrote the words like they looked in his head. You got any to spare? Not words. No, not . . . Hardly anybody, nobody's out anymore."

Any blood to spare, he'd meant. I remembered the first glass of wine that Bradley had offered me, a '99 Sonoma Zinfandel to wash down his rigatoni marinara. The bottle had been cold, refrigerated, as had nearly all the wine he'd served up, even though reds should be kept at room temperature. Contaminated and recorked—of course! Bradley had kept his own stash—for me, for himself—in the restaurant kitchen.

"Let's see what's in the fridge," I said, reaching for my keys. It seemed foolish to let Mitch leave thirsty. Or me, either. "We've got to hurry, or I'll be late for school."

He puttered inside after me. "I see you look, that you're looking like a regular girl again. Who'd you chomp?"

It had been Mitch who'd explained that after my "first bite," I'd be better able to control my blood lust and hide my demonic features—the red eyes and fangs.

"Kieren," I replied, shoving away the memory. The way his breath had become short and ragged. The way I hadn't needed to breathe at all.

"Gonna miss, miss that boy. Too bad he's dead."

I froze with my hand on the fridge handle. Had Mitch heard something? "What?"

He looked confused. "Didn't you drank, drink, suck him dry?"

"No, he's . . ." Thank God Mitch had only been assuming. "I stopped in time. Kieren's alive. He's safe." Or at least he had been the day before.

Leaning against the butcher block, Mitch scratched his stubbly chin. "Huh. That's, it's really something, Miss Quincie. It's . . . something else."

I suspected from his tone that Mitch had killed the first person he'd fed from and no doubt more since. I didn't have high hopes that he'd ever adjust to a low-key preternatural existence. Mitch had barely scratched by as a human being.

I'd heard what Miz Morales had said about vampires and souls and inevitable damnation, and my foray into Kieren's Wolf studies had only confirmed her words.

I knew I couldn't let Mitch go on the way he had been, that I might have to take the axe from the safe and hunt him down. But, like me, he hadn't chosen his fate. Maybe together we could find our way, at least for the time being. At least until I found some means of preventing the baby-squirrel eaters from turning toothy like us.

Rooting around, I counted three bottles (labeled *chef* in black ink), hopefully enough to get us through the school week. Once Sanguini's reopened, I'd arrange for a steady supply of animal blood. But for now, we'd have to rely one last time on Bradley.

I grabbed a bottle, yanked out the cork, and sniffed, confirming that the house Cabernet had been spiked. As a human, my nose hadn't noticed the distinction. Now I had a heightened sense of smell, if only when it came to blood.

"Grab a seat, Mitch." I poured him a tall glass and myself a shot.

"This Bradley's blood?" he asked.

"Probably," I said, repulsed by the thought, then more repulsed by other possible alternatives. "But we should drink it. There's nothing more he can do to us."

Mitch slowly blinked his Santa-blue eyes. "No, no, I don't know, Miss Quincie." He coughed. "You think so, do you?"

ACADEMIC ANXIETY

I spent most of first-hour Econ scribbling every word Mr. Wu uttered or wrote on the board. He kept talking about the elasticity of supply and demand. He might as well have been speaking ancient Sumerian. No wonder I was getting a D+.

Under the circumstances, school felt like an extraordinary waste of time. But the last thing I needed was the counselor calling the Moraleses, who might well, in turn, reduce my hours or even forbid me to work at the restaurant so I could study more.

After the bell rang, I shuffled to stand in front of Mr. Wu's desk. He hated students. He ridiculed questions, denied hall passes, and God forbid you fell asleep during class. Rumor had it he was a Marine.

Mr. Wu held up a finger, instructing me to wait until the room cleared, and I braced myself for a tirade about my having missed so many days.

Once we were alone, he leaned forward and whispered, "Your boyfriend, he's the one who beheaded the blood-sucking vice principal?"

I tried to guess which answer would help my grade. "Yes?"

"With the blood-sucking vice principal's own battle-axe?"

"Yes," I said, surer of myself.

"Good for him! Good for you! And *this* is why your Econ grade is abysmal, because you two have been locked in battle against the undead?"

"Definitely," I agreed, and happily enough, it was sort of true.

"Mrs. Levy told me all about it this morning in the faculty lounge. Here, take this." He handed me copies of his lesson plans from the classes I'd missed. "And here's my card with my home number on the back. If you have any questions, give me a call."

*   *   *

Mrs. Levy beamed at me and continued passing back essays while I took my seat. I vaguely remembered the assignment, a response to "The Lottery."

Later, while the other students looked over her comments, she called me to the front of the room. "It's a relief to see you safe, though I missed Kieren today."

I shifted my weight. "Me, too."

"I also missed him at Travis Reid's funeral," Mrs. Levy added.

I struggled not to lose my patience. Kieren had been mine, but not all mine. Other people cared about him, and Mrs. Levy had fought by his side.

Lowering my voice, I explained, "So far as I know, Kieren's okay. He, um, transferred to a fancy prep school up north." It was what the Moraleses had decided to tell people.

"So far as you know . . ." Mrs. Levy didn't look satisfied, but she didn't push it, either. Switching to teacher mode, she began making notations on her desktop calendar. "Well, you have missed a lot of school. You owe me a few papers and several journal entries."

I opened Frank to record my make-up work.

"I'll need to see an essay on 'The Lottery,'" Mrs. Levy went on. "Oh, and one on *Metamorphoses* and its retellings. You flunked the quiz on 'Young Goodman Brown,' but given the circumstances, if you want to write a paper on it . . ."

God, I had no time for this! Why did the Moraleses have to be so responsible? For all of Uncle D's drawbacks, he'd hardly glanced at my report cards.

My Chem teacher had ditched us for a conference in Houston and the sub had no clue, so class had defaulted into a study hour. Better yet, since I'd elected to do work-study in the afternoons, it was my last class of the day.

Which brought me to Kieren's locker. I doubted he'd left anything too personal in there, anything that screamed "werewolf," but it seemed prudent to check.

I waited until after the fourth-hour bell, glanced both ways, and then slammed the combination lock into the door, breaking it loose. Supernatural strength could be handy.

Opening the door, I smelled the garlic before I saw the long rope of it dangling from the coat hanger. I pinched my nostrils closed and waved my hand to clear the air, though I honestly couldn't tell if the scent was awful because I was a vampire or if it was awful because it had mixed with that of—I spotted Kieren's gym bag on the shelf—overly ripe workout clothes. He must've forgotten to bring them home to wash.

Shaking my head, I smiled, remembering Kieren for who he was—a real fur-and-flesh-and-bone boy—instead of for the fact that he was gone.

Beyond that, the locker was mostly empty. There hadn't been a need to bring a coat to school yet, and shifters ran on a hotter body temperature anyway.

I'd return the stack of honors and AP textbooks to the office, and—thank you, Kieren—put the handwritten class notes in his English folder to good use myself.

The folder felt bulky, and flipping it open, I noticed a thick envelope shoved into one of the divider pockets. *Welcome to the University of Texas!*

It took me a minute to process. Kieren had applied to U.T., and he'd been in the first round of admitted students. Regardless of his mama's fatalistic attitude, Kieren had been holding out hope that he'd come to manage his shift before it was time for him to leave, that his future would be here in Austin with me.

I closed the folder, knowing I'd always treasure the letter—proof that I, not the Wolf pack, had been Kieren's true dream.

HELP WANTED

*I*n Sanguini's kitchen, I poured myself a taller glass of blood wine than I'd had that morning. My body seemed better able to metabolize (or whatever) it than when I'd been human. The effects still felt slightly intoxicating—my fangs descended once. But I could concentrate.

I retrieved Kieren's vampire fact sheet from my backpack. I read it. I reread it. I chanted it. Sang it, proclaimed it, and eventually memorized it. Then I turned on a gas burner, lit it on fire, and dropped it to burn to ashes on the stained concrete floor.

I had to get organized, to make checklists. It was how I'd handled everything since my parents' fatal car accident, back in middle school.

Maybe I hadn't figured out the solution to Brad's mass-infection coup. At least not yet. But I could do some basic, everyday things that needed to be done, and that would make the world seem slightly less overwhelming.

In the manager's office, I called to order the installation of a security system, including indoor and outdoor video cams. Then I bought a couple of mirrors for the restrooms and checked the incoming résumés on my laptop.

Because Sanguini's had so quickly become famous, or at least infamous (what with Vaggio's murder and all), chef applications had zipped in from across the country. Plus, I'd counted two Canadians, an Australian, a Parisian, and someone from the restaurant at the Four Seasons México in Colonia Juárez. Oh, and a chef from Scotland, another from Poland, and a one-time *Iron Chef* contestant from Tokyo.

Only one woman, though, which was disappointing. She'd included a scanned-in magazine clipping. "The Top Chef in the Southeast," according to the headline. Apparently, butter had been her ingredient of choice.

The article was dated not long before I was born. From the black-and-white photo, Nora Woodworth looked to have been anywhere from her midforties to midfifties at the time and projected a down-home charm.

According to her résumé, she'd recently spent over a decade working as a personal chef at a private estate in Whitby Estates, Illinois. The cover letter explained that Nora's previous employer had passed away last spring and she had newly relocated to Austin.

I had a good feeling about her. But obviously, a homespun type couldn't play the sexy vampire chef.

Applications for manager were fewer, less interesting, and mostly local.

Checking messages, I found a slew of condolence notes—along with offers to bring by casseroles, tamales, and honey-baked hams in response to the e-mail I'd sent yesterday.

I replied individually to Sergio, the veteran expeditor (and, hopefully, my new work-study adviser), asking that he meet me here tomorrow afternoon to help review applications so we could start scheduling interviews. Then I sent a reassuring note to the whole staff, saying that I was staying with friends and coping as best I could.

After clicking SEND, I made a call.

"Zaleski here," was the answer.

"Detective Zaleski," I began, "this is Quincie—"

"Did that Bradley character show up again?"

Only in my nightmares. "No, nothing like that. I was just wondering . . ."

"Yeah?"

If I was stereotyping werebears, I hoped he wouldn't take offense. "By any chance, do you happen to have any family members interested in the growing field of restaurant security?"

The main phone rang. "Sanguini's: A Very Rare Restaurant."

"It's me, Clyde. I'm at the back door."

I slammed down the receiver, burst out of the office, and poured on the speed through the back hall and the restaurant kitchen, skidding on the concrete floor.

Throwing the door open, I found Clyde yawning wide on the step and yanked him inside.

"Take it easy!" he hollered. "Watch the shirt!"

"Kieren," I said, letting go. "How's Kieren?" I knew better than to ask "where."

"Chill." Clyde crossed his hirsute arms. "I dropped him off near Denton. He's jiffy, believe me. Yesterday he inhaled two orders of barbecued beef ribs, a pulled pork sandwich, and a tub of coleslaw from some hole-in-the-wall joint in Waco. He says howdy, and that you shouldn't worry, even though you will anyway."

Denton was about an hour past Dallas. "He's on foot? Alone?"

Clyde strode past me into the kitchen. "There's a safe house outside town."

"What's a safe house?"

He paused, and I could tell he'd thought it was something Kieren and I had discussed before. "A house that's . . . well built."

It sounded more like part of an underground railroad for werepeople wanted by human law enforcement. It was a relief to know that such a thing existed.

"Can you get a message to him? Tell him he's not a murder suspect anymore?"

Clyde did a double take. "Come again?"

He listened carefully as I explained. Then he said, "Sorry, it's not like Wolves clue in lowly Possums on their secret hideouts."

It had been worth a try.

"He'll be fine, though," Clyde added. "Kieren's the smartest fur-face I know."

It was nice that Clyde had stopped by. But why? After all, the last time I'd seen him, he'd called me "unholy" and "hussy" and threatened my neck with a battle-axe.

I waited the Possum out, let the silence become uncomfortable.

"Look," Clyde began again, "here's the deal: when I dropped Kieren off, I . . ."

"You . . . ?" I prompted in a gentler tone. I couldn't help feeling for the guy. Yesterday he'd missed the funeral of one of his two best friends. And he'd said good-bye to the other one only a few hours ago.

The Possum continued, "I told Kieren that if there was anything I could do . . ."

I couldn't help smiling. "And he asked you to look out for me."

Clyde bristled. "Yeah, something like that."

Classic Kieren.

HER MAMA'S DAUGHTER

*T*he next day, in Sanguini's dining room, Sergio shook hands in turn with two bearded, massive men who had to have been relatives of Detective Zaleski. Both were over six-six and three hundred pounds each, and their distinguishing features were all about hair—from the furry toes peeking out of their brown leather sandals to the manly tresses flowing down their wide backs. Joining them from the kitchen, I said, "My new bouncers, I presume?"

*   *   *

Sergio had already sorted the most promising faxed and e-mailed applications into two piles, one for the chef position and one for the manager job. I could trust him to vet professional qualifications. My priority: whether the candidates had heartbeats. We would not be hiring any more murderous vampires on my watch. "How goes it?"

With a flourish, Sergio deposited his own application for manager on the desk. "I don't expect any special favors, lamb chop, but you know how much I love this place."

I couldn't imagine a more qualified or better-fit candidate. Sergio had helped Uncle D with payroll, and he'd been Vaggio's number two in the kitchen (and archnemesis at the poker table) for some thirty years. Especially after all the chaos, it might reassure the staff if one of their own took over.

Then, in a flash, I remembered Sergio raving about Bradley's chilled baby squirrels, which meant that in just a few weeks he'd join the legions of undead. God, what if I couldn't save him, save any of them? I had a sudden, terrifying image of my old buddy Sergio, overcome with blood lust, draining his longtime partner Raúl.

I fought rising panic. I'd stayed up past 3 A.M. the night before, trying to decipher a book with a bat etched into the cover, using an online French-English dictionary. But Kieren's cheat sheet—assuming it was accurate—was still the only solid information I had to go on. Demonic infection, eternal damnation. So far, none of the news was good.

For now, though, Sergio was still a human being, which, hell, was more than I could say, and he looked so hopeful. "I'll have to run it by the Moraleses, but . . ." I reached over the desk to hug him. "You've got my vote."

Sergio brightened. "Want to grab a bite to celebrate? We could—"

"I'd be happy to keep you company, but Miz Morales packed my lunch this morning." I tried to lighten the moment. "We're talking thinly sliced smoked white turkey with fresh Wisconsin cheddar, iceberg lettuce, German mustard, and olive-oil-infused mayo in a whole-grain tortilla." I'd stashed the untouched wrap in the restaurant fridge.

"Tell me about the side!" Sergio prompted, enjoying our familiar game.

"Lightly salted sweet-potato chips," I obliged.

Menu was my first language.

STAR-CROSSED

*O*nce Sergio had packed it in for the day, I polished off the open bottle of blood wine and slipped the last one into my backpack, protecting it with a frozen cooling sleeve. Then I realized that Miz Morales, as a Wolf, could probably smell the blood-spiked alcohol, no matter where I tried to hide it in the house.

Damn. I'd already blazed through two boxes of breath mints so no one would notice my "drinking" problem.

When I opened the door to leave, Clyde was there, standing on the back step, poised as if to knock, with a teenage girl I only vaguely recognized. Her short, spiky blond hair had been streaked pink. A small silver hoop hooked her left eyebrow. She wore a ton of black eyeliner, no lipstick, a political T-shirt, and artfully torn black jeans. No big deal. About a quarter of the people at my school dressed that way.

"Something I can do for you two?"

"Aimee's here about the dishwasher job," Clyde announced.

Finally, some good news! I opened the door wider and slid my backpack to the floor. It had to be over ninety degrees outside. "Y'all thirsty?"

As I grabbed glasses, Aimee trailed in after Clyde and hopped onto the kitchen island bar stool next to his. In a bored voice, she asked, "Is it true that you're a vampire?"

What? "I . . ."

"I told her," the Possum admitted, reaching into his back jeans pocket.

"Clyde!" I banged the glasses onto the counter. Right then, I wanted to kill him, *really* wanted to kill him. Seize his throat and slam him into the ceiling. Poke out his beady eyes and sauté them in olive oil with chives.

"Look," the Possum began, holding up a palm-size wooden cross. "Kieren may think you're hunky-dory, but if Aimee takes this job, she has a right to know the risks."

"Loosen up, both of you," Aimee said. "I'm not afraid."

"I am," I replied, rubbing my temples. "You should be, too."

I took my time, counting backward from fifty as I poured the water and set the glasses in front of the sophomores. The flash of fury had frightened me. I'd thought my mood swings had ended once my transformation was complete—apparently not.

What's more, though Clyde's cross didn't have a supernatural effect on me, his wielding it like that hurt my feelings. "I'm supposed to be home for Dr. Morales's famous chicken tortilla soup in"—I made a show of checking my watch—"seventeen minutes." I adopted an alpha stance that would've made Kieren proud. "So, tell me, Aimee, why risk your young life washing dishes for the undead?"

I made eye contact with Clyde, and he fumbled the cross.

Aimee snatched it away. "I need money. Between U.T. and St. Ed's, nobody's hiring high-school kids. And you know, there's a lot less to live for with Travis gone."

She'd lost me with that last part.

"Aimee and Travis had this sort of unspoken love," the Possum explained. "You know, the kind where everybody else can't understand why they don't just get together."

I was familiar with the concept, but . . . "You and Travis?"

Travis had been nobody's idea of a heartthrob, and Aimee was seriously cute. But in fairness, the 'dillo had also been a total sweetheart. It made me think more of Aimee that she'd liked him. I hoped that he'd known. "You're human, right?"

"You got a problem with that?" she snapped.

"Me? Hell, no. But it is unusual." Typically, were-people didn't date or mate outside their own kind. Meara and Roberto were an exception, Kieren and I, an even bigger one, though we'd never technically dated.

"Travis and I were paintball buddies," Aimee announced as if that explained everything. "Besides, who're you to talk? A vampire smitten with a Wolf."

"Is there anything you didn't tell her?" I asked Clyde.

He sipped his water. "Travis had already clued her in on the shifter scene."

"Just like that?"

"What?" The Possum smirked. "You thought only your and Kieren's forbidden, unspoken, mutual yearning had been special enough for him to confide his true self?"

Actually, I had.

"At least Aimee isn't a damned and depraved hellion," he muttered.

Nice. "Just wait," I began, suddenly resigned. "Once the baby-squirrel eaters turn toothy, everybody'll be romancing the dead."

Clyde and Aimee traded a look and exclaimed, "What baby-squirrel eaters?"

Had I meant to say that out loud? Maybe. Maybe on some level I knew I couldn't handle it all by myself, that I had to tell somebody. I pulled up a bar stool and started talking. Because of what I was, I hadn't felt like I could trust anyone with the whole truth. But these two already knew so much, and despite their attitudes, neither had walked out yet.

Once I finished the story, Clyde went crazy. "How could you let this happen? How could you have been so stupid? How —?"

"Shut up!" Aimee yelled at him. "Everyone who tasted the squirrels?" she asked me in a softer voice. "Even a little bite?"

I nodded, wondering who Aimee might've known who'd dined at Sanguini's. Most parents hadn't let their high-school-age kids come to the restaurant — too scary after Vaggio's murder, too sexy what with all the leather and chains, lace and feathers.

"What can we do to stop it?" she pressed.

"Well, I've been looking through Kieren's books —"

"Most of which you can't read, for a cure that may not exist," Clyde shot back. "That's kick-ass, Quincie. Really. You rock."

I'd about had it with his sarcasm. "Do you have a better idea?"

The Possum crossed his furry arms. "We go down every name in the reservation book, hit the Web, get their contact info, then call and ask if they ordered the chilled baby squirrels. We can say it's a consumer satisfaction survey or something. That way we'll have a working list of the infected."

"To do what with?" Aimee asked.

I knew what Clyde was thinking before he said it.

"At least we'll know where to point the stakes."

Before I could add that he wasn't totally out of line, Aimee pushed him off his bar stool. "It won't come to that," she insisted. "Don't worry, Quincie. We'll help you."

SECRET WEAPONS

*T*he following afternoon, it occurred to me to grab the burnt-orange sports bottle from the break-room cabinet and fill it with Bradley's blood wine.

My stash had held up better than expected, mostly because Mitch hadn't stopped by since Wednesday. That worried me, but I'd seen no new reports of murders on the lakefront or anywhere else.

"I've scheduled initial interviews," Sergio announced. "But rushing like this—"

"Xio's a single mom. Jamal is putting himself through U.T. They live on—"

"Tips." Sergio smiled at me. "You know, your mother was the same way. She always took care of her staff first."

The highest praise. Embarrassed, I ducked my head and flipped through today's applications. "We'll be okay, though, right? I mean, we've got some solid candidates."

The office phone rang, and Sergio snagged it. "Sanguini's." He paused. "Sorry, he's moved on." After hanging up, the new manager responded to my quizzical look. "Another one," he said, "asking for Bradley."

"Another one?"

Thankful that I could sip chicken broth, I made it through dinner. Miz Morales dished about her latest wedding, to be performed in Klingon with full makeup and costumes at the Sheraton downtown. The groom was the son of a local tech millionaire, and the bride was one of Dr. Morales's former engineering TAs.

Meanwhile Meghan glowered at me, gripping her spoon like a weapon.

After fielding cheers for clearing the table—a compulsion I'd picked up sometime between my first steps and mastering the alphabet, I headed upstairs to Kieren's room.

The books were gone. So was the map of the Western Hemisphere.

Miz Morales knocked on the door. "Big change, isn't it?"

"What . . . ?" I'd almost asked: what did you do? "What happened?"

"Surprise! Roberto and I packed up Kieren's desk and books while you were at school. We'll get to his closet early next week." She strolled in. "This is your home now, Quincie. You need to make it your own space. I can help you decorate, if you want. We could start with new linens."

"Where did the books go?" I asked, turning in place. The house didn't have an attic, and I doubted the Moraleses would dump such valuable old texts in the garage.

"What do you think?" she went on. "Paint? Wallpaper? The house is so white — the walls, the carpeting. It's starting to bother me."

I made an effort to sound casual. "The books?"

And failed.

"Sorry, Quincie," she said. "I can't say."

Sorry Kieren had to go away. Sorry his books had to go away. Sorry they'd just taken away the only slim hope I'd had to foil Brad's mass-infection scheme.

I volunteered to clean out Kieren's closet, saying I might want to keep a T-shirt as a keepsake, and Miz Morales had been quick to agree.

It felt wrong, sorting through his clothes. It's not like he'd died. I wished I knew whether he'd already reached the pack, whether he'd managed to prove himself. I might've been biased, but I couldn't imagine anyone being smarter than Kieren.

I shucked shirts off their hangers, folding each and placing it in a growing stack on the water bed. Kieren had dress clothes, church clothes, but for the most part he'd kept his wardrobe simple. Jeans, shorts, and T-shirts, short-sleeved or sleeveless.

He hated the heat. I wondered how much farther north he'd gone from Denton, whether he preferred the climate of his new home.

Reaching for a much-faded Ice Bats shirt that had fallen on the carpet, I noticed a couple of two-liter plastic jugs marked HOLY WATER that had been tucked into a corner of the closet behind a baseball bat, tennis racket, and fencing foil.

How long had Uncle Davidson been a vampire? How long after his transformation had we lived under the same roof? I'd never guessed that he was a danger to me. I wonder if even he realized that or if, after the initial bout of blood lust, Uncle D had convinced himself that he was no longer a threat. That he could exist, passing as human, without potentially murdering the people he cared about. Just as I was doing.

The jugs looked so innocuous on the floor of the closet, not far from my red cowboy boots. I touched Kieren's crucifix beneath my shirt. I had the Moraleses to consider, my employees, my neighbors and classmates.

A moment later, I slipped into the upstairs bathroom and began rummaging through the medicine cabinet. I spied a nearly empty four-inch-tall bottle of cherry cough syrup and an expired tube of concealer about the size of my forefinger. I rinsed them out until the tap water ran clear. Then I took both to the closet to fill with holy water.

Now I'd always have a handy means of self-destruction.

Once I'd replaced Kieren's clothes with mine, I texted Aimee and Clyde, asking that they hit the public library the next day and look for anything they could find on the undead, demonic magic, or related transformations (it was worth a try).

In the meantime, I'd see what I could find on the Web, and then we'd meet on Sunday afternoon to compare notes.

I logged on to Kieren's PC, keyed in the password (Brazos), checked his bookmarks, and zeroed in on the shopping folder. When I clicked MAGICAL TOOLS, the screen seemed to shimmer. It took me a second to realize it wasn't the computer.

I closed my eyes and, opening them again, saw spots. I tried once more, and this time, seemingly projected images filled my mind.

I stood in the entryway of Bradley's two-and-a-half-story Arts-and-Crafts house.

He was there, laughing on the landing, impeccably dressed in his gray toasting suit and toying with the antique bowie knife that used to hang above his fireplace. "Weapons and witchcraft . . ." He lifted a shiny black dress shoe to the stair rail and leaped neatly down to the foyer. "Baby, who do you think you're trying to bump off?"

Before I could reply, Brad pointed the blade at my mouth. "Go ahead. You know you want to."

Just like that, at his whim, I did. I couldn't resist. I felt the way he wanted me to. Tempted. Tantalized.

Moving closer, I leaned in to kiss the sharp knife point and tasted blood.

Still seated at Kieren's desk, I realized that my fangs had pierced my lower lip. I wiped it and stared down at the red smear on my finger, trying to make sense of the dream. Or had it been a delusion? I could've sworn that I hadn't fallen asleep.

primo

HAPPY PUPPY DAY

*W*hy don't you cry?" Meghan demanded from the booster seat behind me. "Don't you miss him?"

Driving the Moraleses' Chevy through the Hill Country, I tilted the air conditioner vent upward, hoping to cool off my little passenger. "Brazos?"

Brazos had been all love and loyalty, playful in his blue bandana. If Bradley had committed no other crime, I still would've hated him for poisoning Kieren's dog.

I peered at Meghan via the rearview mirror. "Of course I miss him, and I know you do, too. But your parents found a breeder who has two German shepherd puppies for you to pick from. Don't you want a new puppy?"

"No."

I itched to turn the car around. I had answers to find, and with every passing hour good people like Sergio were more at risk. Besides, my dead heart seemed to clench whenever I spotted a beige SUV like Brad's (who knew there were so damned many of them?). But when Miz Morales had asked if I'd take Meghan to pick up the new dog, I couldn't refuse. Roberto had an engineering journal to edit, and given tonight's full moon, Meara had been reluctant to leave the house.

What I was doing mattered, not only to Meghan's morale but also to her family's safety. By tonight, any sightings of a Wolf on the Morales property could be explained away by a harmless family pet.

I also had a theory that—even though Wolves supposedly didn't feel the full moon's pull until adolescence—its influence was making the cub a bit mouthier than usual, and the last thing we needed back home was Meghan testing her mama's patience.

Besides, Aimee and Clyde had been researching vampirism at the public library since the doors first opened this morning. Maybe their luck would be better than mine.

"Kieren," Meghan clarified, interrupting my thoughts. "Did you hurt him? Did you make him go away?"

The memory rushed back. *That night at Sanguini's. The chef's wager. His dare. Biting deep, gulping thick blood, grasping smooth leather. Kieren's hips nestled tight between my thighs.*

"Quincie!" Meghan screamed.

A horn blared. Our car had wandered over the yellow center line, only yards from an oncoming station wagon. As I swerved back into my own lane, the wagon barely missed us. Gripping the wheel, I shouted, "You okay? Meghan? Meghan!"

She nodded, tears welling in her big brown eyes, and that's when I fully appreciated that she was anything but okay.

Baby Meghan. What was it that the Moraleses had told her? That Kieren had gone away to school? That she'd see him again someday? She was only four; another fourteen years without her much-idolized older brother probably sounded like an eternity. If there was anything I understood, it was how much the idea of forever without Kieren could hurt.

Worse, she'd seen me—red eyes, fangs extended—the one night the blood lust had nearly won. She had the smarts, the instincts to recognize the threat. And now I was her acting chauffeur. Poor kid. That didn't exactly say "happy puppy day," did it?

Around the next bend, I turned in the dog breeder's gravel drive, punched in a key code to open the gate, and we rolled across the cattle guard.

At the top of the hill, I spotted a homey log cabin on steroids—probably a three- or four-bedroom, fronted by a long front porch, complete with rocking chairs and hanging baskets of marigolds and geraniums. It looked nice and wholesome and like somewhere that a pre-school girl-beast and her undead babysitter could have a pleasant afternoon.

After putting the car in park, I unbuckled my seat belt and twisted in the driver's seat to face Meghan. When I reached for her hand, she cowered in the booster seat.

I wouldn't tell her that I hadn't hurt Kieren. I'd never been a good liar.

At the same time, I couldn't lay on her the blow-by-blow of the night I nearly sucked her big brother dry—albeit with his permission—and have her skip away thinking that had been a good thing. "Did your mama tell you that I talked to Clyde?"

Meghan brushed imaginary lint from her Barbie T-shirt. "Clyde?"

"Yep, Clyde. He drove all the way past Dallas with Kieren, and he told me that your brother's appetite is bigger than ever. He ate two whole orders of barbecued beef ribs, a pulled pork sandwich, and a whole mess of coleslaw at some joint in Waco."

"Waco on the way to Tío Carlos's house?" she asked, somewhat reassured. Then, just as fast, her hopeful expression fell. "Kieren had coleslaw without me."

I might not have known how to prevent the rise of Brad's undead army, but this was a tragedy I could deal with. "How about we visit the dogs, pick out your puppy, and grab some take-out coleslaw on the way home?"

Later, we left with both remaining puppies and the mother German shepherd.

THE BEAST WITHIN

*I*t's not hard to fake eating solids when you're offered soup. But that night, Dr. Morales served grilled catfish, the take-out coleslaw, and Cajun-style dirty rice.

After some small talk about varmints on the roof— probably squirrels, maybe raccoons—and getting the trees trimmed, Miz Morales noticed that I was just moving my food around on my plate. "You're not hungry, Quincie?"

I sipped my sweet tea. "Not all of us have shifter metabolisms."

"Teenage girls." Roberto ruffled Meghan's hair. "I hope you won't give us any of that nonsense when you're her age."

"Me?" In typical werechild form, Meghan had plowed through three fillets and had just launched into her fourth helping of slaw. Having never seen her exhibit so much enthusiasm for a vegetarian dish, I figured there had to be a story there. Something between her and Kieren. When things were better between us, I'd ask.

"You've hardly touched your fish," Meara pressed.

In life, I'd been a proud and notorious foodie, grateful that restaurant work was such terrific cardio. "Actually," I began, "my stomach's acting up. I don't know that I'm catfish-ready at the moment."

She sprung to her feet in full-blown mom mode. "You're not feeling well?"

On the upside, she whisked away my plate, covered it in aluminum foil, and stashed it in the fridge for when I felt better. On the down, my physical condition had become the focal point of the household.

No, I wasn't dizzy. Kind of nauseated. The smell of the fish and Cajun spices was getting to me.

No, my forehead wasn't warm.

Yes, I had the chills, hence my low body temperature.

"You look awfully pale," she mused, and something in her tone made me wonder if she'd guessed the real problem. Miz Morales was making all the right noises, but we both knew my "symptoms" might be medical or mystical.

She suggested that Meghan go help her daddy feed the dogs outside.

(After much debate, we'd decided to name the mother German shepherd Angelina and her pups Concho and Pecos—like Brazos, all after Texas rivers.)

Once they'd left, she presented me with a glass of 7-Up. "Is it cramps?"

"Um . . ." If I hadn't died, my period would've started earlier this week. But according to Kieren's books, vampires—being creatures outside the cycle of life—didn't menstruate. Mostly as a distraction, I reached to clear Miz Morales's plate.

"Oh, you don't have to do that," she scolded, stacking the dishes. "You just sit there and relax. This won't take a minute. Would you like some soda crackers?"

"Maybe later," I said, and then, as she loaded plates and silverware into the dishwasher, I decided to change the subject. "About my uncle's body . . ."

Meara stopped what she'd been doing. "Yes?"

"I've been thinking about what you said, about how he became . . ."

"A different being," she supplied. Her tone grew gentler, and I could tell she felt guilty about her suspicions, especially in light of my recent loss. "At the end, love, that was not your uncle. It was a corrupted, damned thing that had gradually taken his place."

A damned thing. "How gradually?" I asked, thinking back to the way my anger had spiked when I found out Clyde had told Aimee what I was.

I was still too ignorant of the full ramifications of what Brad had done to me. To me and so many others at Sanguini's.

Miz Morales returned to the kitchen table. "It varies, if I'm remembering right—about a year, sometimes less, sometimes more. Then the soul is gone. It's been, well, some time since my own Wolf studies, and I focused on healing, not the demonic."

I glanced at my hand, resting on the table, crisscrossed in scars. Back in middle school—because of a partial shift gone wrong—Kieren's claws had nearly ripped it in two. An accident on a railroad bridge that had involved an oncoming train and that had haunted him far more than me, especially since he'd saved my life in the process.

Yet, despite the extensive damage, I had no trouble snapping my fingers, typing on a keyboard, holding a pen. Evidence of Miz Morales's formidable healing skills.

"When Ruby staked him . . . do you think any of my uncle's soul was left?"

"It's possible," Miz Morales confirmed. "In which case God could still forgive him if —"

"We stake his heart, cut off his head, and stuff his mouth with garlic?"

She covered my hand with hers. "We don't have to have an open casket."

I thought about it, about what my parents would've wanted. "Uncle D was Daddy's little brother."

She patted my hand, the smooth one. "I'll call Detective Zaleski and see when the body will be released. The police may want to keep it longer than usual, for study."

Dissection, she meant.

"Okay," I agreed. "Closed casket."

MOONLIGHT MADNESS

*F*rom Kieren's bedroom window, by the full moon's light, I spied Miz Morales, still in human form, playing with the mama shepherd and her puppies in the backyard.

Meara hadn't even begun her shift yet. I had plenty of time.

I ran downstairs to the kitchen, barefoot in my over-size Longhorns nightshirt.

Roberto had picked up a twelve-pack of chicken legs at the grocery store this week. I could defrost a couple in the microwave and suck the juices dry.

I'd hardly reached for a plate, though, when Miz Morales came back inside, buck naked. Damn. Her shift had been a quick one. I could hear the dogs barking outside.

"Quincie?" she asked.

"Just grabbing a snack. You're in early."

Meara rolled her shoulders. "I'm afraid I panicked Angelina and had to reverse the shift. I'm not sure if it's the change in my scent or the sound of the bones cracking, but they'll get used to it. Dogs always do. Brazos . . ." She shook her head. "How're you feeling?"

"Better," I said, hoping she'd assume I'd eaten while she was out, trying desperately to decide what to say next to Kieren's very naked mother. Talk about awkward. "Is it hard," I began again, "always staying in control?"

Of the shift, I'd meant. Kieren had told me how difficult it had been to regain his wits once he'd begun that partial transformation on the railroad bridge. And on our last night at Sanguini's, for a second there, I'd thought his Wolf might tear me apart.

"You can't be too afraid of making a mistake to be yourself," Miz Morales said, splashing off her face at the bar sink, "to do what comes naturally. But you also have to consider the consequences of completely giving in to the moment." Reaching for a towel, she added, "You know, love, if you ever have any questions or find yourself in a difficult situation . . ."

"About shape-shifting?" I asked.

"About sex," Miz Morales clarified in a matter-of-fact voice. "I remember Sophie saying that the two of you had had the Talk when you were twelve, but now that you're a young woman—"

"Oh! Oh, no, not right now, thanks. I don't need that kind of talking." I almost admitted that, despite my and Kieren's feelings for each other, we'd never really gone there. But I didn't want Miz Morales feeling sorry for me or—

Wait. Why was *she* thinking that *I* was thinking about sex, anyway? How mortifying. Not that I never thought about it. I was sleeping in Kieren's bed, after all, but it's not like he was there with me.

Whatever. I had no interest in discussing the issue with his mother.

"We're both tired," Miz Morales said, drying her hands. "But that's a standing offer. Me, Roberto, Meghan, we're your family now. I know that Kieren's leaving is an adjustment, for all of us, and you're also dealing with the loss of your uncle and the horror of what he became. But please know that you can come to me with anything."

Miz Morales was a first-rate mom, a champ among

moms. But I had a feeling that "anything" didn't include my craving for chicken blood. Let alone human blood. Or that I was trying to prevent the deaths of hundreds of innocents, not to mention their subsequent rise as fiends who might not settle for fowl.

I mumbled "Thanks" and took a step toward the door.

"Quincie . . ." Her predator eyes shone in the darkness. She gestured toward my chest. "That's Kieren's."

The crucifix. It had escaped from under my nightshirt when I ran downstairs. Hadn't it been his grandfather's? What would she and Dr. Morales think if I told them I'd fetched it, discarded, from an empty lot?

Before I could explain, Miz Morales grinned wide. "Looks good on you."

WIRELESS CONNECTION

*U*ncle D had managed to doze through Sunday services without flaming into a human torch, so I suspected I could safely return to my home church or hit Mass with the Moraleses. But instead, because of my "mild flu," both morning services and my afternoon "study date" with Clyde and Aimee had been nixed, and I'd spent most of the day alone in Kieren's bedroom, researching.

I'd settled on the white Berber carpet—beneath the window against the far wall—so the back of my open laptop faced the door, just in case someone with Wolf vision strolled in.

I'd wasted quality time online reading up on anemia, catalepsy, porphyria, HIV, hepatitis, Ebola, bubonic plague, and the effects of smoking on blood pressure. Then there was the folklore about bites to various body parts, burial practices, and the dangers of the dead being leaped over by a black hen. Searching *buy blood,* I found a handful of posts on fish bait and a few more by "living vampires" (human wannabes), most of which suggested making friends with the local butcher.

So far, the only thing all my reading had accomplished was to heighten my appetite. I hadn't had a blood fix since Friday, and a YouTube video of chumming for sharks actually made me salivate.

Checking my phone, I found a text from Dr. Morales, saying the family would be home after brunch with Sergio and Raúl on Lake Travis and asking if I wanted them to bring me home a snack. I passed, but replied that I was feeling better.

Mindful of the dogs barking outside, I resolved to thaw something juicy from the freezer well before the Moraleses got back and then returned my attention to research.

Just ten more minutes. Surely, I could concentrate for that long.

"Bradley Sanguini" had been a stage name. My former chef had gone by Henry Johnson when we'd first met. I keyed that in, trying to replicate a search Kieren had done.

On Sanguini's opening night, he'd confronted me with a printed list of Web links—some leading to articles that dated back to the 1920s—all attributed to Henry Johnson. I hadn't taken my Wolf man seriously. Forty-eight hours later, I was undead.

Today a handful of sites pulled up, but *The Gothic Gourmet* listed "Beyond Sashimi and Tartare: Culinary Expressions of Neovampirism" as "no longer available," and both *Eternal Elegance* magazine and *Underworld Business Monthly* required registration. *Demonic Digest* offered only a preview of Brad's article.

HEARTS AT STAKE: GENDER POLITICS ARISING POST VAMPYRIC INFECTION

by Henry Johnson

Though an unholy union, the relationship between an established eternal and his neophyte consort mirrors that of traditional human marriages in matters of dominance, fiscal responsibility, and daily management as well as the setting of sexual expectations.

"Miss me?" a masculine voice whispered over the air-conditioning.

I stiffened, certain I was alone in the room.

The dogs! From outside in the backyard, the mama shepherd sounded wild, barking and snarling. What had set her off?

Moving the laptop aside, I turned, rising on my knees to peer out the window at the sprawling live oak and surrounding historic neighborhood.

Nothing. God, my whole ordeal with Bradley had made me crazy, paranoid.

Then a fist popped up to knock on the window, and I screamed.

Blood Sisters

*C*lyde raised his head into view and screamed, too. Then he glared at me and yanked Aimee up beside him on the massive tree branch.

Glad I didn't have enough blood in my system to blush, I raised the window.

"Little jumpy?" Aimee asked, falling forward onto the carpet.

Climbing in after her, Clyde looked like hell. His lower lip was split and swollen, his cheek and jaw bruised.

"What happened?" I whispered, though the Moraleses weren't home yet.

Staring at the largely emptied room, the Possum waved me off. "I heal fast."

"A werewolf slugged him," Aimee explained, sitting up.

Clyde limped to the desk chair, and with his injuries, I wondered how he'd made it up the tree. "Kieren wasn't the only trained Wolf scholar in Austin," he said.

I should've thought of that. The city had a loose-knit shifter community made up of runaways and the banished, plus a few werepeople who'd decided to, say, study architecture or business at the University of Texas.

Sinking to perch on the denim comforter, I prompted, "And?"

Clyde's claws sprouted, retracted. "Let's just say you shouldn't quiz a lone Wolf about vampirism if you haven't made up a really outstanding lie to explain why you need that information." He blew out a breath. "Mr. Accommodating wasn't impressed with 'uh' for an answer."

"You didn't find out anything?" I pressed.

"Nah," Clyde said. "I think I was barking up the wrong Wolf. I'd bet my tail that when it comes to decoding supernatural crap, Kieren's the alpha puppy in the Lone Star State. Or at least, he used to be."

"Yeah." I didn't know what else to say. But I couldn't help wondering, had Kieren left Texas altogether? Had he confided that much about his destination to Clyde?

God, I needed Kieren so much. Not only did I love him, but I needed him on a practical level. I was failing at the very thing he'd spent his whole life preparing to do.

I slipped a hand over my rumbling stomach, hoping the sophomores hadn't noticed. Hoping they didn't realize their arrival had further piqued my thirst.

I mentioned that the Moraleses weren't home yet.

"We didn't *have* to climb the tree?" Aimee exclaimed.

"Nice," Clyde said. "I'm going to grab some ice from the freezer for my lip."

"Any leads at the library?" I asked Aimee as he ambled out.

"Yes and no," she replied. "There was the usual victim blaming. Apparently, sinners, alcoholics, suicides, witches, sorcerers, seventh children, highwaymen, plague victims, and the unpopular are more likely to rise undead." She shrugged. "I did fill out a form for an interlibrary loan on an interesting-looking book published in the 1860s by some Hungarian professor. But it'll take at least six weeks for it to come in. Then we'd have to find a translator."

We didn't have six weeks. We had, damn, less than three. It wouldn't help to whine about it, though. Nope,

I was the one in charge. I had to maintain the morale of the home team. Speaking of which . . . "What's wrong?"

Aimee had begun quietly crying. "My cousin and I—she's a food critic for *Tejano Food Life,* we hit the Sanguini's launch party on Friday night. I only went because Travis was supposed to be working, and . . ."

Oh, God. "You ordered the chilled baby squirrels."

So that was it. Aimee was dying right here in front of me. She had been all along. And unlike the hundreds of other victims, she knew it.

"Brad may be a monster, but his honey cream sauce . . ." Aimee wiped her eyes, smearing the heavy black liner. "I practically licked the plate clean."

SELF-SUFFICIENT

I'd felt too self-conscious to defrost the chicken legs in front of Clyde and Aimee, and then, just as the sophomores were leaving, the Moraleses had returned home.

At midnight, in desperation, I jumped from Kieren's window to the front yard, ran to Sanguini's, let myself into the kitchen, and opened the fridge—empty.

Sergio must've cleared it out earlier that day.

Damn. No more blood wine. No more crutch.

Fearful of what might happen if I came across a potential victim, I quickly returned to the Moraleses' house. No way could I start The Banana without waking up Meara, but after dawn, I would drive to the nearest twenty-four-hour grocery store.

At 4:30 A.M., I paced nude on the white Berber carpet, my bare skin prickling in the darkness. My stomach clenched. My throat felt as if I'd swallowed sawdust.

Just down the hall—one door, two—Meghan would be so defenseless. No.

What about the dogs outside? At Kieren's window, my fingernails extended, *tap, tap,* tapping the glass. Hide the bite in the fur, and who would see? I didn't have to take it all. I could stop. Drink the mama German shepherd. Save the puppies. No.

Escape. Quick, out the window, down the tree! Go night-crawling. Why had I come back to the house? How long could it take to find a homeless person? Might as well put them out of their misery. Why should Mitch have all the . . . No.

I glanced at my backpack, remembering the two small bottles of holy water, tucked inside its zippered pockets. Morning would be better. It would. Heaven's light shining high in the sky, even if it'd never shine for me.

I could last a few hours. Try to rest. Yes, sleep would solve everything.

In the upstairs bathroom, I grabbed a full bottle of NyQuil from the medicine cabinet and chugged it down. Then I shut myself in Kieren's closet, a hand gripping the handle of each plastic jug of blessed water.

A breath before sunrise, I sank my fangs, deep and eager, into my own thigh.

"THE LOTTERY"

I found Aimee in the sophomore hall. There was a KEEP AUSTIN BATTY bumper sticker displayed at an angle on her locker. "Hey, how're you doing?"

For so long, it had been just me and Kieren. I didn't know how to act around a new friend, especially one facing this particular nightmare.

"I didn't mean to freak out on you yesterday," she replied. "You're under enough pressure, and I know you're trying hard to fix everything so I don't . . ."

"I won't give up," I promised, trying to project confidence. "We'll find a cure."

"Well," Aimee said, "even if we don't, maybe it's not all bad. Look at you. You're okay, aren't you? You seem totally normal to me."

My thigh still smarted, though the puncture wounds had almost immediately scabbed over, and I'd learned better than to push my luck—or anyone else's—again. Feeding on my own blood had sated my appetite, but I couldn't get by that way indefinitely. "I won't give up," I said again.

Later, after English let out, I handed in my essay on "The Lottery" and checked it off my to-do list in Frank.

Mrs. Levy jotted today's date on my paper. "What did you think of the story?"

"Heinous," I said. "Awful. Stupid. Ridiculous. Hated it."

She glanced up. "I sense a thesis statement."

"Some poor woman's name is drawn, and so her friends and family—"

"Even little Davy Hutchinson," Mrs. Levy said.

"Yes, her own child helps to stone her to death." I reconsidered that. "Or at least someone in the chipper, folksy, yet psychotic mob offered him a few pebbles."

"It's a harvest ritual," Mrs. Levy reminded me.

I snapped my planner book closed. "So what—they're going to use her decomposing body as fertilizer?"

"It's tradition," Mrs. Levy explained. "Their society is built—"

"But Mrs. Adams says that some towns have already called it quits, and Mr. Adams says that the north village is talking about doing the same. Besides, it's intrinsically wrong. Incredibly, obviously wrong."

"Perhaps it's not so obvious to the villagers," Mrs. Levy countered, playing with the wooden apple paperweight on her desk.

"So, this innocent woman has to die just because it's all they know? What a sucky, pointless ending! Why did Jackson write such a depressing story, anyway?"

"But is it a pointless ending," Mrs. Levy asked, leaning forward, "if it makes you feel, if it makes you think?"

"Ask Tessie Hutchinson," I replied.

MONSTERQUEST

*F*rom the office laptop, I studied a live shot—transmitted via new security cameras—of the four finalists for Sanguini's "vampire" chef position.

"You're looking at the most qualified," Sergio said from across the manager's desk, "and the least egomaniacal. Well, you know, by the chef standard."

Not a scary-looking bunch. But when I'd first met Brad, he'd dressed like a Bubbaville 'kicker. He'd tricked me into thinking he'd needed my help to make him over into a dapper and convincing pretend monster when he'd been a real one all along.

It didn't give me a lot of faith in my ability to judge character.

"What about a private detective?" I asked. "Not for all the finalists. But to check out the new chef, you know, during his six-month probationary period."

"Six-month . . . ?" Sergio shook his head. "Listen, lamb chop, I've explained to all of them that, despite your age, you are ultimately the legal owner of the restaurant and that you grew up in the business. I also explained that this isn't a hobby or a phase that you're going through. But, Quincie, you're still dealing with grown-up professionals here. You have to show some respect."

He was right. I knew he was right. But I didn't like it.

"I thought we agreed that Nora Woodworth doesn't have the right vibe," I said.

The job included wooing the hearts and, to be candid, the libidos of the diners. Where most chefs stayed in the kitchen, ours made a grand entrance each night and led the crowd in a toast. I was looking for what I thought of as a swoon factor.

"I mean, she's adorable for her—"

"Quincie." Sergio flicked his graying ponytail over his shoulder. "There are laws against age discrimination."

"Fine." I raised my burnt-orange sports bottle in surrender, appreciative of the fact that Sergio was too old-school to go over my head to the Moraleses. "I'm going to refresh my drink in the kitchen, and then you can send back the first one."

My skin felt tight, my temper short. Later, after Sergio went home, I'd defrost some meat from the freezer, start committing to animal blood.

For the moment, though, the quick fix I'd had from drinking my own had worn off, and all I had to make due with was the plain old house Chianti.

I ruled out the clean-cut candidate after he made a passing comment about his "baby face" because that's an expression people had used to describe Uncle D.

I ruled out the guy with the nose ring when he began waxing poetic about Sanguini's "midcentury" brick building because Brad was an architecture geek.

I ruled out the guy with the hard-to-pin-down accent because of his movie-star-white teeth. Dental hygiene was one thing, but I'd had enough of the dentally obsessed.

Standing in the doorway of what really was his office, Sergio glanced at his watch. "You axed three candidates within forty-eight minutes. We have only one left, and I know you have qualms about Mrs. Woodworth."

A Certain Edge

*D*aggio would've fallen hard for Nora. He had an eye for quality women, prioritized his stomach, and always said you couldn't trust a skinny chef. Plus, they would've shared a complex and layered relationship with butter.

"You've seen our menus?" I asked.

Sanguini's offered two, one for guests who self-identified as "prey" and one for guests who self-identified as "predator."

The prey menu celebrated vegetarian Italian staples—portobello mushroom pâté; mozzarella, gorgonzola, and parmesan ravioli in wild mushroom sauce; eggplant parmesan; and so forth.

The predator menu catered to the most bloodthirsty of carnivores with such meaty dishes as veal tartare; breaded pig's feet in Merlot and onion cream sauce with fettuccine Alfredo; blood and tongue sausages with new potatoes; rice pudding blood cakes; and of course the infamous chilled baby squirrels, simmered in orange brandy, bathed in honey cream sauce. Brad's weapon of choice.

"I don't have the recipes, but the kitchen staff—"

"Don't you fret," Nora said, "I can whip up anything edible from *unagi* to rhubarb pie. But . . ." She adjusted her rose-patterned shawl. "It's not my place to quarrel with the judgment of your previous chef, this Bradley—"

"Quarrel away," I replied, making a note to turn down the air-conditioning.

Nora folded her hands in her lap. "I'll create menus of my own."

I wrote that down in Frank. "Of course the new chef would be welcome to bring his or her own style to Sanguini's, so long as it meshed with the theme." I'd practiced that line ahead of time. "But my staff is counting on our reopening on Friday night, and the freezer is stuffed with frozen squirrel—"

"I work with fresh meat only," Nora informed me. "If budget is an issue, young lady, I'll be glad to make a financial contribution to the cause. As it happens, I left my last position with a generous severance package."

Oh. Well. I had no idea what to say to that. Hold it! Did she just "young lady" me? Oh, my God, she did! "But it can take weeks," I argued, "months even, to develop a signature menu; the critics will be out for blood, and Friday . . ."

Nora reached into her purse and slid two pieces of paper across my desk.

"Scorpions?" I exclaimed. "They're poisonous!"

"I'll take out the stingers," Nora assured me.

"What about the rattlesnake?"

"Fang free. We're just talking about the meat, though I'm contemplating the idea of using the rattles as garnish. As for the tiramisù, I kept that in play for the risk averse."

How considerate. Studying the proposed menus, I tuned her out for a moment. On the prey, I almost protested the garlic, but on second thought, it seemed only fair to give the hunted a fighting chance. On the predator, I couldn't decide who the dove dish would upset more: left-wing peaceniks or right-wing devotees of Noah's ark.

"How 'bout I meet Sergio here tomorrow morning,"

Nora went on, "and we'll look forward to you joining us later for a tasting? Today I'll settle for a tour —"

"Whoa. Wait." Had I agreed to hire her? I liked her. Sergio liked her. But Sanguini's was dangerous. I was dangerous. Not to mention the God-only-knew-how-many employees nearing their pre-preternatural mood swings. And Bradley, who's to say he wouldn't mist in some night, demanding "his" kitchen back?

Was Nora dangerous? Could she even fake dangerous? I didn't think so, and I didn't want anything awful to happen to her. She struck me as someone who'd led a calm, wholesome life.

"I'm sure you're an outstanding chef, and your proposed menus scream 'Sanguini's.' But, um, this particular position involves more than cooking and running the kitchen. The chef is an attraction per se."

Nora reached for my sports bottle of Chianti and took off the top.

"You see, it takes a certain persona, a certain edge . . ." Damn, Sergio had been right. If I didn't learn when to shut my mouth, we'd get sued. "To lead our guests in the midnight toast and convey a . . . Excuse me, what are you doing?"

Nora had taken a four-inch-long plastic vial of dark red liquid out of her large quilted purse and was unscrewing the cap. At the scent of blood, my gums contracted.

❧ Sanguini's ❧

A Very Rare Restaurant

Prey Menu

(select one in each category below)

antipasto

gorgonzola and a selection of Italian olives

roasted garlic with Italian bread and a tasting of olive oils

primo

linguini *l'autumno*
with *romanesco* broccoli, carrots, and sweet corn

wilted wild mushroom soup

secondo

eggplant with sun-dried tomato tarts

baked tomatoes and bell peppers
stuffed with risotto and mozzarella

contorno

asparagus with drizzled basil-seaweed pesto

cabbage leaves
stuffed with mushrooms, wild rice, and leeks

dolce

brandied peaches flambé
over French vanilla ice cream

tiramisù

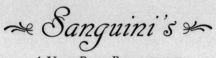

⚜ Sanguini's ⚜

A VERY RARE RESTAURANT

PREDATOR MENU
(select one in each category below)

antipasto

CARNIVORE TASTER:
wild-boar prosciutto, venison blood sausage, duck-liver pâté

wasabi deviled quail eggs

primo

West Texas rattlesnake ravioli marinara

cognac-cream fettuccine Alfredo
with broiled alligator and pine nuts

secondo

three little javelina chops
with rosemary and olives

spit-roasted white-winged dove
stuffed with walnuts, served with olive-leaf garnish

contorno

Chianti-marinated wild mushrooms
sautéed with mesquite-smoked bacon and artichoke hearts

lamb's liver
with parsley, asparagus, and button mushrooms

dolce

kumquat sherbet with frozen eyes of newt
garnished with a newt-shaped butter cookie

THE RENFIELD SPECIAL:
chocolate-covered crickets and scorpions with assorted biscotti

"Pig juice," she informed me, pouring a good two shots into my wine and swirling it around before handing back the sports bottle. "You're looking parched, hon, and, if you'll forgive me for saying so, that's never a safety-first situation when dealing with eternals."

"Eternals?" I asked, reaching—despite myself—to drink.

"Vampires," she explained as if it were business as usual.

BUSINESS AS USUAL

*A*s I toured Nora around the restaurant—she didn't so much as blink at the boar heads or baby squirrels in the freezer—she explained that her previous employer had been undead (though she insisted on using the word *eternal*).

"But why would a vampire need a personal chef?" I asked, carrying my bottle with me. "I can't keep any solids down, and it's been a total nightmare trying to pass —"

"It takes practice to build up a tolerance," Nora told me. "Start small—fruits, berries, Jell-O. They're mostly liquid."

"Really?" When she nodded, I almost hugged her. Not being able to eat wasn't just a social and logistical dilemma. I missed it.

I'd been craving habanera-stuffed olives for days.

Nora glanced at my sports bottle. "You're already acquainted with the grape."

I blushed, busted. Something about her acknowledging what I was, being so apparently comfortable with it, made me feel more like my old self again.

Nora added that she'd cooked regularly for a sizable household staff and her employer's "bleeding stock," whatever that meant. Apparently, it totaled out to more than a full restaurant seating, and for the most part, she'd pulled that off daily for years and without any kitchen help to speak of. Incredible.

"As for this midnight-toast business," Nora went on, opening the refrigerator to case it for future use. "I have no interest in it. But you should have received a résumé from a fellow named Freddy for the manager's position. He's a personal friend and a gentleman of some resources." I was about to inform her that we'd already filled that job, when she added, "The role of vampire chef might . . . amuse him. It doesn't have to be the actual chef handling the part, does it? I mean, wouldn't any human chef be sweaty and frazzled from supervising the kitchen all night?"

"I guess not," I said, clutching Frank for support. "I mean, I guess so."

It wasn't a bad idea, splitting the real and pretend chef jobs. It occurred to me, too, that if Vaggio hadn't been murdered, playing the part—tailored suit, formal cape, devastating cheekbones—would've been beyond him. Well, the cheekbones, anyway. He probably would've enjoyed the show.

Maybe this Freddy could audition. If he worked out, Mama's restaurant would be up and running, and I could devote my full attention to saving the infected.

"Are you positive you want this gig?" I pressed Nora. "I understand that you've been a chef at a sizable private estate. You've done large-scale parties, catering, and other possibly creepy stuff." I wasn't sure I even wanted to know. "But restaurant work can be beastly, and Sanguini's . . ."

Nora held out her wrist to me. "Feel my pulse. Go ahead. It's there." When I hesitated, she added, "I'm not afraid."

I felt for the beat and, after a moment, found it, steady and strong. I appreciated that she trusted me, but on second thought, could I trust her? Or was Nora Woodworth too good to be true? Too comforting, too confident, too savvy about the supernatural?

"I've got my own suppliers for the meat," she declared, not missing a beat, "but I'll need fresh produce." Nora narrowed her eyes. "Now, where's the local farmer's market, and what're the going rates for bribes in this town?"

REALITY CHECK

*I*t occurred to me during Econ that the *tasting* part of Nora's scheduled tasting might be an issue. I remembered Bradley cooking at Sanguini's stove, sampling dishes and spitting out the food. I recalled thinking how gross that was, but it hadn't tipped me off that he was a vampire.

Anyway, I could manage the mushroom soup, maybe the ice cream and sherbet, the olive oils, the pesto, the cognac cream. Forget the pâté. As a human being, I'd adored the vegetarian stuff, but duck-liver pâté? Yuck.

I was intrigued, though, by the quail eggs, the lamb's liver, less so the newt eyes.

Maybe if I took teeny bites, spit the solids into a napkin . . .

Forget it. I needed backup—stat.

After Chem, I had the halls to myself. Everyone else was in class or at lunch. So I ducked into a girls' bathroom and texted Clyde and Aimee, asking them to meet me after school to go to Sanguini's. As soon as I sent the message, my phone vibrated.

"Quincie Morris?"

"Who's this?" I demanded. Hardly anybody outside Sergio and the Moraleses had my cell number.

"We're seeking information on Henry Johnson, also known as Bradley Sanguini. Do you know his whereabouts?"

My grip tightened. "No. Who are—?"

The call died.

I hit Detective Zaleski's number on my speed dial, then filled him in on last week's mystery calls at the restaurant and today's on my cell. "It could've been the same guy. I don't know. We don't have caller ID at the restaurant."

"Be careful," the detective warned me. "Any associates of Brad's could be undead themselves, and this side of hell there's no more unpredictable or depraved form of evil than a vampire."

"Yeah," I replied, staring in the mirror at my own vaguely translucent reflection. "I keep hearing that."

I logged a few hours of homework in the school library, and then Clyde and Aimee met me at The Banana. They'd already put the top down.

Today the Possum's lip had healed up, and his bruises had almost completely faded. Aimee's blond hair had been colored a faded royal blue (like she'd changed her mind and tried to wash it out), which looked purplish striped where the pink had been.

The back of her head was cradled in her laced fingers as she leaned back in the convertible. Her ankles, each tattooed with a tiny skull, were crossed and rested on top of the driver's seat.

As I walked up, she said, "I thought sunlight made vampires go *poof.*"

"This isn't a movie," I replied, lightly knocking her feet down.

At least with these two and now Nora, I didn't have to hide who I was. I wondered, not for the first time, if Kieren was happier with the pack, where he could just revel in being a Wolf, or if he missed me as much as I did him.

As we exited the parking lot, I explained to Aimee

and Clyde that I needed their input on Nora's cooking. "Plus, we finally have a real lead. Her previous boss was a vampire, and she could recognize me as one. Only she used the word *eternal* and —"

"Whoa," Clyde interrupted. "You're trying to tell us that, after Sanguini's first chef was *murdered* by vampires and its second chef *was* a vampire, its third chef has a history of *working* for vampires, and that's supposed to be a good thing?"

"News flash," I countered, glancing back at Aimee's pained expression. "*You* work for a vampire." I hit the turn signal. "Don't get me wrong. I'm being careful. I've been fooled enough. But Nora may know something that can help us."

In the front passenger seat, the Possum made a show of rolling his beady eyes.

"Damn it, Clyde!" I exclaimed. "She at least . . ."

"She at least what?" Aimee prompted.

Accelerating past a bicyclist, I said, "She knows a hell of a lot more about what I've become than I do."

The "Vampire" Chef

The kitchen smelled of marinara and garlic, wasabi and peppers, bacon and chocolate. Tiny bowls of pine nuts, olives, basil, rosemary, parsley, and newt eyes (on ice) littered the counter. Nora bent in front of the open oven, checking the javelina chops.

After I introduced Clyde and Aimee as our dishwashers and taste testers, the Possum made a beeline for the jars of live crickets and scorpions.

"Child," Nora exclaimed, offering her hand to Aimee, "I love your hair!" Then the chef fetched me a refreshed sports bottle of pig's blood from the fridge and announced that, from now on, we'd be serving a new house Chianti with the predator dishes and a Pinot Grigio with the prey. "Underage diners," she added with a meaningful look at me, "will be offered Italian sparkling water or cranberry herbal tea."

After pouring each of the sophomores sample glasses, Nora shooed them out, declaring that the tasting would begin in ten minutes in the private dining room.

I lingered in the kitchen, drinking blood from the sports bottle as Nora bustled around—stirring the soup, taking the Italian bread out of the oven.

Opening my day planner, I tried to think of a graceful way to broach the subject. Then I decided there wasn't one. "Once a human has consumed vampire blood, is there any way to stop the transformation?"

Nora glanced up. "I take it this isn't a hypothetical question."

I shrugged. "It may sound strange coming from me."

"Not really. Most neophytes struggle with 'soul sickness,' as they call it, regrets, even those who ask to be elevated. Who did you bless?"

"Bless?"

"Infect," she clarified, setting down the pan. "Curse with your blood."

My pen slipped through my fingers. "No, I wouldn't. The guy that did this to me, he also did it to others."

Understatement. "I'm trying to help them before it's too late."

Nora washed her hands and began arranging prosciutto in rose formations. "I'm afraid that a dose of eternal blood—be it down the throat or into a vein—is an undeath sentence." She cocked her head. "Now that you mention it, though . . ."

I gave her a moment to gather her thoughts.

"I'm no expert," she admitted, "but clearly vampirism is outside the natural order. If you could remove the demonic magic that triggers the transformation, I suppose the scales might tip back in favor of the living."

"That's it?" I asked. "All I have to do is find a way to break the spell?"

"In theory. And before the victims die. But that's going to be pricklier than it sounds. Remember, we're talking about a vicious and malignant enchantment—nothing on the magnitude of what created Dracula Prime, but still, fierce."

Kieren's notes had referenced the count under MYTHS, nothing to worry about. But Nora had spoken with such conviction that I felt stupid asking. "Dracula who?"

"Prime. Drac One. The eternal villain in Stoker's novel." At my blank expression, she added, "The book is loosely based on truth. You really didn't know?"

* * *

Taking my planner and sports bottle, I joined Aimee and Clyde in Sanguini's private dining room. With its wall sconces, crystal chandelier, painted "castle" rock walls, and midnight-blue carpeting, the room's décor matched the rest of the restaurant. From hidden speakers, Sinatra sang, "That's Life."

Nora followed, carrying an appetizer tray. She set the roasted garlic on the far side of the table from where I was seated, the gorgonzola and Italian olives close by.

I popped an olive in my mouth, very firmly telling myself that I wasn't nauseated. Meanwhile, Aimee spread her duck-liver pâté onto sliced blood sausage as Clyde scooped a tiny quail egg into his mouth.

A moment later, as Aimee began cooing over the food, the Opossum's eyes bugged and he spat the egg back out. Then he grabbed his sparkling water and chugged.

"Mind the wasabi," Nora warned too late.

"Smell this, Quincie," Aimee exclaimed, mopping olive oil with a hunk of fresh-baked bread. "It's carb heaven."

I grinned and told the chef, "I'm digging the Sinatra. We could start with Frankie and later in the evening switch to —"

"Pavarotti," she finished for me.

Kismet. And cheesy, totally obvious, but I didn't care. It was Italian, fun, and most important, not what Brad would have done. Nora brought a new energy to Sanguini's. I only hoped she was what she seemed.

While I lingered over the woody mushroom soup, Aimee grazed across menus and courses from the eggplant on the prey to the sherbet on the predator. It occurred to me that maybe she was eating well while she still could eat at all.

Clyde avoided most of the meat until the Renfield special, at which point he asked if he could polish off the jar of live crickets.

Nora excused herself to fetch it for him.

I said, "Please tell me that's a Possum thing."

Moments later, Nora returned with both the insects and Sergio, who spread his arms wide and asked, "Ready to meet Sanguini's new vampire chef?"

I reminded myself that he hadn't been talking about Bradley. So far, the vampire had kept his word, left me alone. All week, I'd been on the lookout for any sign of him or his precious beige SUV, and nada. Despite the horrendous ongoing fallout from his time here, maybe I'd seen the last of Brad himself. In any case, it was time to give a new Chef Sanguini a chance. I forced a smile and nodded.

An elegant fortyish man—he had to be Freddy— parted the crimson velvet curtains and strolled in, holding a glass of what I hoped was Chianti. He had short, bleached hair and modeled a black single-breasted silk suit, white silk shirt, and black patent loafers. Plus, red contacts and fake fangs, both high dollar and almost too convincing. "Good evening," he said in a voice equal parts irony and menace. "I bid you welcome, my children of the night."

"Nice to meet you," I said. "But maybe dial it down a notch or three. You're supposed to be a vampire chef, not vampire royalty."

Freddy broke form, laughing. "Can't enthrall 'em all." Setting his wineglass on the table, he raised my hand to kiss it. "You must be the legendary Quincie P. Morris."

"Oh, please," Clyde said, crunching another bug.

But Aimee grinned when Freddy bent to kiss her hand, too.

"Poseur." Who said that? No one else seemed to have heard it. Had my imagination kicked into overdrive? Or had it been something more insidious, a symptom of the insanity that Miz Morales had said came with vampirism?

As I got ahold of myself, Freddy presented me with a doctor's note confirming a physical he'd taken that morning. "In case you have any unanswered questions."

Then, as fearless as Nora, he offered his wrist so I could confirm his only slightly elevated pulse.

GUARDIANS

*S*anguini's," I said into the manager's office phone. "This is Quincie."

"Detective Zaleski here. Listen, a young couple—a man and a woman, good-looking, twenty-something, dressed in business suits—have been asking around about Brad. They come off like feds. They're working the antique shops, the Fourth Street and Sixth Street bars. They went on a historical society tour of Hyde Park. I've already talked to your bouncers, but can you alert the staff to keep an eye out for them, too?"

"Sure," I said, taking notes. "Have there been any new victims?" When he hesitated, I added, "Really, I need to know."

Zaleski cleared his throat. "No, but I have flagged a couple of new missing-persons cases. Do us both a favor and stay sharp."

Then he informed me that the number of the mystery caller—the one I'd fielded on my cell phone in the high-school girls' bathroom—had been a dead end.

Nora slid a mug of porcine blood into the microwave to warm for a few seconds. (We'd decided that *porcine* sounded more appetizing than *pig*.) She'd spread out the *Capital City News* on the counter and had been circling various classified ads for rental homes. "A friend of yours came by this morning. Mitch."

Oh, God. "Are you . . . ?"

"Fine, fine," she said. "He just stared at me a moment and then asked to see you. I explained that you weren't here and offered him a full bottle of porcine blood." Nora handed me the mug. "I didn't think you'd mind."

I didn't, but something else was bothering me. "You could tell what he was, like you could tell what I was." I took a sip. It tasted better heated. "How exactly?"

"Well, when I said you weren't available, his incisors came down—big tip-off."

Okay. "But when we first met—"

The interrupting knock was sharp, forceful. Nora and I exchanged a glance. We'd had a security camera installed out back, but I hadn't thought to boot the laptop. Sloppy.

"We might look into a com system," she said.

"Not a bad idea . . ." Motioning for her to stand behind me, I opened the door.

A UPS driver, holding a clipboard, stood there with a huge box.

"Careful, miss," he said when I reached for it. "That's . . ."

I heaved the box onto my shoulder, and a few quick steps later, deposited it on a stainless-steel counter.

". . . mighty heavy."

Nora offered the delivery guy an apologetic smile and shut the door in his face. "What's all that?"

I ripped open the box and began unpacking the supplies I'd ordered—garlic, holy water and wafers, crosses, wooden stakes, knives . . .

The three of us—me and the sophomores—met at a quarter past nine by the lighted tennis court at the neighborhood park. According to everything I'd just read at the public library, midnight would've been a more powerful time. But unless we were working, both Aimee and I were supposed to be home by 10 P.M. on school nights.

I'd spent much of the evening—online and off—researching how to break a spell, curse, jinx, or hex. "You brought the stuff?"

Clyde lifted his cloth tote bag so I could see the herb store logo on it.

"I still think we should hire a wizard," he said.

"You got a copy of the Hogwarts alumni directory?" Aimee joked. She was trying too hard to hide her anxiety, at least while Clyde was around.

"We have no idea how to find a legitimate wizard or sorcerer," I said. "Assuming, in either case, that there is such a thing."

I'd briefly considered trying a cleansing spell, using oils, incense, candles, crystals, or an over-the-counter air purifier, for that matter. But it wasn't Sanguini's . . . it wasn't the *place* that had been infected, afflicted; it was *people,* like Aimee, who'd dined there. A reversal spell—sending the malevolent magic back to Brad—probably wouldn't work, since he was already undead. Plus, every article, book, and online how-to warned that those babies—reversal spells—could come back to bite you in the karmic butt. So a hex-removal spell it was. Maybe there were other options, better options, but hell, I'd only been studying witchcraft since about 5:30 P.M.

As we strolled through the picnic area, Clyde handed the tote to Aimee and announced that he'd forgotten something in the car.

While we waited for him to return, she settled across from me, cross-legged on the ground cover of wood chips in the play area. "Quincie, look!"

I tensed, ready to face the threat. But it was only a raccoon—make that three young raccoons—barreling into the trees. Adorable. "I think we crashed their play date."

Clyde jogged back with his iPod, a couple of small speakers, and a flat stone.

The general idea was that we would light a candle and imagine its flame or maybe the wax or both as the contaminating power of Brad's blood. Then we'd visualize that power disappearing as it burned down. And finally, we could toss whatever was left into the lake or bury it or something. I had two or three chants written down for good measure. One was even in English.

Reaching into the bag, Aimee withdrew a bloodred tea light. About the size of a half-dollar, maybe a quarter-inch thick. Black-cherry-scented. And set it on the stone.

Aimee struck a match and lit the wick.

Clyde hit PLAY on his iPod, and ambient New Age music filled the air—a mix of wood flute, chirping crickets, and hooting owls.

Aimee smirked. "Kumbaya."

The Possum opened his mouth to retort, but then his eyes widened and he pointed over my shoulder. "Fire!"

It took me a half second to realize he hadn't been talking about the tea-light flame. I glanced back at a blazing arch, maybe four feet long, splitting the darkness by the picnic area. I caught a glimpse of a tall, fair-haired male figure. Brad?

I *knew* we hadn't seen the last of him.

"The car," I ordered the sophomores. "Go, run!"

If Brad thought I'd spend eternity playing squeaky mouse to his kitty, then so help me, this time one of us wouldn't walk away. Remembering countless football games I'd watched with Kieren, I decided to just tackle the opposition. I poured on the speed, planting one foot on a bench seat to leap over two tables.

In midair, I spotted a red-eyed bloodsucker that I didn't recognize, totally ablaze, crawling in agony from behind a recycling bin. Looming over him, a stranger who—hang on—*wasn't* Brad wielded a flaming weapon, torch, something!

Oh, God, my target had been *battling* the vampire.

But I couldn't stop. I'd never before run or leaped at top preternatural speed, and, trying to slow down, I tripped in my new Nikes. "Look out!"

The vampire hunter (or whatever he was) sidestepped, dodging the full force of my blow, but I still knocked him off his feet, backward into the air. The flame died, and I glimpsed metal flying from his hand. He crashed into the chain-link fence surrounding the tennis court and fell to the ground, bleeding and unconscious.

Meanwhile, I landed hard, hitting my forehead on a stray tennis ball. Brushing myself off, I climbed to my feet and jogged to the fence.

The sophomores, who had ignored my order to vamoose, were weaving between the picnic tables toward me and the possibly heroic guy I'd just slammed into.

The Possum reached my side first. "Who . . . ?"

"Wow," Aimee breathed a few seconds later. "He's . . ."

"It was an accident," I whispered. "I didn't mean to kill him."

"Don't be hysterical," Clyde said, checking for a pulse. "Nobody's dead." He gestured toward the smoldering ash where the vampire had been. "At least nobody who wasn't dead in the first place."

Aimee asked, "Quincie, did you hit your head?"

That's when I saw the flashing lights of the police cars. Detectives Wertheimer and Zaleski burst out of an unmarked sedan, leading the charge in our direction.

"We're okay!" I shouted, stepping between the cops and my friends. "Don't shoot!" Not that I thought they would, but just in case.

Zaleski shouted for his officers to take five and stormed over. He looked even bigger and furrier outside at night than he had in my house. "What're you kids doing out here?" He pointed to my victim. "Who's that?"

"We think he might be a good guy," I said.

"He's breathing," Clyde added, standing. "Out cold, though."

Somebody radioed in for an ambulance while Zaleski explained that they'd gotten a call from a woman in Travis Heights who'd seen the fire from her rooftop deck. Then he questioned us about what had happened.

I didn't offer much in the way of details.

We'd noticed the fire and decided to investigate.

I'd seen a burning figure. Yes, it had fangs. Yes, I was sure.

Yes, I thought that the unidentified injured man had been fighting him. (I left out our collision.)

Yeah, the three of us "young people" had been fooling around with magic — "A protection spell," Aimee had blurted out.

Yes, we knew magic should be left to professionals and those for whom it was an integral part of their religious faith.

No, we didn't want to risk making it rain toads or bringing the swing set to life or turning Clyde into a heaping bucket of goldfish.

God, I hated being talked at by grown-ups.

Meanwhile, Wertheimer, on a hunt for evidence, found the black-cherry tea light, the pile of smoking ash, and a "very pretty" sword. Even from a distance, it gleamed.

No torch, though, which was weird. Where had the fire come from?

As EMTs strapped the mystery guy onto a gurney, I volunteered to ride with him to the hospital. I had questions of my own to ask. Besides, I owed him an apology, especially since it looked like he might've been defending us from a pal of Brad's.

Rare as vampires were reported to be, I seriously doubted that our all being at the park tonight was a coincidence.

"Not on your life," Zaleski declared. "You kids should be getting home."

"But—"

"Or, Miss Morris, I'm going to have a serious conversation with your new guardians about keeping better tabs on your whereabouts. Especially after dark."

Frederick —

*the Mantle of Dracul
Cordially Invites You to a Gala
in Honor of the Glorious Return of
Her Royal Majesty Sabine
from Her International Tour*

*Sunset
U.S. Midwest regional estate
Whitby Estates, Illinois*

STAY TUNED TO THE ETERNAL NEWS NETWORK
FOR AN OFFICIAL ANNOUNCEMENT
ON THE DATE OF HER MAJESTY'S ARRIVAL.

In the Red

_D_uring English, Detective Zaleski had left a message on my cell, saying that last night the unidentified man had disappeared from the hospital. Even weirder, his sword had apparently vanished from the police station.

"Keep an eye out, will ya? Don't get me wrong. Vigilante or not, he's not in any kind of trouble for taking out that vamp. We just want to chat . . . ask him a few questions . . . maybe try to talk him into applying to the training academy."

*　　*　　*

When I stopped by the school library after Chem, both copies of *Dracula* by Bram Stoker had been checked out.

"By Vice Principal Harding," the librarian whispered from behind her desk. Obviously, he wouldn't be bringing them back. "I'll put replacements on order," she added. "But if you're in a hurry, you might try the public library or the Web. A book that old is in the public domain. You can read it on the Internet."

After school, Miz Morales swung by Sanguini's on her way to meet with a chocolatier. From the break room, I heard Nora loudly greet her at the back door.

Appreciating the warning, I skedaddled to the restroom, dumped the blood from my mug into the sink, rinsed it, popped a breath mint, and zipped back to the floral sofa.

By the time Miz Morales walked in, my orange highlighter was perched over my Econ textbook. After exchanging howdys, she said, "Are you okay, Quincie? It seems like you're always at work. You study and take almost all of your meals here. . . ."

"That's how it's always been," I reminded her.

With a reluctant nod, Miz Morales changed the subject. "Nora mentioned that she's looking for a place to rent. And you know, your house is just sitting empty, costing money." At my questioning frown, she added, "Sorry, love. The restaurant renovation didn't come cheap, and just the expense of reprinting the menus . . . I'm afraid the insurance company is refusing to honor your uncle's life insurance policy."

"He had been technically dead for a while." I picked up my planner book from the coffee table, wishing I was in charge of my own finances. Then I glanced down at my Econ text and reconsidered.

"At least," Miz Morales assured me, "the company is being discreet. I'm sure that once Sanguini's is open regularly again, the books will look better, but —"

"You're going to rent out my house?"

"You can have a few days to get used to the idea."

"Will I be able to take your journal home with me this weekend?" Mrs. Levy asked after English class on Thursday.

I waited until the other students had left. "I can't think of anything to say."

"You can't?" Mrs. Levy leaned back in her chair. "Quincie, this is your journal. It's perfectly acceptable if you need to write about your uncle or Kieren. I just need to see some words on each page."

I did not want to have this conversation. "Kieren?"

"I get it," she said, tapping a pen. "You're not the kind of soggy girl who falls apart because the boy that she cares about suddenly isn't around anymore. You have your own life, your own goals, and other people who matter to you. That's good. It is. But you're still a person, and, well, not to pry, but anyone could see that you two . . ."

That we loved each other. Yeah. I already knew that.

DRESSED TO KILL

On Friday evening, vintage dresses—black and red, chiffon and velvet, satin and silk—hung from a freestanding brass coat hanger that Miz Morales had positioned in Kieren's room. Art Nouveau and gothic filigree costume jewelry lay artfully beside tassel teardrop hair sticks on the denim comforter. I picked up a headband with a small peacock feather attached.

"It's called a fascinator," Miz Morales informed me.

Good Catholic Wolf that she was, having spied me wearing Kieren's crucifix seemed to have quieted Meara's lingering suspicions. A few days earlier, I'd accepted her offer to help me augment my work wardrobe, and in classic wedding-planner mode, she'd eagerly taken off with my sizes and measurements.

Sanguini's wasn't merely a restaurant. It also doubled as a venue for the slinkiest, most glam gothic fashion show in the Southwest. Our seductively spooky hostess, Yanira, along with the waiters, bussers, and ladies and gentlemen of the bar, elevated an otherwise kitschy food-service concept to magnificent theater and cosplay.

Owner or not, I played a nightly role that might be best described as "catchall"—restocking the wait stations, cleaning spills, clearing tables, running food, replenishing hand towels and toilet paper. Not the most glitzy job, but I still had to look like I belonged.

Miz Morales had access to an endless array of eclectic stores and hefty discounts. Her choices for me were on the demure side, not that I minded. Not that I was about to emphasize to my maternal werewolf guardian that—after food and atmosphere—my restaurant's WMD was sex appeal. Of course she'd probably figured that out for herself.

I had to admit I was having fun. It wasn't so much

playing dress-up as doing it with Kieren's mama. I soaked up her affection, her approval.

Miz Morales held up an off-the-shoulder, sleeveless red velvet party dress with rhinestone buttons up the bodice, likely worn for a holiday wedding.

"I like it," I said. "The material's so heavy, though. I may turn into a sweat monster." That wasn't true. I'd noticed that neither heat nor cold bothered me as much as they used to, though I could sweat. But it had sounded like a human thing to say.

Around the coat hanger, I studied a black lace, empire-waist gown overlaid on a black silk slip. Lovely, but when I tried it on, the material bagged at my bust.

"I'll get that altered for tomorrow night," Miz Morales promised.

The last dress—a vintage black chiffon, fell an inch below the knees. The room didn't have a mirror, so neither I nor (luckily) Meara could check out my semitranslucent reflection. But I spun, delighted by how the skirt swirled around my legs.

I only wished Kieren could've seen me.

When I had been drunk on blood wine, my work wardrobe had skewed more toward the sleazy than sexy, and he'd made his feelings about that known. But tonight my ensemble suggested a sassy sophistication. Like the young woman I wanted to be.

"You look too innocent for Sanguini's," Miz Morales observed.

I grinned. "Not for long."

After showering, I blow-dried my hair straight and used an environmentally horrifying amount of hair spray to hold it in a swoosh shape down my back.

Then I slipped the black chiffon dress on, accenting it with the fascinator, earrings, a pair of sheer black thigh-highs, Kieren's crucifix, and my red cowboy boots.

Tucking the vial of holy water along the base of my bra, I called it done.

"Voilà!" I announced. "One spine-chilling Cinderella."

Meara had waited in the bedroom to coo over me, and for a moment, it felt sort of like having Mama back again. Certainly, I'd never played dress-up with Uncle D.

Roberto knocked on the bedroom door before peeking at my ensemble. "Wow," he said. "Who killed *The Lawrence Welk Show*?"

I had no idea what he was talking about.

EARTH ANGEL

*S*ergio led me down the hall to where most of Sanguini's staff had gathered in the dining room. He'd dressed in a black hooded cloak, complete with scythe.

"That's an ominous look for you," I said.

"I've never been management before," he replied.

As soon as we parted the crimson drapes, Mercedes and Simone pulled me into a comforting hug. Both were Fat Lorenzo's veterans, and they'd each left unreturned messages on my cell while the restaurant was closed.

"Oh, Quincie!" Mercedes exclaimed. "Are you all right?"

"Not that you have to talk about it," Simone added. They exchanged an uncertain glance. "I mean, you can if you want to, but you shouldn't feel like you have—"

"I'm okay—really." I'd heard from Sergio that the staff had been buzzing nonstop about Uncle D and Brad. I also suspected that Sergio had asked everyone to keep it out of my earshot, which was fine by me. "You two look amazing!"

Simone pivoted, showing off a crushed black velvet baby-doll mini with a chunky satin bow across the bust and fringe along the skirt line.

Mercedes, who'd streaked her dark brown hair a midnight orange, glanced down at her three-inch spiked boots like she already regretted them. Mercedes, the adventurous one who'd tried the chilled baby squirrels.

As Sergio launched into a welcoming pep talk, I scanned my eerie, come-hither-looking staff, counting five new unnatural hair colors—onyx, glittery navy, deep purple, bloodred, bone-white—a few new tattoos, a few new piercings.

Xio wore a silver corset and black slit skirt with finger-less silver gloves and fishnets. Yanira—also among the unknowing infected—modeled a long nude slip with a crimson netting overlay, accented by a sheer crimson scarf. By apparent agreement, the bussers wore leather on leather and the bar staff wore chains on leather.

Jamal had won Sergio's old job as expeditor, running the food from the kitchen to the dining room. But two of the new waiters had called in that day to quit—no notice.

After Sergio introduced Nora and Freddy, I stepped to the center of the small dance floor. I had no intention of interfering with Sergio as manager, but this I had to say for myself. "I just want to thank everyone for the cards and messages. Your love and prayers were appreciated. I'm sorry I haven't been great about getting back to you. We had to focus on reopening the restaurant ASAP. I hope y'all understand."

"That's what Vaggio would've wanted," Xio called.

And Mama, too, I thought as the staff burst into whoops, hollers, and applause. Forget Uncle D. Forget Bradley. I'd fret the future tomorrow. Tonight was ours!

Now and then, I'd catch sight of a tall, slender, fair-haired man and pause to make sure he wasn't Bradley. Sometimes it would take an extra beat because of the guests' makeup, because of the almost uniformly goth posturing. But no. Except for me, all the vampires here tonight seemed to be make-believe—at least for another two weeks.

By nine thirty, Ol' Blue Eyes was singing "Strangers in the Night," Sergio had ditched the flowing Grim Reaper robe to better navigate the tables, and I was running an order of spit-roasted doves to the bar. I grabbed three more tickets from Sebastian and strode — projecting calm — toward the kitchen.

Talk about an obstacle course! Many of the guests had gone to greater lengths with their wardrobes than the staff. I dodged an open bloodred umbrella, almost tripped over a raven-head cane, and nearly stumbled at the sight of a busty and bare-bellied Vampirella sporting red spandex wrapped around her torso like a slingshot.

As Xio rushed out with javelina chops, I called to Nora, "How goes it?"

"Catching up," she replied. "By the way, we donated the meat in the freezer to a local homeless shelter."

That made sense, and given that the squirrels had been delivered frozen and were never unwrapped, I wasn't worried that Bradley had had a chance to contaminate the leftovers. "Any sign of Mitch?"

"Not since Tuesday," Nora replied.

Three days ago. The media had been quiet. No new killings.

How was Mitch getting by?

*　*　*

Later, I scooped vanilla ice cream, topped it with brandied peaches, and, tray held high, scooted from the kitchen to the dining room.

All the tray tables had been snatched up, but I'd been running food since fifth grade. In the chaos, I decided to wing it. After blowing a quick kiss to Vaggio and Sergio's poker buddies, the Sunday Night Sinners, at table six, I grabbed a flame lighter from the wait station and stepped carefully around the thumping tail of a Seeing Eye dog resting beneath a nearby four-top.

The midnight-blue carpet, crimson velvet drapes, and black leather all helped for sound dampening, but the dinner crowd had still become loud, well lubricated, and guests had the annoying habit of straying from their seats.

Pivoting, I accidentally bumped into one of our massive bouncers. Olek Zaleski, or maybe it was Uri, was hauling away a wannabe Nosferatu in an off-white bodysuit that looked like something out of a black-and-white movie.

The crazed customer flailed his long, pointed fingernails, screaming, "Blasphemy! Blasphemer! You'll pay penance to the master!"

Backing around, I stepped to table nine, where two blue-haired women in their seventies were dining in full-length black gowns with high necks, long sleeves, and lace-trimmed cuffs and collars.

"Evening, ladies." Raising the flame to the first bowl of brandied peaches and ice cream, I noticed what looked like a real human finger bone—complete with a gold wedding band—mounted on red lace and pinned to a bodice.

"It's rude to stare," scolded the woman wearing the macabre brooch.

As the brandy caught fire, the Nosferatu broke free and barreled past me. One of his waving arms slapped my tray up, out of my control.

As the bouncer yelled, "Look out!" I angled to catch it, only to be accidentally knocked off balance by a guy I'd noticed earlier wearing a MY NAME WAS LESTAT name tag.

Falling to the carpet, I shut my eyes and flung my left arm over my head to try to protect myself. Once the flames hit my hyper-sprayed retro 'do, it would ignite like a torch. Now debuting on Sanguini's menu—vampire flambé.

But the impact never came. Instead, the crowd gasped, loud and awestruck, and then burst into applause. Mystified, I opened my eyes.

Standing above me was the young hunter from the neighborhood park—the one I'd sent flying into the chain-link fence and who'd slipped away from the hospital. He'd somehow caught my tray on his fingertips. "Nice crucifix," he said.

HELL SPAWN AND HEAVEN SENT

*W*ithout missing a beat, the personable stranger delivered the flaming desserts to the *Arsenic and Old Lace* grannies, who twittered at him. Then, as I smoothed my chiffon skirt over my knees, he handed the tray off to Jamal and offered me a hand up.

Back on my feet, I found myself confronted by piercing green eyes. A strong jaw and cheekbones, full lips that almost crossed the line to pretty. I'd guess twenty-two years old. Just over six feet tall in a silky white, long-sleeved shirt with a banded collar, black brushed suede pants, and black cowboy boots. He had a bandage over his temple where it had been scratched by the chain link.

The dining room was still at a virtual standstill. Gawkers peeked in from the foyer and bar. Somebody whistled, and Lestat whispered to his date, "Mount Olympus called. They want their Greek god back."

I focused on the newcomer. "What're you doing here?"

His gaze was cautiously friendly and like he was weighing me somehow. He let go of my hand. "I'm Zachary. I'm here about a job."

Sergio stepped between us and hired him on the spot.

Two minutes later, I'd dragged Sergio to the manager's office.

"Are you crazy?" I asked. "Who is this guy?" So much for my vow not to armchair-quarterback business decisions.

"Zachary is a good friend of Nora and Freddy's. He used to work with Nora in Chicago. Freddy called him tonight, saying that we were shorthanded, and asked if he could pitch in." Sergio slipped his cloak back on. "I forgot to mention it earlier."

"You forgot?" I was still stuck on the used-to-work-with-Nora part. In Chicago? For the vampire? But . . .

I'd assumed he was a hunter. At least it had looked that way in the park. "Don't you think he's too charismatic, too good-looking?"

Bam! Sergio brought the end of his scythe down hard on the concrete floor. "Lamb chop, Clark Gable was charismatic. Montgomery Clift was good-looking. We could auction off tickets to see this boy."

As Yani seated Zachary's first table—Lady Macbeth with three fellow Shakespearean-looking types I couldn't specifically ID—I moved to the trainee's side. I liked Freddy well enough and had begun to trust Nora's judgment, but Sanguini's was mine and no way would I just turn this rookie loose on the public unsupervised.

From just beyond the far side of the dance floor, I gestured toward his station. "That party, they'll be predators."

"You can tell just by looking?" Zachary asked.

I reached to adjust my fascinator headband. "Can't you?"

He pointed at a slender girl in a nouveau Gap dress, being escorted on a leash by a macho guy with a fondness for hair gel. "She's prey, right?"

"Don't even get me started on the Little Red Riding Hoods." Handing him a notepad and tray, I added, "You want to tell me what you were doing in the park? Or would you rather talk to Detective Zaleski at APD?"

"Did you *not* want me to save you and your friends from the vampire?" he countered, which pretty much put an end to that conversation.

For all of Zachary's mystery-man persona and splashy looks, the other night Clyde had confirmed a pulse, so he was probably still a living being. It also seemed obvious that if Nora knew what I was, Freddy and Zachary did, too.

I only hoped that the new hire restricted his hunting to *bad* vampires.

Zachary made a few newbie mistakes—confusing the Chianti-marinated wild mushrooms with the lamb's liver (which, granted, was served with mushrooms of a different variety), forgetting who'd ordered what at table ten, briefly hitting the weeds once his fourth party was seated.

Nobody complained. Zachary's tips were outrageous. He seemed good-naturedly resigned to all the attention, even when a petite dark-haired girl (who he later referred to as "a one-night lapse in judgment") slapped him hard across the face.

By midnight, five women, two men, a zombie of ambiguous gender, and a couple in their midfifties had all propositioned him, shamelessly and in front of me.

It was entertaining, watching the restaurant swoon. But frankly, I preferred my men with a little more hair on them.

*   *   *

Because of the distraction that was Zachary, I'd worried that Freddy's debut entrance as Chef Sanguini would be anticlimactic. I shouldn't have.

It wasn't just the black silk suit and fake fangs. It was in the curl of Freddy's lip and the come-hither aggressiveness of his stride. He had a cynical edge that Zachary didn't. An impishness juxtaposed with high-brow breeding that Bradley could've only hoped for. Freddy projected nefarious charm and unapologetic regality.

He didn't prattle on. He didn't spout hypocrisy about entering freely or of one's own will. He raised his wineglass as if it were a challenge.

"Welcome to Sanguini's," Freddy began. "To the prey, I say, welcome to your last night among the living." He met my eyes. "To the predators, I say, welcome home."

Then Sergio fired up the instrumentals to "Nessun Dorma" on the speakers, and Freddy burst into song — gorgeous, *soaring* song — and brought down the house.

Swinging a heavy arm around my shoulders, Sergio leaned in. "We did good?"

I laughed and kissed his cheek. "We did terrific!"

A half hour or so later, a young woman in a navy suit flagged me from a nearby two-top. She had one of those (probably fake) artfully placed moles over her upper lip that supermodels referred to as a beauty mark. Her similarly dressed companion wore his light brown hair in an outdated mullet, much in the fashion of a '90s country pop star.

"May I help you?" I asked, realizing that they matched Detective Zaleski's description of the couple that had been asking around about Brad.

The woman gestured to Freddy. "That's not him, and he's not in the kitchen."

"Who?" I asked, already knowing the answer.

"Where's Bradley Sanguini?" her companion demanded, grabbing my hand.

And there it was: the lingering question.

What with my own superpowers, I didn't feel especially vulnerable. But I didn't appreciate the attitude, either. "Bradley Sanguini was make-believe. The individual who played that role is no longer employed here."

"Let go of her," Zachary said from behind me.

"This is why we have bouncers," I whispered, glancing over my shoulder. "The big, burly, hairy men — go fetch them."

Yanking my fingers free, I addressed the table in a grown-up voice that would've made Kieren proud. "Sanguini's strictly forbids any touching of the staff."

In fact, Sergio had instituted the policy earlier this evening because it had become a hassle trying to discourage guests from running their fingers through Zachary's hair.

Zachary himself had made no move toward the werebears. "Quincie, I think—"

"Excuse me," I said, turning. "You haven't even filled out a W-2 yet. Is this some kind of male ego thing? Do you have a problem with working for a teenage girl?"

"Me?" Zachary exclaimed. "Really, no. I'd happily pick up your dry cleaning if that's what it took to get the job done." His gaze flicked past me. "Oh, crap."

When I turned to look, the two-top had been abandoned. "Where'd they go?"

"They disappeared," Zachary replied, "literally."

More like dissolved into mist.

After tipping out the bussers and bar, I touched base with APD while Zachary grabbed a bowl of linguini, a loaf of Italian bread, and a glass of Pinot Grigio, and met me in the private dining room. "Did you know those two?" he asked. "The real vamps?"

"Never saw them before." I took a sip of porcine blood from my U.T. sports bottle and opened Frank to take notes. "You?"

Zachary speared some *romanesco* broccoli. "They were after . . . What was his name?"

"Brad," I replied, noticing he'd sidestepped the question. "Also a . . . you know."

"They didn't seem especially into you or the restaurant beyond that."

True. They had flagged *me* over, though. "You don't think we'll see them again?"

Zachary shrugged. "When it comes to your kind, I've learned not to assume."

Bristling at the *your kind,* I demanded, "How do you know what I am? How does Nora? And Freddy, does he know, too?"

"We're sort of in the business of knowing." Zachary twirled a forkful of linguini. "Don't get me wrong. Nora's a first-rate chef. You saw how well Freddy worked the crowd, and I'll try not to drop food on anyone. But it's fair to say we're tapped into the goings-on of the underworld."

"And cryptic answers?" I replied, writing it all down anyway.

Zachary didn't take the bait. "This Brad, he's the one who—"

"Killed me?" I suggested, though what he'd done was worse than that.

Zachary's voice softened. "Nora mentioned that you two weren't on good terms."

I had no intention of rehashing everything that had happened.

"And you don't associate with other vamps?" he added.

I shook my head. "Really, no."

Zachary seemed to consider that. He downed a few more forkfuls of pasta before gesturing at Frank. "They have electronic things that do that, you know."

"It was a gift from Kieren." I hated the catch in my voice. "You won't meet him. He, um, transferred to a prep school up north."

Zachary stared at me for a minute. "Yeah, I had someone who . . . transferred up, too. Now I just hear things. My friend Joshua, he keeps me posted on how she's doing."

Oh. Zachary was in love with someone, someone he'd lost, too.

For a while, we sat quietly together. I toyed with my dangly, red-drop earring. Zachary polished off his veggie linguini and a full loaf of Italian bread and washed it down with white wine. Then he ducked out, and I smiled when he returned with another full serving of the same meal. It reminded me of Kieren.

Zachary's voracious appetite, combined with his astonishing reflexes and the way he looked, meant he had to be some kind of shifter. A big Cat probably, given his height, grace, and build. The golden brown mane suggested a werelion. True, he had no shadow of a beard, no hair on the backs of his hands. But Ruby was a Cat of the Cougar-ish variety, and in human form, she hadn't been noticeably hirsute, either.

There was something he wasn't telling me. But Zachary had a quality (apart from the looks) that was irresistibly likable.

A moment later, he asked, "What is it, Quincie?"

"What is what?"

"The reason you're sitting here with me instead of hovering over cleanup."

"I do not hover." Actually, I did. "Well, now that you mention it, I saw what you did in the park the other night, and given that I'm—"

"I'm not hunting you," he said. "I'm here to help save your soul."

So that was the deal with the Chicagoans. Just what every undead teenage restaurateur needed—Jesus freaks! "And the vampire you torched, was he an atheist?"

"It wasn't like that. Protecting you and your friends was all that mattered. That vampire . . . his soul had eroded away a long time ago. There was nothing left to save."

SORCERY AND SECRECY

*Y*ou're sure you don't want lunch?" Miz Morales touched up her frosted plum lipstick. She had a rehearsal dinner in Round Top tonight and would be gone until late Sunday.

I'd only been living here for eleven days, but already, her leaving reminded me of when Daddy would go on trips to academic conferences and archaeological sites. The Morales house had started to feel like home for real.

"Quincie?" she prompted.

As Meghan squeezed yellow mustard onto her third chili-cheese dog, I replied, "Nora served up hearty leftovers last night after close."

"And you're still full?" Miz Morales pressed, twisting the lipstick tube closed.

"Pretty much." Not really.

She let it go. "Roberto will be here if you need anything. Well, he'll be glued to the U.T.–Tulane game, but you know . . . Next weekend we could go shopping—"

"Thing is," I said, trying not to hurt her feelings, "I don't want to redecorate Kieren's room. I miss his books." Leaning against the counter, I added, "Without them, it's like *he's* more gone somehow."

Miz Morales grabbed her purse. "Wolves have secrets—"

"I get that." I felt bad trying to manipulate her, but it's not like I was outright lying, and there were lives at stake. "But with those old texts . . . I don't even know how to read German or Latin or Tsalagi or Hindi. Really, Ye Olde English is beyond me. I miss the smell of the books, though."

"I know what you mean," she said in a gentler tone.

Miz Morales smoothed the cub's hair. "I have to go to work, but you can play with the dogs or watch football with Daddy, and Quincie will be here most of the day."

Meghan looked up at her. "Can I go to Didi's house? Or Ethan's? Or—?"

"How about you make this easy," her mama answered, "and stay here?"

Meghan glared at me and pushed her plate away. It was an impressive show of bravado, coming from someone so small.

My fault that she didn't feel safe in her own home.

"ALL SORTS OF QUEER DREAMS"

*A*fter Miz Morales drove off, I confirmed that the still-pouting Meghan had curled up on the white leather sofa in the great room and was watching superhero cartoons with her stuffed toy bunny, Otto. Then I made my way back upstairs to Kieren's room.

Nora had said that *Dracula* was loosely based on truth. The fact that Vice Principal Harding had checked out both copies from the school library only seemed to back her up. The Chicagoans might be religious loons, but that didn't mean they were totally off base.

Not that—given the arcane nature of Kieren's research books—I imagined that a well-known classic novel, available in most libraries and bookstores, held the key to undoing Brad's mass-infection effort. But it might be useful for background info.

In an Undead 101 sort of way.

I logged on to my laptop and found a searchable site with the text. First, I skimmed an accompanying article long enough to learn that the story had been written in letters, diary entries, newspaper articles, a ship's log, and something called a "phonograph diary." Then I started in on the novel myself, taking notes in Frank.

The story begins with Jonathan Harker, a young English lawyer. He's traveling from England to Castle Dracula in the Carpathian Mountains.

On one hand, he's organized and thorough in writing down the details of his trip—Mrs. Levy would award him an A for journal entries.

On the other, he seriously cannot take a hint. A hysterical old woman gives him a rosary for protection. Other peasants cross themselves, point two fingers at him (to guard against the evil eye), and mutter words like *Ordog* (Satan), *pokol* (hell), *stregoica* (witch), and *vrolok* and *vlko-slak* (werewolf or vampire?). Dogs howl outside his window, and he's having "all sorts of queer dreams." But he goes to the castle anyway. Idiot.

I paused to dig my English journal out of my backpack,

grabbed a pen, and retreated with my laptop to Kieren's water bed.

I scribbled as much as I could remember about my own recent "queer dreams"—dancing with Bradley on Sanguini's dance floor, his cool mouth on the creaking twin bed in his basement, my kissing the blade of the bowie knife in his foyer.

Then I began reading again.

Along the way, Jonathan takes a coach ride from hell, complete with howling wolves and a ghostly driver who can mysteriously control them.

"Enter freely and of your own free will," Dracula finally greets him.

Brad had used that line—"Enter freely and of your own free will" (or some variation of it)—on me twice. Not long after we first met at Sanguini's, and again when I went to his house.

Black-on-black wardrobe aside, nobody would mistake the count for a sex symbol. Dracula is an old, scrawny, tall, and thin man with "waxen" skin, red eyes, a hook nose, and sharp white teeth, mostly hidden by his long white mustache and pointed beard. He has a heavy accent, bad breath, long fingernails, and hairy palms.

His manner is courtly, though. Aristocratic.

The visit starts off cozy, and I'm charmed by how much Jonathan misses his fiancée, Mina. But before long, Jonathan figures out that he's a prisoner, that he needs to be a *lot* more careful shaving, and that the castle's other residents are three ruby-red-lip-licking, baby-eating, voluptuous female vampires with silvery, musical laughs.

In Frank, I noted that Dracula looked younger after drinking blood and had a thing about sleeping on dirt. Neither clicked with what I knew about the undead, but Nora had said the novel was only "loosely" based on truth. I wished I knew which parts were "loose" and which were solid. What I wouldn't have given for Kieren's personal library. Not to mention Kieren himself.

"Why do you miss him so much?" a voice whispered. *"So much more than me?"*

STILL WATERS

I walked in on Clyde snacking on crickets and watching coverage of the U.T.–Tulane game in Sanguini's break room. "Did Nora say you could eat those?"

In reply, the Possum crossed his high-tops on the coffee table, leaned his head back on the floral sofa, and dropped another squirming insect into his mouth. "What do you think?" he asked before swallowing.

"I think that's disgusting," I said, feeling only vaguely hypocritical. Taking a seat beside him, I downed another spoonful of the surprisingly tasty porcine-blood-and-raspberry gelatin that Nora had concocted for me.

"When are we trying the hex-removal spell again?" Clyde asked.

"Because it went so well last time?" I shook my head. "Detective Zaleski was right. We don't know what we're doing. We might make things worse."

"What's left then? Prayer? Because—"

I patiently explained what Nora had told me, adding, "So, I'm reading *Dracula* to try to find out—"

"That's your master plan?" the Possum replied. "Homework?"

"And what genius idea do you have?"

Clyde didn't have an answer, not that I'd expected one. I saw no reason to explain that studying Stoker wasn't the sum total of my working strategy. I'd been trying to feel out the Chicagoans, trying to gauge whether we could confide in them. It was hard, being subtle, what with time running out. But I wouldn't repeat the mistake that I'd made with Bradley, not with so much and so many at stake.

That said, it seemed best to leave Clyde out of it. At least for the time being. The Possum's interpersonal skills were even worse than mine.

During the commercial break, I asked, "Do you suppose that, wherever he is, Kieren's following the 'Horns this season?"

Clyde shot me a look. He popped another cricket into his mouth, swallowing it whole. "You never talk about him."

I shrugged, finishing off my Jell-O. "Neither do you."

"I'm a guy. It's different."

What was it with people? Everyone wanted me to talk, share, bond—first Meghan, then Mrs. Levy, and now Clyde.

I snagged the remote from the table and lowered the volume. "What's your point? You think I'm deficient because I haven't gone catatonic?"

"Catatonic?" he shot back, fishing out another insect. "Try *panting*. Wasn't that you trailing after that Zachary guy last night?"

Was *that* what this was about? "I do not pant." I set my empty bowl on the coffee table. "For your information, Zachary's in training. He needed my help."

"Sure he did."

I started to say that I followed all the new-hire waiters in case they got weeded, but it's not like I owed some sophomore part-time dishwasher an explanation. "What do you know?" I replied. "You were in the kitchen all night."

Clyde held up the jar, selecting his next victim. "I see things. When Zachary came in to drop off and pick up his orders, you were always right there, chirping at him."

I could not believe he'd just said that! Maybe Clyde and I had never been close. Maybe Kieren had been our only real connection. But I'd thought we were starting to become friends. "You honestly think I don't care that Kieren's gone, that after spending our whole lives as friends, I've already moved on to some other guy?"

"Give 'im hell, baby!"

My fangs came down. "You think . . ." I narrowed my red eyes. "You think that inside I'm just singing, 'La, la, la, Kieren who?'"

Clyde glanced at me, dropped his cricket, and scrambled off the couch. "Whoa!"

"You do, don't you?" I went on, snatching the abandoned insect from the cushion as I stood to face him. "Well, you know what, you little weasel?"

I crushed the bug and felt its guts ooze between my fingers. "It's all I can do to think about anything else. Kieren's bedroom is now my bedroom and his bed is my bed and his parents are my parents and his little sister—"

"I get it, I get it!" Clyde raised his hands in surrender. "Relax." He took a breath. "You stay here. I'll go get you some more ungodly disturbing Jell-O." He paused. "You might want to wash your hands first."

I grimaced at the gooey guts on my palm, the tiny broken cricket leg lying off to one side. Poor cricket. Suddenly, I didn't know why I'd gotten so upset.

I'd heard it again, though. The voice. Brad's voice?

As quickly as my temper had flared, now I felt utterly deflated. "Yeah, okay."

While the skittish Possum scooted out to refill my bowl in the main kitchen, I took his advice and washed up in the break-room sink.

"Better?" I asked once I looked and felt human again.

Clyde, who'd returned to perch on the edge of the couch, cautiously handed me my gelatin. "Better. You could probably play off the look as makeup, fake teeth, and colored contacts, like Bradley used to do. Nobody would think twice about Sanguini's owner in a vampire getup." He was on the verge of babbling. "But why go there if you don't have to? I mean, unless it's a marketing thing."

I had another spoonful of Jell-O, determined to clamp down on my mood swings.

"You mentioned Meghan," Clyde said. "How's she doing?"

"She misses Kieren, of course. But it's more than that. Meghan knows. I think she doesn't know what she knows, but she knows she knows something."

The Possum clicked off the TV. "What?"

"The cub knows that I'm not the girl I used to be."

MISSING MIRANDA

*A*t sunset, Sanguini's rose again. The waitstaff arrived, chatty, upbeat, and, as usual, looking decadent. Jamal had the shape of a bat shaved into his hair. Mercedes and Simone had braided black-glitter-sprayed faux orchids into theirs.

Even better, Sergio had called in Fat Lorenzo's veteran server (and Jamal's cousin) Jamie, so we were no longer understaffed.

The first guests through the front door looked fresh off the *Rocky Horror* stage. Other themed parties of two or more included dark faeries, shuffling zombies, and one that I seated myself: a collection of self-proclaimed literary types—an Edgar Allan Poe, a Mary Shelley, a Sir Arthur Conan Doyle, and a pair of ladies calling themselves the Brontë sisters.

"No Bram Stoker?" I asked the community college English teachers.

"Too obvious," Poe explained, gesturing as a tall, bearded, red-haired Stoker walked by, formally dressed for the late 1800s.

Our staff had maintained the vampire theme. But I liked that the guests felt free to interpret the world of Sanguini's.

"Excuse me, miss," called a woman at the next table. "Who's the urban cowboy?"

Tonight Zachary had gone with a shiny navy-blue cowboy shirt over black jeans and black boots that reminded me of Kieren's. "He's our new waiter."

"Is he going to ride a mechanical bull?" asked her friend.

We didn't have a mechanical bull. "Not tonight."

The first woman replied, "He can ride me anytime."

I pasted on my most professional smile and excused myself.

Coming up on midnight, I found Chef Frederick Sanguini in the break room, standing in front of the new full-length mirror, fussing with his bleached hair. He'd added a red gerbera daisy to his lapel. "For irony," he'd claimed.

From behind him, I appreciated the sharpness of Freddy's reflection. It was challenging, trying to make sure no one spotted my own fuzzy image, but we'd had to make some accommodations for the staff, given our emphasis on costuming.

Moving away from the mirror, Freddy raised his white wine. "Hello, my dear."

"You don't drink red?" I asked, reassured by the thought. Bradley had almost always had a glass of what I now knew was blood wine perched between his long fingers.

Freddy made a face. "I'm happy to do it for the toast, but the tannins give me a headache." He took a sip, set down his glass, and removed his wire-frame glasses. "I probably shouldn't be saying that to a teenager, bad role-modeling and all."

"It's okay," I told him. "When it comes to drinking, I'm a lost cause."

"That's not what I hear." Returning to the mirror, he put in his right contact lens, blinking rapidly. "Nora said you'd given up alcohol, voluntarily sworn off human blood."

I raised a finger to silence him and then checked behind the doors to the kitchen and hallway to make sure no one was listening. "What do you know about it?"

With both red contacts in place, Freddy adjusted his black silk jacket. "I know it's a good sign." He glanced at the wall clock—two minutes till—and relaxed his stance. "You've already heard that Nora, Zachary, and I have all lived and worked, to varying degrees, within eternal high society."

I'd known that the other two had been employed by a vampire. I figured out that there must've been a hell of a lot more bloodsuckers in the world (or at least in this neighborhood) than the general public realized. But I'd had no idea that there was enough of an undead *society* to distinguish between high and low.

"We've been open about that," Freddy added, spinning to check himself out in the glass one last time. He frowned. "Do you think the red silk shirt is too much? I don't look like the Joker, do I?"

"The red brings out your eyes," I said. Bradley could never have pulled off that outfit—too shiny for his height or something.

Freddy seemed to consider my opinion, nodded, and then moved to lean against the back of the sofa, careful not to wrinkle his clothes. "We're not sure how much you're ready to hear, but we won't lie to you. We want you to trust us, and we understand that, after everything you've suffered, that's going to be hard. Just know that you can come to us if you have any questions or fears about what you've become or what happens next."

I'd been braced for a sermon, not whatever that had been. Again, I was tempted to confide what Bradley had done to the baby-squirrel eaters. But reassuring words or not, this was still the first real conversation that Freddy and I had ever had.

I moved to skim the newspaper spread open on the coffee table. Ads for three-bedroom rental houses had been circled. I remembered Nora, looking for the same, and what Miz Morales had said about leasing my home.

"You're all planning to live together?" I asked Freddy. I'd been trying to figure out the Chicagoans' relationships. Not that age was everything, but Zachary looked like he was in his early twenties, Freddy about twice Zachary's age, and Nora could've been my grandmother.

"For a while," the pretend chef replied. "We've been through a lot together. Nora and I feel that especially Zachary needs our support, a sense of belonging in this world."

I took a seat at the nearby six-top and began folding crimson napkins into the shape of bats. "He mentioned something about an ex-girlfriend."

Freddy examined his manicured fingernails. He'd had extensions applied but kept accidentally breaking them off. "Not ex, not exactly. I'll have to let him field that one."

Just then, Sergio peeked in from the hallway. "Showtime!"

"We'll finish this later," Freddy said with a jaunty salute on his way out.

Reaching for another red napkin, I remembered Zachary explaining that the three of them were in the business of saving souls. Now I was less sure about what he'd meant, but I knew mine was in jeopardy—not to mention Mitch's—and then there would come the next wave: Aimee, Sergio, Yani, Mercedes, the mayor, and hundreds more.

I wondered, though, whether the new hires could use some saving, too.

Mostly to placate Clyde, I'd suggested to Sergio that Simone should follow Zachary tonight. But she begged off, saying she'd already lost so much in tips from when we'd had to close. Then Sergio had pointed out that most of the servers probably felt the same way, and that he'd rather not put anyone on the spot. So it had been up to me again.

This time I'd given the new-hire more space so he could get into the flow without having to make small talk with me. But I had noticed that, as friendly and upbeat as he acted with his own tables, Zachary kept scowling as he made his way around Sanguini's for order drop-offs and pickups at the kitchen and bar.

At half past midnight, I stopped him, coming out of the men's restroom. "What's with you? Half the time I glance your way, it's like you're sucking a lemon."

"How can you do it?" he countered. "Glamorize the demonic, after what happened to you? Joke around about people becoming predators or prey?"

Apparently, Zachary was the self-righteous zealot of the group. I'd braced myself for something like this, but it still stung.

Maybe he had a point. But the vampire theme hadn't been my idea in the first place, and now I had enough to worry about without being lectured.

"You said you wanted to help," I began, "and I could use some help right now. But if you've changed your mind, fine. *Adiós.* The door's that way."

As I brushed past him, Zachary called, "Quincie! I—I didn't think it would get to me like . . . We'll talk later, okay? I'll explain what I can."

After close, I had the key in the ignition of The Banana when I happened to glance up and notice the masculine figure standing on Sanguini's roof. My mind went first to Bradley, as it too often did. Then the moonlight broke through the cloud cover and I realized it was Zachary, standing against the heavens. What was he doing up there?

I jumped out of the convertible, and after scanning the parking lot and alley for witnesses, set my hands, fingers spread, against the one-story brick building. Hadn't Kieren's notes on vampiric powers mentioned something about climbing ability? And Jonathan Harker had reported Dracula wall-crawling in a lizardlike fashion.

A second of concentration was enough to unleash my clawlike nails, and reaching upward with my left, I could somehow easily support my body.

Fascinated, I rose in a blur, swinging onto the roof.

"Intoxicating." That voice again.

"Having fun?" Zachary asked, his arms crossed.

Behind me, the neighborhood was dark, shadowed by large trees. Looking ahead, the neon and headlights created a commercial kaleidoscope. "Are you?"

"I . . ." He yawned. "You should be careful about that, tapping into the demonic magic. Letting it loose."

"I didn't let anything loose. I just climbed up a wall." I glanced down at my hands, one smooth and one scarred. The nails looked normal again. "I thought you were going to explain yourself," I prompted. "What got into you tonight? What are you doing up here?" I frowned. "And what's that you're holding?"

He strode across the roof and handed me a wallet-size picture.

I moved forward where the light was better. "This is her, your girlfriend?"

"Miranda Shen McAllister," he replied. "Her junior-year photo."

She had freckle-free skin, blue eyes, and nearly black hair. Chinese and Scottish heritage, not that you could always tell by names, but her looks matched. "She's pretty." Such a lame, superficial thing to say. I handed back the picture.

"My girl." Zachary's fingertip traced her heart-shaped face. "This was taken before she became a neophyte."

Oh, God, no wonder he was so pissed about Sanguini's vampire theme. Not to mention obsessed with saving neophytes. I remembered how Freddy had mentioned Zachary needing extra TLC. I should've guessed.

"Miranda had been shy," he said. "An only child. Bullied at school. Nothing like you—so sure of yourself."

He thought I was sure of myself? I must've been doing a better job of faking it than I'd thought. Or at least of covering up my insecurities by keeping busy.

"Her parents had just broken up," Zachary continued. "She had a gerbil named Mr. Nesbit and a best friend that she loved like a sister. Miranda's mother made her crazy sometimes. Most of the time. She'd dreamed of becoming an actress. Then . . . *then* doesn't matter, except for the few weeks we had together. Her soul was flown upstairs. And now we're apart."

Upstairs as in heaven? So she was *dead* dead, not undead, not anymore.

"I know we just met," I said, touched, "but if it helps to talk . . ."

He slipped the photo into his shirt pocket. "Does it help you, talking about Kieren? It can't be easy dealing with your new existence, what happened with your uncle and Brad, and Kieren's leaving, too."

"How did you—?"

"The staff here loves you, Quincie. They're worried. When you're not around—"

"They talk." Nora had told him I was undead, and that, plus Sanguini's gossip mill, had hinted at the rest of the story. I didn't blame the Chicagoans for asking around about me, especially Nora, given what had happened to Vaggio in the kitchen.

Zachary kept his gaze steady, waiting for an answer.

"No," I admitted. "It's not easy." And then, I wasn't sure why, I started telling Zachary all about the two of us. About Kieren and me. Not the werewolf-vampire thing, but other, more important stuff. How Kieren had always talked to me like I was just as smart as he was. How he was so serious but, after my parents' death, also the first person to make me laugh again. How nothing ever felt totally real or complete until I told Kieren about it, and that trying to go on without him had been a walking nightmare.

How sometimes I couldn't tell what was real anymore.

Later, when I returned to Kieren's bedroom, most of his books had reappeared on the shelves. Thank you, Meara! She was still at the wedding in Round Top, but she must've called Roberto from the road, and he'd taken it from there.

I hadn't inventoried the library, so I couldn't tell what might still be missing. But I did spot the pristine copy of *Dracula*. The Moraleses had dismissed it as fiction, too.

HOME AND FAMILY

On Sunday afternoon, Nora, Freddy, and Zachary met me at my house for a tour.

She presented me with a porcine-blood Popsicle. "Here you go!"

I couldn't help being amused. With Nora on the job and Sanguini's open six days a week, my liquid diet had become far less challenging.

On the way upstairs, Freddy paused to admire a painting by an artist from Léon who'd been a friend of my parents'. "Your father was an archaeologist?"

"An academic," I replied. "Not so much with the whip and fedora. He traveled a lot. If you don't like the baskets and rugs and stuff, I could pack them up."

"Oh, no!" Nora exclaimed. "Don't even think it."

Seeing the house through their eyes, I felt a pang of loneliness. I missed my parents. I even missed Uncle D. "When my mama was alive, there were plants everywhere. But they've died off over the years."

The Moraleses had made a couple of runs for more of my clothes and a few family treasures—my parents' wedding album, Grandma Morris's Bible, my engraved silver baby spoon from Vaggio—but this was the first time I'd been home since the police had come for Uncle D's body and the cleaning service had done its job. The lilies from Brad, I'd noticed, had been removed.

"You're welcome to look around."

Freddy and Nora strolled into the master bedroom, chatting about closet space.

Zachary, who'd been oddly quiet, chose my room instead. He looked extraordinarily male in contrast to my canopy bed with its calico-print bedspread, the eggshell-ivory-painted nightstand and dresser, and my moth-chewed Oriental rug.

I sank into the rattan chair in the corner as he studied the space.

"Mrs. Morales mentioned something to Nora about a finished attic," Zachary said.

"You don't want my room?" I teased. "You could take down the canopy if it's too girly for you. Really, I don't mind if—"

"It's not that." He briefly studied a picture of Mama on my nightstand. "Your room is *your* room. You may need it back before our lease runs out."

"The Moraleses expect me to live with them at least until graduation, and —"

"Quincie . . . as time goes on, it may not be safe for them to have you there."

It wasn't like I hadn't thought about that. I still carried the holy water with me everywhere. I remembered too well biting my own thigh.

Zachary rested his hand on one of the bedposts. "They don't know, do they?"

"No, they don't."

"And they have a daughter?"

"Meghan," I said. "Kieren's baby sister. She's four. She knows about me. Or, I mean, she suspects, but she's so young. Right after I transformed, she saw me . . ." I gestured to my face. "You know. I was pretty out of it."

"But you didn't drain her," Zachary said, brightening a bit.

I looked down at my blood Popsicle. "I ran away to the lakefront instead."

I was sure he'd heard about killings on the hike-and-bike trail bordering the lake. Mitch's work, I suspected.

I didn't want to have that conversation, though, or point a finger at my old friend. Not yet, anyway. Besides, there hadn't been a new murder reported in nearly two weeks. I took comfort in the fact that it was a start.

At least until Zachary said, "You know, even angels are fallible."

There was something about the way he said it. . . .

But then I remembered: Jesus freak.

HER DADDY'S GIRL

*L*ater, I sprawled across Kieren's denim comforter and opened *Dracula*.

The focus shifts from Jonathan, still trying to escape the castle, to his fiancée, Mina, and her vivacious friend, Lucy, who's received three marriage proposals in one day.

One of the suitors is her choice and ultimate fiancé, the Honorable Arthur Holmwood. The other two are Dr. John "Jack" Seward, who works at an insane asylum, and a Texan named Quincey P. Morris.

My name. Or at least my name if I'd been a boy, though somehow I suspected that his *P* didn't stand for *Patrizia*.

My parents had always told me that I'd been named for a generations-ago great uncle and described him as "a Texas war hero." It had never occurred to me that they'd been talking about the War between Good and Evil.

I'd always been so focused on the restaurant, Fat Lorenzo's and then Sanguini's. The Crimi family legacy. But this was my family history on Daddy's side.

In England, Mina worries that she hasn't heard from Jonathan and frets over Lucy's sleepwalking. A ship carrying fifty boxes of soil wrecks onshore. A dog, which goes missing, is the only survivor.

One night, as Lucy is sleepwalking at a nearby cemetery, Mina follows and sees something shadowy hovering above her friend.

When Mina reaches Lucy, it's vanished, but Lucy's neck has been punctured. The two wounds are tiny. Mina writes them off as pricks of a safety pin. (Really.)

Over time, Lucy's health gets worse. Dracula is obviously "visiting" her. (By *obviously*, I mean to me, not to the characters.)

Then Mina is called away to nurse Jonathan after his ordeal at the castle, and Jack contacts Dr. Abraham Van Helsing to request his help with Lucy's condition.

Van Helsing, who's a total windbag, is upset about the wounds on Lucy's neck and the fact that she needs several blood transfusions. The donors are her former boyfriends, Quincey included, and also Van Helsing himself.

The transfusions have an oddly sexual vibe. Like all the men have become Lucy's lovers because their blood flows in her veins.

Each time, Lucy improves for a while and then weakens again. Van Helsing seems to get what's happening and tries to protect her with garlic flowers to ward off the monster, but he doesn't tell anyone else.

One night a wolf smashes through Lucy's window, and her mama, who's also been sick, dies of a heart attack.

Finally, Lucy's fiancé, Arthur, is summoned to her deathbed, and when he bends to kiss her good-bye, Van Helsing tears him away. "Not on your life!" Van Helsing says. "Not for your living soul and hers!" And then: "He stood between them like a lion at bay."

At first, Lucy doesn't take that well. "A spasm as of rage flit like a shadow over her face. The sharp teeth clamped together." But later she's thankful.

Before death, Lucy's gums have already begun to retract, and her teeth are noticeably sharper.

It hadn't been that way for me, or at least I hadn't noticed any changes in my smile before I'd died. I hadn't been weak, either, just moody. One moment I'd felt emotionless, the next euphoric.

Not long after Lucy dies, news reports begin to appear about a "bloofer lady," who's been attacking village children.

Finally, Van Helsing tells Jack, Arthur, and Quincey that Lucy has vamped out (he really should've mentioned it earlier), and the four of them confront her in her tomb.

As a vampire, Lucy is no longer sweetly high-spirited (and kind of a bubblehead). Instead, she's as wanton and voluptuous and evil (or so she's described) as the female vampires at Castle Dracula. "Never did I see such baffled malice on a face, and never, I trust, shall such ever be seen again by mortal eyes. The beautiful color became livid, the eyes seemed to throw out sparks of hell fire, the brows were wrinkled as though the folds of flesh were the coils of Medusa's snakes, and the lovely, blood-stained mouth grew to an open square, as in the passion masks of the Greeks and Japanese."

What's more, "the woman, with a corporeal body as real at that moment as our own," can "pass through the interstice where scarce a knife blade could have gone."

Plus, in keeping with her early fangs and blood-lusty behavior, she's been working her sultry thrall for a while. Quite the undead achiever, not that it helps her.

The men stake Lucy, cut off her head, and fill it with garlic.

It's Arthur, her fiancé, who hammers home the stake. (How romantic.)

That's when they decide to hunt down the count. (About damned time.)

Along the way, Mina and Jonathan, now married, return to England. He's still shaky from his ordeal at the castle.

The heroes study one another's journals, correspondence, and whatnot. Mina—who gets bonus points for being able to work the newfangled gadget that is the manual typewriter—compiles and organizes all the information for them. She also pulls the sobbing mess of guys together despite their grief over Lucy's death.

The men spend quality time tracking down the count's fifty boxes of Transylvanian soil, purifying them with holy wafers. Meanwhile, Dracula moves on to Mina, who looks "too pale" for a while before anyone figures out what's going on. (Didn't they just go through all this with Lucy?)

One night, Mina and the count are discovered together. "Her white nightdress was smeared with blood, and a thin stream trickled down the man's bare breast, which was shown by his torn-open dress. The attitude of the two had a terrible resemblance to a child forcing a kitten's nose into a saucer of milk to compel it to drink."

White nightdress . . . like the one Bradley had chosen for me?

Beyond that, hmm. I didn't get it. Van Helsing suggested that anyone preyed on by a vampire would turn into one, but he also tried to protect Lucy with the garlic flowers. He didn't immediately give up hope for her.

With Lucy herself, the transformation process seemed to be triggered by the count's bite (I thought), but I also knew some kind of transfer of blood was required, and Mina apparently did drink. Like a kitten.

Kieren had labeled "Dracula and his spawn" as Carpathians, a whole other breed of undead. Modeling my notes on Kieren's cheat sheet, I compiled a list of the count's unique qualities.

What Makes Dracula Special

Dracula: unattractive, undead Transylvanian count

Origin: "They learned his secrets in the Scholomance, amongst the mountains over Lake Hermanstadt, where the devil claims the tenth scholar as his due." —Van Helsing

Allies: Renfield (bug-eating madman in Jack's care), three female vampires

Qualities: no reflection or shadow; bad breath; can't eat

at all; victims show physical signs of vampiric infection prior to undeath

Powers: the usual (the full gamut, and immediately after rising) plus:

- Can vanish and "become unknown."
- Can change size (dramatically).
- Can enthrall victims and control minds. "When my brain says 'Come!' to you, you shall cross land or sea to do my bidding. And to that end this!" — Mina Harker quoting Dracula
- Can affect the weather (fog and thunderstorms).
- Can command the rat, owl, bat, moth, fox, and wolf.
- May look younger after feeding.

Weaknesses:

- Can't enter a household unless initially invited.
- Can only change form at noon, sunrise, or sunset; loses powers during daylight.
- May only cross running water at low or high tide.
- Must sleep on soil of his homeland.
- Holy wafers, crosses, crucifixes, wild-rose branches, garlic (huge turnoffs).

Methods of Destruction: sacred bullet, the usual (stake, beheading). Fire?

Spiritual Status: damned. The staking, beheading, garlic-mouth ritual is in play.

I twisted Kieren's crucifix on its chain. He'd written off the Carpathians as myth. Just like he'd written off several undead attributes that appeared in the novel—the ability to enthrall or control human minds and those of some animals, weather-related powers, the need for homeland (and/or unhallowed) soil, throwing no shadow or reflection (my reflection and shadow weren't sharp, but they were visible), and so on.

The way I figured it, either Stoker had decided to use his creative license to weave in several well-known misconceptions, or the count and his fellow Carpathians had been both real and a more powerful breed of vampire, created with a different spell from the one that had transformed me, Mitch, the vice principal, Uncle D, and even Brad.

A different spell from the one I hoped to break.

It was sort of interesting in a Goth-lit geek kind of way, but it didn't help in my quest to save the baby-squirrel eaters.

Rubbing my eyelids, I decided I was wasting my time. Besides, anyone could tell from the exhausting foreshadowing where the story was going.

"You would not kill yourself?" Van Helsing asks.

"I would," Mina says. "If there were no friend who loved me, who would save me such a pain, and so desperate an effort!" Then: "She looked at him meaningly as she spoke."

So Mina would die, and the men would destroy her the same way they had Lucy, only this time it would be her husband Jonathan's turn to drive a stake into the heart.

Forget that. I had more important things to think about. I tossed the novel aside.

MASTER AND MADNESS

Bradley glanced at both dress watches on his wrist. "He's running late."

"Who?" I asked. "Who's late?"

I was in his 1920s parlor, seated in a leather club chair, wearing my black leather bustier with a matching mini-skirt, sheer thigh-highs, and my red cowboy boots. My curls had been pinned up, and a glass of Cabernet was perched in my gloved hand.

Brad lounged across from me in his toasting suit, accented by a red lily boutonniere. I could detect a hint of eyeliner and lip liner, a dash of blue-gray blush on each hollowed cheek. I hated to admit it, but he looked magnificent.

Brad laughed. "You might say I'm in my prime."

How annoying that he could read my mind.

Black candles burned in the fireplace, and two more blazed on the mantel, illuminating the box-framed bowie knife, again hanging above. He'd previously displayed clocks up there, three of them, all antique. Now they were gone.

"You've found a new boy," he added, shaking his head. "A golden boy. And to think, I just got rid of the other one. That inconsequential fur-ball."

"Zachary?" I asked. "Is Zachary late?"

"Too late," Bradley answered. "They're all too late. You're my doll now." The doorbell rang, and he rose. "Finally!"

I set my untouched drink on a side table and twisted to see who it was, surprised when Mitch walked in, dragging a large burlap bag. "Special, it's special. I'm special delivery, delivering, just like you asked, master."

"Don't call him that," I scolded. "You don't have to call anyone that." I certainly wasn't about to.

Then I heard a soft moan come from the bag. It sounded like a smothered puppy. I recognized the image from Stoker's story, the count bringing a child to feed his three thirsty women. I heard laughter. Tinkling, inhuman. Mine?

The ring of my cell phone, recharging on the nightstand, jolted me awake. It was Freddy. The Chicagoans had decided to rent my house.

SOUL SISTERS

I slipped into the noisy high-school cafeteria and met Aimee and Clyde at a long, empty table toward the back, behind the band kids' table.

Both of them had a series of new tattoos circling their necks—a repeated half-inch design of a cross. They didn't mention it. I didn't mention it. I didn't blame them, either. I knew I could be dangerous. Plus, those two bloodsuckers who'd shown up at Sanguini's last Friday night were still out there. That said, I wore Kieren's crucifix against my skin. Hopefully, if the need arose, the sophomores' tattooed crosses would be more effective on other vampires than they were on me.

Clyde had brought his lunch. Given his taste for insects, I decided not to ask what had been rolled into his corn tortilla. In the cafeteria line, Aimee had grabbed chicken fingers for herself and a Dr Pepper for me.

After filling them in on Stoker's Quincey P. Morris, I added, "Which is kind of nifty, if you're me, anyway, but I don't think it'll help us save the infected. I didn't see anything in the novel that—"

"We can't give up," Clyde insisted in a low voice. "Shouldn't we at least warn people? The media or the government or—?"

"The media?" I said. "Can you imagine how fast word would spread? Do you want to see the words 'vampiric pandemic' in a headline?" I leaned forward. "Do you have any idea how Sergio would react if he found out? Or Mercedes? We served at least one little kid the chilled baby squirrels, a five-year-old boy."

"Besides," Aimee said, waving a chicken finger, "the infected are still human beings. They don't deserve to be rounded up or persecuted."

At that, Clyde looked ashamed, and I realized Aimee had finally told him.

"I *haven't* given up," I assured them. "I've already tried to talk to Nora about it once without, you know, really letting on, and I'm getting to know—"

"Try speed dating," Clyde said. "We're running out of time."

"And we can't afford to make things worse!" I exclaimed. Lowering my voice, I added, "I know what's at stake. I know we're getting desperate. But aren't you the least bit suspicious? Think about it: I need a chef, a waiter, and someone to play Chef Sanguini. *Voilà!* I need to rent my three-bedroom house, and they're looking for a three-bedroom house to rent. I'm a brand-new you-know-what, and they're savvy about—"

Across the multipurpose room, someone dropped a tray, and everyone applauded.

"You rented them your house?" the Possum asked.

"Clyde," Aimee said, handing him my cup. "Go refill Quincie's Dr Pepper."

"It's still full."

"Go!" she insisted.

He took his time getting up, moving away from the table.

"Maybe it's not my place to say so," Aimee began, "but from what I hear, you're a walking tragedy. Your parents died in a car accident a few years back, and then last month that Vaggio guy—"

"He was my grandfather," I explained. "I mean, not really. Not like—"

"I get it." Aimee sipped her chocolate milk. "Your honorary grandfather is murdered, and it turns out that your uncle was at least partly responsible, and then he dies." She paused. "Twice, technically. Plus, there's your own . . . situation to deal with. And finally, Kieren high-tailed it to—"

"That fancy prep school up north," I supplied.

"Not to mention the burden of trying to save everyone like me."

"You're not a burden."

"I'm just saying," she went on, "the universe has to balance out. When bad things happen and happen and happen, well, good things have to start happening eventually."

I could tell she was thinking about herself and Travis, too.

"The karma owes you new people to care about," she concluded. "Your heart already trusts Nora and the new guys, or no way would you let them live in your home. Believe me, Quincie, it's your own thick head getting in your way."

I didn't know much about karma, and I doubted that Aimee did either, but . . . "You're saying that the universe owed me Nora, Freddy, Zachary, and you."

She grinned up at the Opossum, who was back from the soda fountain. "What about Clyde?"

"What about me?"

I took a long drag of Dr Pepper. "Let's not go crazy."

Aimee laughed. "What do you think he is?"

"Clyde?" I asked.

"Zachary."

With a mouthful of who-knew-what, Clyde replied, "Werelion."

Aimee nodded. "I was thinking Lion, too."

"The hair," we all said at the same time.

secondo

GONE BATTY

*D*ue to a clothes-shopping trip with Miz Morales, I didn't make it to Sanguini's until almost sunset. She dropped me off in my newest work outfit—a classic little black dress with sheer black hose, black-and-white checked pumps, and a pillbox hat that Miz Morales had said reminded her of Jackie Kennedy.

In the kitchen, Nora's staff was in full prep mode, and she'd put Zachary to work churning vanilla ice cream. The chef exclaimed, "My, don't you look spiffy!"

"Freddy around?" I asked.

"Not yet. I expect we won't see him until after ten."

Maybe Freddy or Zachary knew more about demonic magic than Nora did. But I'd have to wait to catch one of them alone later.

The chandeliers sparkled, Sinatra crooned, and the staff looked succulent, but so far at a half hour past sundown, Yani had seated only four tables, including the six-top dressed as the Sopranos. According to the reservations roster, we were booked solid.

"Where *is* everybody?" I muttered, wandering into the foyer.

"Surprise!" exclaimed a guest with long black hair, wearing a long black dress with a plunging neckline accented by a simple pendant.

"What do you think?" asked her date, turning to greet me. He sported a pin-striped suit, white shirt, black tie, and a vaguely familiar dark mustache. With his hair combed down and over—

"Gah!" Meara and Roberto! "What are y'all doing here? Like that?"

"We're Morticia and Gomez," she replied. "From *The Addams Family.*"

"It's supposed to be ironic," he added, which did not help at all.

They were here. At Sanguini's. For dinner. Which technically would've been fine, fine, fine, except that werewolves hated vampires and something at Sanguini's was wacky tonight and Kieren's parents should not dress like that. It was almost worse than seeing Meara naked in the kitchen. Almost. "Oh, too bad! We're all booked up."

Dr. Morales leaned to peek into the dining room. "I see a few free tables."

There had been a big question mark in that statement. Even though only one of them was a shifter, they were both parents. They could both smell trouble.

Yanira glided back in. "Welcome to Sanguini's! Are you predator or prey?"

From the she-wolf and the king of the grill, their "predator" answers came as no surprise. "Zachary's section?" Yani asked me, leading them into the dining room.

"No, are you kidding? Give them to Xio. She knows what she's doing."

With that, I waved cheerfully at the Moraleses and made a beeline to the bar area. "Xio?" She was flirting with Zachary, who looked politely bored. "Xio!"

As they turned toward me, I said, "Xio, the restaurant is practically empty. My new guardians were just seated, and you have to go out there and be perfect so that they don't think I need any more of their 'help' here at Sanguini's."

She fluffed her hair. "Not a problem."

Zachary said, "You don't think they're just trying to show their support?"

I frowned up at him. "Of course they're trying to show their support. But they're also checking up on me, and—"

"Quincie," Sergio called from the dining room, "can I have a word with you?"

From the sidewalk, Sergio and I tried to look nonchalant as we cased the eco-activists who'd set up camp in our parking lot. Two or three blocked each space. They wore black mesh ponchos with prominent BADL logos.

The Bat Anti-Defamation League.

The world's largest urban bat colony made its home under the Congress Avenue Bridge, a few blocks north of the restaurant. BADL had been suspicious of Sanguini's negative PR effect on the city's beloved eco-mascots since before we'd first opened.

It was unfair and vexing. I personally considered myself bat-friendly.

Back in the day, Uncle D would've asked Vaggio to handle it, and Vaggio would've just slipped 'em a fifty and told them to get lost. I suggested that strategy.

"They're trespassing," Sergio countered. "Let's call the cops."

"If it goes live on the police scanners, the media will be—"

He gestured at the news van. "BADL already sent out a news release."

Just then, I noticed Miz Morales stolling toward us in her Morticia getup. "Do you need any help?" she asked Sergio, like I'd become invisible.

That's when I realized that, owner or not, I wasn't getting full blame or credit for anything at Sanguini's, which was fair enough, considering the fact that, day to day, when it came to most of the management stuff, I wasn't the one in charge. Except . . .

"Everything's fine," I said. "Sergio has the situation under control. Don't you?"

"Oh, yes, yes," he assured her. "Thanks for the offer, Meara, but I'd hate for your wasabi-deviled quail eggs to get cold."

"They're already cold," Miz Morales countered. "I—"

"You're the top wedding planner in the city," Sergio said, "and I'm so pleased that you and Roberto could join us tonight, but this isn't the Junior League crowd."

Not everyone could get away with reprimanding her like that, however gently. But, to my surprise and relief, Miz Morales made a nonapology apology for overstepping her bounds and headed back toward the restaurant.

Eyeing the BADL protesters, I suggested, "Talk to Aimee." She did have that KEEP AUSTIN BATTY sticker on her school locker. "I suspect she speaks their language."

By 8:30 P.M., I'd failed to catch Freddy alone, but thanks to Aimee, Sergio had agreed to designate all proceeds earned tonight from table seven to a more reputable and reasonable local bat-preservation organization.

Meanwhile, Clyde had needed help with the dishes. So I'd covertly taken a picture of the Moraleses with my cell phone and then ditched the pillbox hat and little black dress for an old T-shirt and jeans that I'd stashed in the office filing cabinet for just such an occasion.

"Hey, Quincie!" Zachary called over the din of clanging pots, water sprayer, and frantic chatter. "You free after work?"

Clyde leaned closer to me. "Remember, a Lion is still a Cat. Shifters can be dangerous, too." He was obviously thinking of Ruby.

I nodded, not wanting to rehash last weekend's argument. "Yeah, but . . ."

Brad had caught me off guard. He'd been older—much older, utterly diabolical, and he'd had Uncle D on his side. Plus, I'd been more vulnerable after Vaggio's death, especially given that Kieren had been a prime suspect.

My consequences had been more dire than most, but a lot of girls had trusted the wrong guy once. I didn't intend to make a habit of it.

"Quincie?" Zachary called again, his tray held high.

"But what?" the Possum prompted me.

"I'm not that naive human girl anymore."

SAVIOR

*A*fter clocking out, Zachary retrieved a sword that had been stored with a White Sox cap in his break-room locker. He left the cap where it was.

I made sure no one else was around and asked, "Is that a costume prop or the sword you stole from the cops?"

He looked offended. "It was mine in the first place."

Fair enough. "And it's in your locker because . . . ?"

He winked at me. "If I wore it in the dining room, I'd bang the scabbard into a table every time I turned around."

Sergio had abandoned his scythe and hooded robe for similar reasons.

On one hand, it made me nervous that Zachary was capable of stealing something out of wherever they kept evidence at APD. On the other hand, it suggested that maybe he could be useful in ways that went beyond waxing poetic about my jeopardized soul.

Outside, the sidewalks had nearly emptied, but one last appreciative whistle trailed Zachary down South Congress.

"It doesn't seem to faze you," I said. "All the attention, I mean." I admired that about him. A lot of guys—Brad, for example—would've soaked it up.

"My heart is spoken for," Zachary replied.

Miranda again, poor guy.

The warm air felt sticky, like the sky ached to rain. Central Texas had been suffering from a drought since last spring.

Making our way past renovated motels, neon-lit storefronts, and music clubs, Zachary and I talked shop. About BADL, the customer whose hoop skirt wouldn't fit between the tables, the drunken grad students singing "Mamma" along with Pavarotti.

Zachary teased, "I didn't realize restaurant owners washed dishes."

"My mother always did whatever needed doing," I

explained, shifting the backpack strap on my right shoulder. "And I do, too."

"You talk about your mom a lot," he said. "Not so much your dad."

"It was always easier with him." I glanced at a newspaper kiosk. According to a headline, some teenagers had gone missing outside San Antonio. I paused, wondering briefly if Bradley had something to do with it. Shaking off the thought, I added, "I never felt like anybody expected me to be an archaeologist when I grew up."

"Do you really want to run the restaurant someday? Or was that your mom's—?"

"People always ask that. I guess . . . it's harder now. With Sanguini's vampire theme, smelling all the food I can't eat, it's like I never have a chance to forget what I've become. But the restaurant isn't work to me. I never dread going or feel sorry for myself because I'm there so much. I guess I'm not really the wannabe-homecoming-queen-where's-the-party-this-weekend-will-you-sign-my-yearbook type." There was more to the social side of high school than that, but he didn't argue.

"Basically, it's your whole world."

"Basically." At least without Kieren, my family, or a heartbeat, but I didn't say so out loud. Mama had hated whining as much as she'd loved Fat Lorenzo's, and I'd inherited that, too.

Faced with the boisterous late-night crowd outside All the World's a Stage—the costume-shop owners had decided to stay open around the clock through Halloween—Zachary led me to the other side of the avenue.

We stepped up on the curb, and I brightened when Mitch appeared directly in our path from behind a giant yucca. Tonight his cardboard sign read:

FREELANCE BLOODSUCKING
LOCAL CELEBRITY
UNDER NEW MANAGEMENT

All of the words were spelled right, too. He seemed fine, for him, anyway. Apparently, I'd been worried about nothing. "This is my friend Mitch."

Zachary extended his hand. "Good to see you, buddy."

Mitch batted it away. "Where did you come from?"

"Zachary's new at Sanguini's," I explained, suddenly wary. "He's a waiter."

"Golden boy." Mitch spat at Zachary. "Leave, leave her alone."

"Mitch!" I exclaimed.

He dropped his sign and ran into the street, almost knocking down a Harley rider, then blending into the costume-shop crowd.

"Alone," echoed a voice only I could hear.

I frowned. "He's not usually like that."

"Yeah, I know. He's a sweetheart of a guy. Or at least he was before."

As we resumed walking down the hill, past more funky shops and restaurants, I asked, "How do you know Mitch? You just moved here."

"We've met in passing a few times. I've lived in Austin before. I was homeless myself back then."

"You?" I asked. From their clothes and the way they carried themselves, I'd figured all three Chicagoans were pretty well off. "You were homeless?"

Zachary shrugged. "It can happen to anyone."

Like I hadn't known that. "Well," I began, peering at him sideways, "you don't have to sound so damn pious about it."

He laughed. "I don't, do I? It's strange. Being with you brings back a lot of memories, not all of them good. You're more assertive than Miranda was. You know, before the vamp took her. But she's not much older than you. She's also from Texas — Dallas. She bossed me around all the time, too."

You'd think we were the only two girls he'd ever met.

We rounded the corner of a sprawling gated stucco apartment complex before escaping into the quiet of the old Fairview neighborhood, headed toward the Moraleses'.

As the sidewalk dead-ended, I bent to retie my new Nikes. "It was awfully coincidental," I began, tentative, "you and Nora and Freddy all moving to Austin, fitting in perfectly to those open jobs at the restaurant—"

"Coincidences are rare. I'm not sure I even believe in them anymore."

Straightening, I asked, "What do you believe in?"

"Old love songs, best friends, the collected works of J. R. R. Tolkien, crispy pork egg rolls with just the right amount of grease, the Big Boss, and eternity."

"The Big Boss?"

Zachary pointed up, as if to heaven.

"Pious," I teased.

We moseyed down the winding residential street, past cottages, bungalows, artsy modern houses, and a B and B whose owners had had their dead lawn sprayed green.

"Listen, Quincie," Zachary began again, his hand resting on the hilt of the sword. "I know this isn't easy to talk about. But I was wondering about the night you first rose undead."

I paused on the sidewalk, and so did he. "What about it?"

"Well, you mentioned the lakefront."

Mitch. He was looking for confirmation that Mitch was a killer vampire.

I took a few steps and shook my head. "I don't want to discuss it."

"Quincie—"

"No." I faced him. "Look, the Moraleses' house is just another block down. We're both tired, and I don't feel like talking anymore."

He opened his mouth to say something, but I cut him off. "Good night, Zachary."

"Good riddance."

"Stop that!" I exclaimed.

"I'm sorry," Zachary said, assuming my rising frustration was all about him. "I didn't mean to . . . I'll see you tomorrow." He turned to leave and retraced our steps, pausing to glance back at me as a sports car passed by.

I waved a little. Then he waved back, and we were almost friends again. Almost.

Earlier tonight, I'd assured Clyde that I wasn't naive anymore. I'd felt so confident right then, but now, I wasn't sure what to think.

Moving on, I noticed a scarecrow seated on a hay bale on the porch of a lime-colored cottage. A homemade-looking ghost hung from a tree branch. Plastic tombstones littered the yard. The one closest to the street read RIP. A tempting thought.

As I rounded a bend, from within a row of tall hedges, a viselike grip seized my wrist and began dragging me around and onto the nearby front lawn of a deeply set-back Spanish Colonial. It was the suit-and-tie vampire with the mullet 'do from Friday night.

"Zachary!" I shouted, remembering that he had his sword with him.

I twisted my wrist free, grabbed the strap of my backpack, and swung it, knocking my assailant into the air. Seconds later, as Mullet Man climbed to his feet, a heavy mist solidified into his dressed-for-success female companion, the one with the beauty mark.

"I told you," I said. "I don't know where Brad is, and I don't give a damn."

Slowly circling, their arms spread like basketball guards, the vampires didn't bother to answer. Just my luck. I had all these spiffy new superpowers and no idea how to use them in a fight. The holy water stashed in my pack and bra might work as a weapon, but I needed to keep my hands free. *"Zachary!"*

Suddenly, he was there—winded from running, furious at the scene, and with his sword drawn. "As a member of Her Majesty's gentry," Zachary began, "this girl is entitled to certain rights under the Mantle."

Oncoming headlights caught my eye, and Mole Woman tore a thin branch off a pecan tree. She sprang, her makeshift weapon aimed at my heart.

Zachary neatly stepped between us, bringing up the blade of his sword—his suddenly *flaming* sword—and slicing her diagonally in two. The body fell in pieces, combusting, and I turned to see Mullet Man run off toward the city.

"Duck!" Zachary shouted, and I fell forward onto the dry grass as his fiery weapon flew overhead.

I pushed to my knees to witness the male vampire struck, to watch the flames engulf and decimate his dead body.

Within seconds, smoke swirled from the ground where each soulless monster had been destroyed. Impressive. A little too impressive. There had been no torch that night at the park when I'd collided with Zachary. It was the sword all along.

I'd been comfortable with the idea of him as a shifter. I lived with shifters, called them friends. I loved a hybrid Wolf. Werepeople were natural, like humans—only stronger, faster, with keener senses, and able to change form.

As Zachary moved to my side, I said, "What you just did, that was magic."

And not black-cherry-scented-tea-light, would- you-like-some-herbal-tea-bags-with-that-packet-of-lemon-bath-salt magic. We were talking destructive magic. Demonic magic? Was *Zachary* magic, or just his sword?

Like he had on his first night at Sanguini's, he offered me a hand up.

This time I stood on my own. "Don't touch me."

"Quincie," he began, "I can explain."

The oncoming car had veered off at the V in the road. A neighbor's dog was barking. The upstairs lights of the

Spanish Colonial had all been turned on. We had to get out of there, but should I be going anywhere with him?

"It's not what you think," he said. "I, um . . ."

I'd officially had *enough* of mysterious, good-looking, older guys from Sanguini's who weren't what they seemed. I ran from my self-proclaimed savior, ignoring his calls, into the night.

CATCH ME IF YOU CAN

*A*s the laptop booted, I could hear animal paws—too small to be a shifter—padding around on the Moraleses' roof. I hadn't noticed them before, but I hadn't been on full alert to the same extent, and I didn't have Meara's hearing either.

Varmints, Roberto had called them.

Angelina had stuck her head out of Meghan's room as I'd come up the stairs that night, but she and her pups were quiet.

I keyed *flaming sword* into a search engine, clicked a link on related mythology, and started reading. After making a page of notes in Frank, I tried the keywords again. As I scrolled a bit, a reference to the Garden of Eden caught my attention.

Without pausing to think too hard about it, I went to the bookshelf for Grandma Morris's Bible and turned to Genesis.

I recalled the reappearance of The Banana in Sanguini's back lot . . . the first time I'd seen Zachary, battling a vampire not far from a certain failed hex-removal spell . . . the way he'd saved my hairspray-shellacked head from the falling tray of flaming brandied peaches and ice cream . . . how he and his friends had filled the open jobs and leased my house and invited me to move back to my bedroom whenever.

I remembered Zachary standing against the hazy neon of South Congress on Sanguini's roof and the way he'd been so protective of me against the Mullet Man and Mole Woman, both in the dining room and in the neighborhood.

A flaming sword.

I heard a skittering from above and a *woof* from down the hall. Glancing at the ceiling, I kissed the leather-bound Bible and returned it to its place on the shelf next to my parents' wedding album. Then I crossed to the window, crawled outside, and began scaling up the front of the Morales house.

Even though I'd come up to the roof planning to confront Zachary, it still delighted me to find him there, sitting with what might've been the same three young raccoons from the park. One walked across his lap while the other two sniffed around.

"You're not a werelion," I announced, pushing up to stand.

"Are you trying to start an argument?" he began. "Because I never said I was."

I crossed my arms. "How about this one: you're an angel."

"What?" he replied, not meeting my gaze. "Who? What?"

Nice comeback. Raising my voice, I replied, "I said —"

"Shhh!" he scolded. "Kieren's mom might hear us."

"You want to play it that way, fine," I said, opening my arms wide. "Catch."

I free-fell backward off the two-story McMansion, and before I could panic or doubt, strong arms scooped me up safe. I glimpsed enormous white wings and then was plopped down barefoot on the dry grass in the side yard, faced with a very cranky angel.

"What were you thinking?" His wings had vanished, apparently at will. "You could've broken bones, severed your spine, ended up in a wheelchair or with permanent brain damage. Do you *want* to spend your supposedly immortal existence in a vegetative state?"

"I *knew* you'd catch me," I exclaimed, bouncing on the balls of my feet. I hadn't been this bubbly about anything since before I'd died—no, before that, since before my parents' accident. A real live angel, and we were friends. Sort of.

"I'm not infallible." Zachary began rubbing his temples. "I can't believe I just blew my secret identity again. No wonder I'm—"

"Why are you following me around?"

"I belong to you," he said. At my double take, he clarified. "I mean, I'm your guardian angel. Newly assigned. Middle management didn't bother to float me a background file or anything so I'm having to sort of wing this. No pun intended."

I bent to retrieve a dog-chewed Frisbee from the dry grass. I'd remembered the cherubim with the flaming sword who'd guarded the Tree of Life, and I'd done my time in Sunday school. But I wasn't a biblical scholar or even that regular of a churchgoer. "Vampires get guardian angels?"

"Up until now, only natural beings with souls—like humans and shape-shifters—were assigned guardians. But we're the first match in . . . let's call it a pilot program involving neophyte vampires, those with at least some of their soul still left."

Thinking that over, I tossed the Frisbee at Zachary, who snatched it from the air. "Why would I be the first?"

"Beats me," he replied. "I'm not the all-knowing one." For a long moment, he frowned down at the plastic disc in his hands. "But I can already tell that you, the *real* you, are worth saving." He studied me. "You're a sweet, smart, very hardworking girl. You're funny, and though you hold most of them at arm's length, anyone could see how much the staff at Sanguini's means to you. How important it is to you to stick with your family business. And despite what you've become, you're making a sincere effort not to kill anybody."

"Uh, thanks," I said, not sure all of that had been a compliment.

Headlight beams from a passing pickup truck illuminated the side yard, and Zachary motioned for me to follow him past the veggie garden, toward the back of the property. "Quincie, I'm glad that you're happy about this. But it's only fair that you know — I don't have a great track record. I'm not even a fully powered GA. For the foreseeable future, I've been banished from the celestial plane. For a while, I lost my wings, and even now I'm earthbound, stuck in corporeal form."

I took a giant step back. "You're a fallen angel?"

"Not fallen," he insisted. "Slipped."

I stayed where I was. "Like Lucifer?"

"Not like Lucifer!" he exclaimed, indignant.

I almost apologized, but then he tossed the Frisbee

back and added, "Except maybe for a bit of pride. Besides, Lucifer didn't just slip. He fell. All the way down."

As I fumbled the catch, Zachary went on, "That doesn't have to happen to us."

I believed him. I did. And it was all so amazing. Aimee had been right. It was time for good things to happen again. "There's something I have to tell you," I said. "It's about Brad, about what he did—"

"Quincie!" Dr. Morales called from the back door. "Is that you out there?"

Damn. "Tomorrow," I whispered. "Tomorrow we have to talk."

When I stepped into the kitchen, Dr. Morales asked, "Everything okay?"

"I thought I heard something outside," I said. "Um, raccoons. It turned out to be some baby raccoons." I suppressed a smile. "Can't sleep?"

"Can't stop thinking about Kieren," Roberto admitted, plugging in the coffeepot. "Wondering how he's doing. It's different for Meara. She knows about pack life. She knows what it means to manage a shift or not. She was raised with certain ideas about life as a wereperson. I respect all that. I do. But . . ."

"You never wanted him to leave in the first place," I realized out loud.

Dr. Morales's eyes went misty. "He should've had a chance to play football and graduate with his class and . . . You both deserved more, better than what you got."

He gave me a big dad hug, and I just went with it.

Now, There's a Metaphor

I hadn't been able to get ahold of Zachary yet that morning, but Clyde and Aimee met me before school on the front steps. At my request, they'd stopped by Sanguini's on the way and picked up a fresh sports bottle of porcine blood, courtesy of Nora.

I took a drag and relayed what had happened the night before.

As students flowed by, Clyde settled next to me. "A flaming sword?"

Aimee, leaning against the handrail, smirked.

"It's not funny!" I exclaimed, biting back a grin. I felt giddy, more hopeful than I'd been in ages. "Y'all believe me, don't you?"

"You could argue that a lightsaber is a flaming sword," Aimee said loudly, and it was then that I noticed gossip queen Winnie Gerhard lingering above and behind us on the stairs, pretending to do something on her cell phone.

"A lightsaber is a *laser* sword," I insisted, also projecting.

"Have you two ever played D and D?" Clyde put in.

A moment later, Aimee said, "Winnie's gone, but our geek cred is sealed forever."

"Who cares about her?" I exclaimed. "What do you think?"

"You're sure he wasn't a werepelican?" Clyde asked.

"No way! There would've been feathers all over his face, and he would've lost the arms completely." I glanced up. "Aimee?"

"I want to believe."

It was then that I remembered Zachary muttering something about his secret identity. I'd been so excited about the whole "angel" part that it had completely slipped my mind. For what it was worth, though, I suspected that Clyde thought I was crazy and Aimee knew how to keep a secret.

* * *

Due in part to preternatural energy, I was almost caught up in all of my classes, English included, though my teachers had the pesky habit of assigning new work.

As I made my way out of class, Mrs. Levy passed back my journal. "Glad to see you're writing again. You have a real knack for the Gothic. Those vignettes—"

"They're not fiction." Flipping through, I was pleased to see all "plus" marks.

At her startled expression, I added, "I didn't mean that exactly. Of course they're fiction. But they came to me as dreams. I wrote down what I remembered."

"Dreams?" my teacher repeated. "With that level of detail? That's remarkable. You reference the bowie knife specifically. Do you have a background in weapons?"

"I . . . no, I don't." That was weird.

"You do know that it's one of the knives mentioned in *Dracula*?"

"Oh." I shoved the journal in my backpack. "That must be it. I've been reading *Dracula*." Though, come to think of it, the nightmares had begun before I'd started the novel, and I didn't recall any knives in the story. "You've read it?"

Mrs. Levy raised an eyebrow. "Ah, yes, Eastern Europeans. Scary."

I wasn't sure what she meant. "Is it true that the count was related to Attila the Hun? He seemed awfully proud of that."

"What do you mean by *true?*"

Zipping up my pack, I said, "Never mind. It doesn't matter. I hate the book. It's even worse than 'The Lottery.' All the girls die."

"Not Mina," Mrs. Levy replied. "Mina Harker doesn't die."

"But didn't Mina drink Dracula's blood?" I asked. "Lucy died and became undead, and it's not clear if she even drank. But she had to have, right? And anyway, how could Mina drink and survive? That's impossible."

"You're not done reading it yet?" Mrs. Levy asked.

"I gave up. It was obvious where it was going." Or so I'd thought.

"But if you haven't finished," my teacher began again, "how do you know about the bowie knife? It's not mentioned until the end of the story."

KICKING IT, OLD-SCHOOL

*A*fter Chem, I left another message for Zachary and then tried Sanguini's main line. When Nora replied that he hadn't been in yet, I asked if she and Freddy were angels.

She chuckled. "That boy, he told me that you were wise to his game. Just as well. You could both use someone to talk to. As for Freddy and me, we're human, through and through. But it's nice of you to ask, hon. I'm flattered."

I couldn't just sit around waiting for Zachary. Shutting my cell, I jogged across the school parking lot to The Banana and nearly flattened two innocent squirrels on my way down Congress Avenue, through the Fairview neighborhood, and back to the Morales house.

Grateful that no one was home, I hurried upstairs to Kieren's bedroom and grabbed *Dracula*. Then I launched myself onto the water bed and picked up the story where I'd left off. It wasn't long before I saw it.

Mina is still making suicidal noises about having become a proto-vampire, and Van Helsing says, "Until the other, who has fouled your sweet life, is true dead you must not die. For if he is still with the quick Undead, your death would make you even as he is. No, you must live!"

I read it over and over. If I understood right, Van Helsing was saying that until Dracula was destroyed, Mina needed to stay alive. Otherwise, if he was "still with the quick Undead" when she passed away, she'd become a vampire like him.

So — flipping the logic — that also meant that if Dracula were destroyed *before* she died, then Mina would . . . might . . . be cured of the demonic infection and live on as a human being.

Van Helsing tries to bless Mina by touching her forehead with a holy wafer. But the wafer burns her skin, which only freaks her out more.

I set down the book and lifted Kieren's turquoise-and-silver crucifix from my chest. Bending my neck forward, I touched the metal briefly to my forehead.

Nothing happened.

The vampire hunters identify a house in Piccadilly as one of Dracula's lairs. Arthur and Quincey leave to find and "sanctify" more boxes while the others wait at the house for the monster. Shortly after the two men return, Dracula arrives, only to escape again, though Jonathan almost stabs him with a kukri knife.

Later, Mina goes to Van Helsing. "I want you to hypnotize me!" she says. "Do it before the dawn, for I feel that then I can speak, and speak freely. Be quick, for the time is short!"

Mina is psychically linked to Dracula, and by hypnotizing her, they discover that the count is leaving the country.

It's kind of a letdown. The legendary Count Dracula's master plan to evade Dr. Van Helsing's crack team of vampire hunters is to mail himself home in a box.

Mina can't understand why they don't just say good riddance. "But why need we seek him further, when he is gone away from us?"

Van Helsing explains, "Time is now to be dreaded, since he put that mark upon your throat."

Back to the bite again. Hmm, maybe the transformation process from human to undead worked the same for

Carpathians as for regular vampires—by blood inges-
tion or transfusion—but Van Helsing didn't really know
what he was talking about.

Or maybe he was being ridiculously cryptic or poetic
or both.

Anyway, there was still time to save Mina.

Ever more vampy, she joins the chase, helping to
track the count via Van Helsing's hypnosis. The heroes
worry that the mental connection works both ways, so
Dracula can spy on them through her. But finding the
villain fast matters more.

It was profoundly disturbing to consider. Despite
my flickering fear that the vampirism was simply costing me my sanity, I couldn't help feeling more and more
that Brad was truly whispering into my mind, invading
and manipulating my dreams and maybe even my waking thoughts. I felt a chill, realizing that—from a certain point of view—he might be with me here and now.
Within me here and now.

Before leaving, Mina again asks for promises that, if it
comes to it, they'll destroy her—using the same staking-
beheading-garlic ritual that freed Lucy's soul. She's
damned enthusiastic about the whole thing: " 'Euthanasia' is an excellent and a comforting word! I am grateful
to whoever invented it."

After more hypnotism, much lapping water, a fair
amount of hand-wringing, and a great chase, we're back

at the castle in the Carpathian Mountains. Van Helsing manages to dispatch all three of Dracula's dentally (and otherwise) endowed groupies.

The heroes finally intercept the box containing the count, fight off some gypsies, and *voilà!* Jonathan shears through the count's throat with his kukri knife, Quincey Morris stabs the heart with his bowie knife, and the Nosferatu collapses into dust.

Bradley told me once that any well-established vampire—over fifty or so—can turn to dust and regenerate, but . . . whatever. Our heroes think they've won.

There's a price, though. Uncle Quincey. He dies from a battle wound. But not until noticing that the holy-wafer scar on Mina's forehead is gone.

Her life and soul are saved.

"Oh, God!" Quincey says. "It was worth for this to die."

Would slaying any vampire free those he'd infected but had yet to transform? Would slaying Bradley cure the baby-squirrel eaters who'd tasted his blood?

Or did it only work that way with Carpathians?

I couldn't wait to talk to Zachary. He'd admitted to not being all-knowing, and okay, I got that. But he had to be some kind of expert on the undead. Why else would— had he said "middle management"?—heaven itself assign him to me?

I logged on to the Web, found the searchable text of *Dracula,* and double-checked. Neither knife had been mentioned earlier in the book. I'd read *kukri* and *bowie* for the first time today. Skimming back over my notes, I circled the references.

I'd seen Bradley with a bowie knife once before the nightmares had begun. That day he'd drugged my Cabernet, carried me to his basement, dressed me in the gauzy white nightgown, tied me to the bed frame, and tasted me with his fangs.

"Yes."

Him again. Fiercely ignoring the voice, I remembered being hungover when I arrived at his house. I remembered mentioning his collection of clocks and how we'd chatted about time . . . about how neither of us believed in squandering it. But I'd noticed the knife, too, hanging box-framed over his fireplace. And I—who'd known nothing much about weapons—had recognized it as a bowie knife.

Me. Quincie P. Morris. I had *specifically* identified it.

Could it have been the same knife as the one mentioned in the novel?

I'd bet Sanguini's on it.

Bradley had acquired the bowie knife that Uncle Quincey had plunged into Dracula's heart. And worse, even before I'd died, he'd somehow been affecting my mind.

Like the count had affected Lucy and Mina's. But how?

He wasn't a Carpathian. And I would know. He'd made me, and I could cross water, sleep in a clean bed, and wear a crucifix — no problem.

BAD NEWS

Sporting my school clothes, I arrived late to work, asked Yani to reassign Zachary's tables, and invited him and Freddy to meet me in the private dining room.

I didn't love telling them about my "dreams" and the whispering voice or showing them my notes and journal. But I felt wacko-nuts-ridiculous explaining my theory that Bradley had created some kind of psychic link between him and me—like Dracula had with Mina—and that, furthermore, Brad had somehow scored the bowie knife my generations-ago uncle had used to kill the count.

Which, come to think of it, seemed awfully coincidental. It sounded a whole lot more farfetched out loud than it had in my head.

The Chicagoans listened without interrupting, though, until after close that night.

I'd wanted Nora there, too, but she was busy in the kitchen.

I wanted Kieren there, for so many reasons, but that was never going to happen.

As I spoke, Freddy stood up to pace on the midnight-blue carpet. He'd taken off his black silk jacket, taken out his red contacts and fake fangs.

"What do you think?" I finally finished.

Zachary tore off a hunk of fresh, warm Italian bread and dipped it in olive oil. "I can only guess what you went through with this Brad—"

"You can guess?" I asked, more defensively than I'd intended.

"It's just that," he began again, "you're seventeen years old. Your entire existence has been turned upside down. It would be only normal if—"

"I'm having some kind of post-traumatic brain melt?" I struggled not to lose my patience. "Think about it. How would I recognize the type of knife?"

"Your father was an archaeologist," the angel said. "When you were younger, he might have shown you a picture. Or maybe you saw one in a museum, and—"

"I get that it sounds strange, vampires who can play mind tricks—"

"No, some can," he informed me. "Neophytes, even. Miranda . . ." He cleared his throat. "It's not that uncommon."

Freddy, who'd said nothing up until that point, stopped pacing and pushed up his wire-frame glasses. "The ability to enthrall their victims, face-to-face, yes. And granted, there's a mystical connection between eternals and those humans they've blessed—like an invisible preternatural umbilical cord. But, Quincie, what you're talking about . . . and I don't say this lightly . . . is a power of Dracula Prime."

Hadn't I just told them that?

Freddy drew his slender frame straighter. "It's long been debated whether the count was truly or at least wholly eliminated by Van Helsing and his friends. A legend among eternals states that Dracula's uncanny abilities somehow survived his presumed destruction—split and lingering within the weapons that killed him."

"The knives!" I exclaimed.

"And," he continued, "if Brad managed to find a spell that would let him access those powers, even just the half housed in Morris's knife—"

"Is that possible?" Zachary asked, dropping the bread. "Not the spell—I've seen my share of magic—but the part about the weapons. You're saying Drac Prime's psychic skills have been trapped all this time in the Morris knife?"

"It's not unthinkable," Freddy replied. "Count Dracula studied sorcery. He took being an eternal to a far more horrifying level, spawning a new, more insidious breed."

"The Carpathians," I said, relieved to have at least that much confirmed.

Freddy nodded. "Of which Dracula is believed to have been the first and last, though he sired others who predeceased him. They were closely related to eternals like you, my dear, conjured into being when the count tampered with the original spell that first created vampires. Or rather, the curse."

I double-checked my notes. "So there really are *two* kinds of vampires?"

"Only two?" Freddy rested his hands on the back of an empty chair. "Quincie, a staggering variety of supernatural blood drinkers have flourished throughout time and around the world—Babylonia, Russia, Serbia, ancient Greece, Brazil . . ." He glanced at Zachary. "Don't they teach children anything in the public schools?"

I didn't bother to ask who'd educated him. "In the novel, Van Helsing says the count studied at someplace called the Scholomance."

"With Lucifer," Zachary put in, reminding me of last night's conversation. "Some slip; some fall."

The two men went quiet, and I could tell by the way they traded looks that they were trying to decide how much to tell me.

"The kukri knife turned up earlier this year," Freddy finally admitted, sitting down again. "The bowie knife was believed to have been lost to the ages. Fortunately, the vast majority of eternals don't take the legend seriously."

Zachary sipped his sparkling water. "I don't think the individual now in possession of the kukri knife realizes that it's more than an antique. Let alone that it houses half of Drac Prime's powers."

That had been a carefully worded statement. "You don't think he's experimented with it?" I asked.

"She's wary of sorcery," Freddy explained, "or at least of its price."

Noting the gender pronoun, I wanted to ask who we were talking about. But then again, maybe it was better if I didn't know. We couldn't risk having Brad rip that information out of my head. If I could help it, he wasn't getting anything else from me.

Zachary pounded the table. "If this Brad does have Morris's bowie knife and he's able to use it to tap *any* of Drac's abilities, we have to stop him."

"And before he gets ahold of Harker's kukri knife," I agreed. "Given that he knows the legend is true, I'm sure Brad is looking for it."

Worse News

$\mathcal{C}$lyde peeked through the heavy red drapes into the private dining room. "Have you told them yet?"

"Not yet," I replied. "Shouldn't you be washing dishes?"

He bared his pointy teeth and went back to work.

"There's more?" Zachary asked.

Glancing from one new ally to the other, I swallowed hard and then explained what Bradley had done with the chilled baby squirrels. I didn't name names, but I did admit that some of our employees had been infected. "The victims should begin to transform in about a week and a half."

"Good Lord!" Freddy exclaimed. "Why didn't you say something sooner?"

"You're kidding, right?" I exclaimed. "Think about it. Three total strangers with mysterious ties to the demonic show up just when I need them. Normal people don't have a history with vampires. Normal people don't think that vampires exist anymore. If I hadn't realized last night—"

"Quincie." Zachary reached for Frank and turned to the October calendar, tapping where I'd circled the 11th. "It's okay."

Freddy nodded, holding up a hand in surrender.

"What matters is this," I said in a rush. "According to Stoker, Mina's life was saved when Dracula was destroyed. If we could hunt down Brad, his victims—"

"Are likely still doomed to undeath and damnation, just like any of those blessed by common vampires," Freddy said, drawing his PDA from his pocket. "It's true that, with Dracula Prime, the transformation of his spawn—including Mina Harker—became dependent on his continued existence. However—"

"Can we please not use the word *spawn*?" I muttered.

"Yes," Zachary agreed, shooting his friend a look.

"Of course," Freddy conceded. "But even though Brad might be *using* some Carpathian magic, *he's* still a typical eternal." At my puzzled expression, he added, "To whatever degree, Brad may have managed to co-opt those powers of the count contained in Morris's knife. But Brad's still Brad. Those abilities are not inherent in him. He transformed you, for example, and you're not a Carpathian. Neither is he."

"Though from what you're saying," Zachary put in, "if Brad gets ahold of Harker's knife, too, then he might as well be a Carpathian. He'd have all their strengths."

Damn. "So, there's no hope?" I asked. "The infected are doomed?"

"There's always hope," the angel assured me.

THE SCENE OF THE CRIME

After work, I parked The Banana on a residential street near the Pease Mansion. I'd brought the standard battle-axe that Kieren had used against the vice principal. The angel had worn his holy sword. Meanwhile, across town, Freddy was looking into the issue of Harker's knife and how we could prevent Brad from acquiring it.

As I locked my car door, I asked, "How does Freddy know so much about vampires?" I'd expected Zachary to be the one with all the answers.

"Freddy was born and raised among human servants of the worldwide vamp royalty and aristocracy," Zachary replied, coming around the convertible. "It's a pitiable subculture, supporting truly revolting dictators. Walking away isn't usually an option. But for most of his adult life, Freddy managed to stay on the outskirts of eternal high society. Finally, here in Austin, he's left it completely."

"Except," I said, "for playing the vampire chef every night at Sanguini's."

As we started on foot through the Old Enfield neighborhood, Zachary explained, "It's for a good cause. Freddy has always had to be something of a chameleon. Blending in, suiting others' expectations to survive. But now, aside from the midnight toast, he has the freedom to be himself. And working with us on the side of good . . . That's something he's always longed to do."

I thought about that as we hiked in the dark to Bradley's two-and-a-half-story 1920s home, entering the backyard through a side door in the tall wooden fence. The cops had been here already, but the angel had wanted to take a look for himself, and I'd insisted on coming along.

With Zachary, I didn't have to pass for human like I did with the Moraleses, with most of the world. And I didn't have to be the one in charge, like I was at Sanguini's and with Aimee and Clyde. Maybe I should've been awestruck that he was an angel, and it still caught me up short. But Mama used to say that God was always with us, and Zachary had explained that guardian angels were everywhere, all the time; it was just that they seldom showed themselves. So I kept telling myself that the whole thing was business as usual.

The back gate was unlocked, and a glass-paned back door offered a partial view of Brad's kitchen. Peering in, I didn't see any sign of activity.

Meanwhile, my GA (AKA guardian angel) had slipped off his shirt—leaving him bare-chested in the moonlight—and wrapped it around his hand.

Despite my devotion to Kieren, I still had eyes. I couldn't help noticing Zachary's shoulders, chest, abs . . . the inch-wide cherub inked into the skin over his heart. "You have a tattoo? Are you allowed to have a tattoo?"

"It wasn't entirely my fault," he replied, punching through a glass pane. "There was tequila involved."

"Are you crazy? What if there's an alarm?"

"We'll find out soon enough." Reaching in, he opened the door.

No alert sounded.

"Show-off," I whispered. "I could've just forced it open."

Inside the kitchen, I studied the Viking range, stainless-steel appliances, and the silver Colonial chandelier hanging above the marble island. I could almost imagine Bradley at the stove, sautéing porcini and veal kidneys in a veal stock reduction. That's when I realized my hands were trembling, and I tightened them on the axe handle.

We skulked through open French doors and the empty dining room into the empty parlor. No leather club chairs, no antique clocks, no bowie knife above the mantel.

Nothing in the sunroom or in the foyer or in the tiny restroom under the stairs or in any of the bedrooms or baths on the second floor.

Nothing in the attic with the pitched roof or out on the south balcony.

"He's not here," I whispered.

"Aren't I?"

Damn. Brad might've kept his promise and left, physically left Austin. But what difference did it make if he could still penetrate my mind?

Hauling the axe, I marched down to the basement door. I thundered farther down to the unfinished, windowless concrete room containing the antique iron-frame twin bed. I heard my GA following me, calling my name. But I couldn't stop. Wouldn't.

I swung the blade into the rusted bed frame. "Damn."

I swung the blade again. "Damn him."

Again. "Damn him to hell!"

Again and again, though I couldn't feel it, not in my arms, back, shoulders.

Though I couldn't feel it, not in my heart or mind.

I swung the blade until, finally, the frame was nothing but scrap metal, and then I sank to my knees on the cold, gray floor. Crying.

I didn't know how to be what I was now. Brad's fault, and in some dark corner of my mind, I blamed him even more for leaving me to deal with it alone. But then again, I wasn't alone, was I?

Zachary reached for the axe, and I let him have it. He set it aside and knelt, wrapping me into a hug. For a second, I stiffened, not wanting to be touched. But it was such a safe and comforting embrace, like I'd skinned my knee and he was the doting big brother. Like Kieren was to Meghan.

"I hate Brad," I whispered, hiccupping. "I hate him. I hate losing. I lost myself."

"You're not lost, Quincie," the angel insisted. "You're still here."

"I'm dead. Mama and Daddy are dead. Vaggio's dead. Uncle D. And I'm a dead, *dead* thing. A dead, dead ruined thing."

"Quincie," Zachary said, gently raising my chin. "Quincie, look at me. Everybody who ever loved you still loves you. Your parents still love you. Vaggio still loves you. Your grandparents, too. I promise you, kiddo: the love never goes away. You just have to give yourself permission to feel it."

I pulled back, blinking at him. "That's how it works? For real?"

"For real." He almost smiled. "Trust me; I've got connections."

A WING AND A PRAYER

On Wednesday, I walked in on Zachary and Freddy, seated at the table in Sanguini's break room, folding napkins into bat shapes. It was a job that Nora and Sergio typically assigned to people who were getting on their nerves.

"We fly," Freddy said.

"We drive," my GA countered. "It won't help to get there before—"

"We have money," Freddy replied.

"Not buy-a-plane money!"

"We don't have to buy—"

"You want to fly commercial?" Zachary countered. "With weapons? Do you have any idea what my supervisor upstairs would say if my sword was lost in checked luggage? Especially after that last fiasco, when it was confiscated by the cops?"

When I laughed, Freddy looked up. "Quincie, we have a working plan to beat Brad to Harker's kukri knife, and you would be a big help—"

"You don't have to," the angel put in, tossing a napkin aside.

"But if you don't come along," Freddy added, "Zachary can't either because his first duty is to you, as your guardian." At my GA's glare, Freddy shrugged. "It's true."

"Go?" I asked, joining them at the table. "Go where?" I paused. "Oh, wait. Never mind. I'm not supposed to know, right? So Brad can't find out through me."

I hated the thought of leaving Sanguini's, especially with so many of Brad's victims scheduled to rise in just over a week. But there was nothing we could do to stop that now. All we could hope for was to limit the powers at Brad's disposal before he could call the baby-squirrel eaters into his service.

"Quincie," Zachary replied, "we can find another way, if—"

"I'm in," I replied.

HOT BLOOD

*S*ergio didn't mind my taking some time off. "You should get out more," he said in the manager's office. "Young girl like you, there's a whole world waiting."

More like a whole underworld. "You sound like Vaggio," I said. "He used to always tell me not to forget that I was a teenager. What are you going to do about Freddy?" Somebody had to temporarily take his place for the midnight toast.

"Mercedes!" Sergio exclaimed, clapping his hands together. "She's been begging me to let her play the vampire chef, and you know, she's so fashionable, so witty—"

"So sultry in a Jane Russell kind of way," I said, quoting what he always said.

I could hardly imagine either of them in the midst of their initial blood lust. God, Mercedes had a brown belt.

THE ROAD TO HELL

*T*onight was First Thursday, which meant all the shops on South Congress would stay open late. Parking had already become nightmarish, and the ninety-something-degree heat had no effect on the already impressive foot traffic.

Outside Sanguini's, Nora paced around the empty lot next door. "Quincie, do you know who owns this property?"

I shook my head. "When Uncle D decided to remodel Fat Lorenzo's, he talked about buying it, but the budget ran dry. Why?"

"I think it could be turned into a wonderful garden. We could grow our own vegetables. It would bring more green onto the street."

She wouldn't be coming on the trip. We'd all agreed on that. But I could count on her and Sergio to take care of Mama's restaurant while I was gone. It occurred to me, though, that staying behind might be harder, and not just emotionally. "You may be getting a frantic phone call from the Moraleses tomorrow."

Nora nodded. "That's all right."

"Miz Morales can be—"

"That's all right, too." She rested a hand on my shoulder. "Hon, I'm not promising they won't be out of sorts when you return. But I'm not going to tell them where you're going, both for your sake and theirs."

That had sounded ominous. Whoever had Harker's knife, I somehow doubted she'd roll out the red carpet. Given Brad's mental eavesdropping, I understood why I couldn't know more about what lay ahead. But that didn't make it any easier.

Truth was, we might not make it back.

Kieren and I used to talk every day. How strange that I could cease to exist forever, and he might never find out. God, I hoped he was okay.

Zachary's car had to have been the largest SUV ever manufactured. The design looked almost military, but its sparkling black paint with red racing stripes was all glitz.

After loading up Nora's care package, I turned to say good-bye to Clyde and Aimee.

The Possum ran a fingertip down the hood. "Hello, Mystery Machine."

"We're going with you," Aimee announced. "Our parents think we're spending the weekend at a youth retreat near Bastrop, sponsored by your church."

I was flabbergasted. "Who'll wash the dishes?" Not my snappiest reply.

"We found a couple of people willing to fill in at the last minute," Clyde said.

I marched past him to the back door of the restaurant and opened it to peer into the already frantic kitchen. "Mrs. Levy? Mr. Wu?"

They waved from the sink.

"If we all die," Clyde called, "Sergio will have to hire replacements anyway."

Zachary drove, Freddy rode shotgun, and I sat on the first passenger bench next to Aimee, who had Clyde on her other side. So Bradley couldn't track us, I'd offered to travel blindfolded. I felt stupid riding in the SUV that way, but he'd too often slipped into my thoughts and dreams for us to underestimate the threat.

About three minutes out, it occurred to my GA that (a) his windows weren't tinted and (b) driving with a blindfolded teenage girl in the back might look suspicious to people in passing vehicles. Consequently, Aimee and I traded places, putting me between her and the Possum.

From the sound of the traffic, I could tell we'd gotten onto a busy highway, probably I-35. I tried not to dwell on it.

It had been Clyde who'd realized that we couldn't listen to the radio beyond the Austin stations' broadcast range because the DJs and ads would clue me (and, again, possibly Brad) in on our location.

The car, which Zachary had proudly referred to as a 1987 Impaler, had no CD or MP3 player. But Freddy had brought along his old Blondie, Pat Benatar, Billy Joel, and Pink Floyd tapes, if only for background noise.

"When we get there," Freddy was saying, "Quincie, and *only* Quincie, is going with us to retrieve the kukri knife."

Clyde said, "Fine by me," as Aimee exclaimed, "No way!"

"It's not negotiable," Freddy insisted. "Any argument, and we let you off at the next exit."

After a moment, Zachary added, "We both admire your loyalty."

"But," Freddy reminded us, "there's a possibility that, if you don't do as we say, you could die or worse." He paused before muttering, "Assuming we're not arrested first for taking three minors across state lines without their parents' permission."

"I'm already dying," Aimee announced, just like that.

"She ordered the chilled baby squirrels," I clarified.

"I've got—what?" she added. "Maybe a week left as a human being."

Zachary exited from the highway, explaining that he needed to speak with Aimee alone for a while, and a few minutes later, when they got out of the car, I could hear a fast-food intercom system in the background.

Meanwhile, Freddy broke out Nora's care package of bread sticks, pine nuts, walnuts, Italian sodas, and porcine blood.

"No crickets?" the Possum complained.

We talked and drove and drove and talked. Aimee's mood had improved. She chatted about fantasy novels with Clyde and Zachary, who apparently had the reading tastes of a teenage girl. We all gossiped about people at Sanguini's, and Freddy pitched the intriguing idea of opening a catering branch.

Hours later, I fell asleep listening to "Love Is a Battlefield."

"*A blindfold,*" *Bradley observed.* "*Baby, I had no idea that you were into that sort of thing.*"

Refusing to play, I asked a question that had been weighing on me. "*Before you lost your soul, were you a good person?*"

"*I was ordinary,*" *he answered as if that had been the most horrible thing in the world.* "*A short-order cook, the son of poor Russian immigrants. But soon . . .*"

"*You want to rule the monsters of Texas,*" *I said.*

"*Not just Texas,*" *he replied.* "*Not just the monsters. And mostly you.*"

GOOD INTENTIONS

$\mathcal{S}$tay close," Freddy ordered as I tore the dark silk from my eyes and jumped down from the SUV. The evening air felt chilly, in the upper forties. "Stay very close."

We'd been careful. I hadn't so much as glanced out my hotel-suite windows, and even before we'd checked in last night, every magazine or other hint of the locale had been removed from my room.

We'd left the sophomores at the hotel but dropped off Zachary a minute or so earlier, maybe a block away. Or on the other side of an immense property.

Beyond "north," I had no idea where I was. A vast parking lot with an upscale clientele. Porsches, Ferraris, Rolls-Royces, Lamborghinis . . . a fleet of limos.

"Remember, you are a predator, as lethal as lovely, and tonight you must pass as an aristocrat as well. I regret not having had an opportunity to better prepare you, but that might've tipped off our mentally intrusive opponent. Perhaps it's better this way, though. You're quite poised for your age. To the extent possible, be silent. When in doubt, raise a disdainful eyebrow. On the off chance that you should encounter—"

"My God!" I stared up, up, *up* at a magnificent white stone castle—at the arched windows, the red-capped towers, the red dragon on the black flag. This was no scaled-down amusement park attraction. It was the real deal. Again, I exclaimed, "My God!"

"Not even close," Freddy replied. "This, my dear, is the U.S. Midwest regional estate in Whitby Estates, Illinois. The subdivision is entirely controlled by eternals."

Should he have told me that? "Brad—"

"May well have already deduced that you've been moving north, but our having left from Texas didn't give him much to work with. It would've probably come up once we got inside anyway. Try not to worry. For the most part, eternals travel long distances just like humans or werepeople—by car, bus, plane, train, or boat. With any luck, we'll be in and out before he has any hope of intercepting us."

With any luck.

Freddy extended his arm. "You might as well know that both Nora and Zachary used to live and work here. They don't like to talk about it."

Resting my fingertips on Freddy's tux sleeve, I paused at the sound of not-too-far-away howling and scanned a distant wall of evergreens.

"Sentries," he explained, leading me through rows of parked cars toward the castle. "Don't mistake them for werepeople. Those are eternals in wolf form who guard the property, its residents, and guests."

"What's the plan?" I asked in a quiet voice.

"I'll finesse your cover, and you'll make sure that I'm not sucked dry. We blend, making every effort to avoid Her Majesty and her personal staff."

I nearly tripped over my taffeta skirt. "Her Majesty?"

"She'll be the one surrounded by sycophants." Glancing at his wristwatch, Freddy added, "In one hour, at precisely 11:30 P.M., we'll pay a visit to the security guard, claiming that your ruby-and-sapphire bracelet has been stolen—"

"I'm not wearing a bracelet—"

"Which will make it that much harder for him to track it down. Our job is simple. Divert the guard from the security cameras to give Zachary a chance to make off with Harker's knife."

"Isn't that stealing?" I asked. "Is he allowed to do that?"

"I think you'll find that our Zachary, despite the best of intentions, is somewhat predisposed to bend the rules."

I took comfort in the fact that we'd prevented Brad from learning the knife's location through me. But then again, he might have found another source of that information.

"Once the angel exits with the knife, be it through a door or window," Freddy said, "the new metal detectors will sound. Be ready for anything."

"Wait." I stopped in place beside a shiny black stretch limo. "If you know these high-society bloodsuckers, why not just *ask* them for Harker's knife?"

"Don't say 'bloodsucker' or, for that matter, 'vampire,'" Freddy insisted, urging me forward. "Here, it is 'eternal,' and—don't forget—the story of the knives is considered a myth. We don't want to do anything to change that impression." He leaned in, further lowering his voice. "We most especially do not want to reveal to the soulless eternal queen that she holds in her possession the key to fifty percent of the most formidable vampiric abilities that the underworld has ever seen."

"But—"

"The devil you know," he muttered mostly to himself, "is still a devil."

Through the arched doorway, strolling beneath a soaring ceiling and past white stone walls, I was reminded of Sanguini's, except these weren't faux painted.

"A first-rate reproduction," he whispered. "And higher-tech than it looks."

We'd arrived late to the party. As Freddy tilted his head at a door marked SECURITY, I could hear the festivities ahead. Voices, laughter . . . techno rock?

The hallway smelled faintly of cigar smoke.

We made our way past massive dragon-themed tapestries and luminous paintings of Paris to a large courtyard crowded with exquisitely coiffed guests, most of whom were showing fangs.

With my free hand, I tried to pull up the strapless top of my forest-green gown. I felt conspicuous, showing off so much freckled cleavage. I hadn't picked out the dress. When we'd arrived at the hotel, it had been waiting for me in my suite, courtesy of Freddy. For tonight, he'd also nixed my wearing Kieren's turquoise crucifix and presented me with a pair of black pearl earrings.

"Va-va-va-voom!"

"Go to hell," I whispered.

Bar tables dotted the glamorous crowd, flanked by a buffet on one side and the raised stage on the other. The band wore boxy, shiny outfits in primary colors and moved like robots. Red, blue, and yellow lights flashed from the stage and surrounding rooftops.

I noted the glittery yellow linens, the six-foot-long dragon ice sculpture. The empty iron shackles hanging from chains fastened to the surrounding four stone walls.

"First the Louvre . . . ," Freddy said with an amused sigh, pointing.

At the center of the yard, a lit glass pyramid, about eight feet tall, stood on a slightly raised circular platform. I supposed it was art.

"I can only imagine what Her Majesty had to say about that," he added, scanning the crowd. "She's brilliant but pragmatic, very old-school, utterly vicious, occasionally petulant, and fancies herself quite the critic."

"It sounds like you know her pretty well," I said.

Freddy shrugged, "Before leaving town, I was the premier event coordinator to the eternal hierarchy." His gaze swept the courtyard. "It appears that I haven't been easy to replace."

An elegant man approached, holding a glass of blood wine in one hand and a smoldering cigar in the other. "Feeling nostalgic?"

"Still the faithful lapdog?" Freddy replied.

My fingertips tingled, tempted by the bouquet of the drink, and then I noticed the stranger's face, build. He looked like Freddy. Not just a passing resemblance. Identical. Exactly alike, except that the twin's hair wasn't bleached, he wasn't wearing eyeglasses, and he was modeling black tails and a diamond-rimmed Rolex.

"I will have you know," the brother began, "that I'm no longer serving the Mantle in the capacity of personal assistant. I'm the head of the dynastic transition team."

"So you're a personal assistant with a better title. You're surrendering your soul for that." Freddy leaned toward me. "Quincie, this is Harrison, a lost cause."

Surrendering? So Freddy's brother was a vampire, had *chosen* to become a vampire. Like Uncle D.

Harrison puffed on his cigar. "She's an eternal. I can smell the blood on her."

I saw no reason to confide that I'd been drinking warmed *porcine* blood.

"Who is she again?" he added. "I don't remember her from the guests' files. Don't tell me she's a rogue."

"No, no," Freddy replied, reaching for his handkerchief. "Nothing like that. She's simply an as-yet-unregistered neophyte." He began cleaning his lenses. "Emphasis on the *neo*. The eternal that elevated Quincie abruptly left town—"

"Without paying taxes on her?" Harrison looked me up and down, apparently unimpressed, before returning his attention to his twin. "Ah, and so you dragged in this little charity case hoping I'd finesse her papers in the midst of this grand celebration in honor of Her Majesty's glorious return from her international tour and—"

"You don't mind, do you?" Freddy asked.

"Not so much," Harrison replied. "These aristocratic bastards still treat me like servant meat. Come on, we can take care of the forms in my office."

"Quincie," Freddy began, "why don't you enjoy the party? I'll deal with this. My brother and I may end up chatting awhile. Family reunion, you know."

What was Freddy doing? Where was he going? Hadn't his own words been "stay very close"? Then I realized: it would be a hell of a lot harder pulling a fast one on the security guard with Harrison hovering over us. I'd have to handle the job by myself.

As the twins abandoned me to the party, I heard Harrison say something about the queen's already having scheduled tonight's event planner for execution.

HELL ON EARTH

*M*y last major social event had been the eighth-grade spring fling.

Granted, I'd hit a handful of weddings with Kieren, helping out Miz Morales with her bridal clients, and of course Sanguini's launch party had been a total blowout. But with those, I'd had jobs to do, clearly defined roles. Truth was, I didn't have practice mingling, let alone at an upscale undead social affair.

The scent of human blood rose from hundreds of wineglasses, and I had to struggle to think straight. I debated taking refuge inside the castle, but Freddy had mentioned security cameras, and I didn't want to draw the guard's attention too soon.

Weaving through the international, multilingual crowd, I tried to appear uninterested as I overheard talk of fashion in Milan, drug trafficking in Colombia, and human trafficking in South Asia. It was all I could do not to turn and look when someone mentioned a "Zachary" and "the End Days."

"The exalted mistress fears God," muttered a man in a top hat.

"Bit late for that," his female companion cheerfully replied in a British accent.

Hardly anyone looked over age forty, but that was a lie. I'd appear seventeen forever. At twenty-seven, folks might write me off as fresh-faced, at thirty-three as having great skin. But how soon would I need to become a makeup expert or disappear for twenty years only to return again as "my daughter"? How could I run Mama's restaurant that way?

Still, as a freak in the human world, it was freeing to be just one of the crowd. Was this the glittering underworld that Brad had hoped to introduce me to? In my gown, I felt almost like a princess. And, really, what was so awful about that?

A few steps later, a bald man with large gold hoops dangling from each earlobe caressed my cheek. "What's this? New blood? Tell me, sweet. Who's your master?"

"Master?" I asked, drawing back.

"Who do you belong to?" he clarified. "I might make an offer of purchase." Glancing at my teeth, he added, "Too late, I see. Pity, that. No offense."

With a bow, he moved on, and I realized that my fangs had descended.

That's when the music stopped, and a woman on-stage rang a small silver bell. "Treats for everyone!" she announced in a shrill voice. "Suicides, fresh and delicious!"

The crowd politely applauded as a line of teen and twenty-something captives, wearing nothing but translucent red knee-length sheaths, snaked through the nearest arched door until they circled the courtyard. The shackles on their wrists and ankles, the chains connecting them, had been forged from red tissue. A tribute to the iron hanging from the walls? The prisoners looked forlorn, rabbity, but utterly resigned.

Suicides, the announcer had said. They had entered freely and of their own will.

The bell rang again, and the guests rushed to choose their respective prey—some courtly in their seduction, others tearing into the first available victim. It was like a

Victorian parlor game, set amid a mouthwatering orgy of slaughter and desecration.

A gaunt boy, a suicide with hair like straw, ripped off his tissue shackles and sobbed. Loud. Grating. He'd changed his mind. An eternal seized his neck and broke it.

Sanguini's had never seemed so wholesome. I couldn't believe that Freddy had left me alone here. It was clearly no place for a seventeen-year-old virgin vampire.

Meanwhile, human servants huddled in the middle of the yard, making an impressive effort to maintain their flow of small talk. "Have you tried the wild prawns?" "Will the governor be indicted?" "Does it usually snow before Thanksgiving?"

Just then, I overheard someone mention another familiar name. "Miranda?" I asked a nearby servant girl. "You said something about a Miranda?" Could she have been talking about Zachary's Miranda?

"The former regent," came the reply. "Miranda was our ruler, however briefly, before the current Majesty ascended to the throne. She was famous for her temper — Miranda, I mean — even before her father formally presented her to eternal society. And then there was the angel! How is it that you haven't heard the stories?"

Oh, my God! Zachary was in love with the dead undead vampire queen! How was that possible? I'd assumed she'd been like me, a regular girl, an unwitting victim, not . . .

I stared, mesmerized by the spectacle in the courtyard—at an eternal on his knees, nursing blood from a vein below his victim's rib cage. As he gripped the backs of her thighs, the girl being bled jerked her hips forward, long blond curls falling across her tear-stained cheeks. Then she threw her head back again, and another aristocrat claimed her open lips with his own.

"Temper?" I choked out, forcing my attention back to the pretty servant. "What were you saying?"

Just then, she presumed to run her fingertips down my bare arm, and I found myself intrigued by her bold-ness. Her dress resembled a toga. Her dark hair had been twisted with shiny gold ribbon and secured in loops. "You're a neophyte!" She moved to press her breasts against mine. "Drowning in the guilt, cutie? Is that why you're not sampling the freebies?"

Freddy had told me to blend. "That's right. I'm new around here. You were saying something about . . . the late Queen Miranda?"

"The Dragon Princess, they called her—before she ascended to rule, of course—but then the angel appeared and . . . it all happened so fast. She abdicated almost imme-diately upon taking the throne."

"The angel?" Right, *Zachary.* God, I'd almost forgotten what I was doing here! What time was it? Had he already made off with Harker's knife?

"I know, angels crashing eternal galas." Taking my hand, she raised it to her creamy throat. "My mistress says it means that the End Days are nigh."

I felt her pulse, wild with anticipation. Her heartbeat, *beat, beat,* urging me on.

"She won't do it."

"Miranda?" I asked, losing my concentration.

"My mistress! She won't let me drink. She only blesses the boys. She's afraid of the competition. That's not you. You're a modern woman, newly risen."

"You *want* to drink?" I asked. "To become like me?"

Gray eyes shining, she breathed, "We'll be BFFs."

Best friends forever . . . The thought of Kieren sobered me.

"No, thank you." Had I blown my cover, turning her down? "It's nothing personal. I'm just not in the market for a new best friend."

The girl looked stricken. "Please."

"The lady said no," a raspy voice interrupted. "Run along. If your mistress finds out about this . . ." She'd already hurried away.

The new arrival's neatly trimmed mustache and mirrored sunglasses fit well with his cream-colored tux and cape but made it hard to judge how old he looked.

Colorful flashing lights reflected off his hair. Was it red or blond? I couldn't tell.

"You'll have to forgive them, all of them. The aristocrats, the personal assistants, the wannabes . . ." He shrugged at the blood orgy. "The pathetic, self-sacrificing party favors. And this. Tonight *this* is considered the height of eternal culture."

As the musicians switched to classical music, the overhead lighting lost its colored tint. "Oh, that's better." He gestured to a bar table in the corner. "My, the queen is in a lousy mood."

We wove through the milling servants. His fingertips brushed my shoulder blade, and I experienced a rolling wave of dizziness. With that slight touch, the gala— reality itself—seemed to fall away. The people and the monsters, the castle and the moon.

The edges of the world grew fuzzy, distant. Silent.

We stood facing each other, me and my charming companion—a hot wind tossing our hair and clothes—on a narrow wooden suspension bridge that swayed above a boiling crimson sea. The plank beneath my feet creaked. Others were missing.

Lightning streaked the cloudy sky above. I looked ahead, behind, and saw no sign of shore. If I fell, I'd fall forever, but at least I had him. I knew him, didn't I?

The water below us began to churn, and I gripped the

*rope railing. Then the stranger tore open his dress shirt,
used a pointed nail to slash his fair skin, and—cupping the
back of my head—pulled my lips to the trickling wound.*

*With no thought of refusal, I nursed like Mina had
from Dracula's breast.*

Like a kitten.

*How unfair that I'd been made to settle for filthy pig's
blood when here nectar ran free! Why shouldn't I seek
solace?*

*No, more than that. Why shouldn't I relish what I'd
become?*

"Baby, I knew, sooner or later, we'd be together again."

Baby? Who called me that? I hated it. Who?

*Damn Bradley's mind tricks! He'd clouded my abil-
ity to recognize him. Had he already beaten Zachary to
Harker's knife?*

Thoughts of the angel released me from Brad's thrall.
I shoved him away, slammed the point of my dress boot
into his groin, and spat his blood into his face.

He grunted, staggered, staring at me—all wounded
surprise—and disintegrated into mist a split second
before my fist would've shattered his face.

Now I understood. True, the courtyard boasted its
share of temptations, but Brad had been mentally stok-
ing my blood lust. God forbid that he fight fair.

I wiped my wet, sticky mouth. What time was it?

A barbarian in a smoking jacket slid his hand over my hip. "My turn?"

I crushed his wrist before throwing him into the glass pyramid. It cracked, changing the light in the courtyard, quieting the revelers, the musicians, shifting all attention to me. Where was Freddy? Zachary? What was I supposed to do now?

"*Mademoiselle* Quincie," came an accented voice from behind. "I am Philippe, Her Majesty's consort, and I bid you welcome in the name of the Mantle. Please accept my most humble apologies for the indignity that you have suffered as our guest."

A few jaws dropped at that as he slipped his scarred hand around mine, like I was a little girl who needed to be led away from a playground skirmish.

I wasn't positive, but I thought that by "consort" he meant "boyfriend," only in a fancier, more grown-up kind of way. The eternal queen's boyfriend.

Why was he being so nice to me? I'd crashed this party and made a terrible scene. Still, kudos to Her Majesty. With his silver bat-head cane, long gold braid, and the small medal at his collar, Philippe looked extraordinarily elegant.

"*Mademoiselle,*" he began again, "what happened to your hand?"

"Claws, werewolf," I blurted out, still shaky, as the other guests turned their attention elsewhere. I figured if he could ask, so could I. "What happened to your hands and face?"

"Fire, rabbi," he replied, meeting my eyes as if we were friends now, or at least understood each other's scars. "Shall we go see the exalted mistress?"

It was gracious of him to ask. "Sure. Why not?"

THE DEVIL YOU KNOW

*P*hilippe escorted me into a soaring throne room, flanked on both sides with red velvet curtains—like the ones at Sanguini's, only much, much longer—and lit by a dozen candelabra. He stepped away as Freddy and Zachary rushed to my side.

Neither looked injured, thank God. But clearly our plan had been a total failure.

"Presenting Quincie," Harrison announced.

Freddy ignored his twin. "Are you all right, my dear?"

I was not all right. I'd completely lost it outside—my self-control, my mind, myself. I didn't know who I'd been for a while there in the courtyard. If that was a preview of soullessness, I'd happily chug down a two-liter jug of holy water the very minute I wasn't needed anymore. I'd shower in it. I'd dive right in.

"Did Brad hurt you?" Zachary wanted to know.

Had they run into him, too? "I can't talk about it now."

Meanwhile, Freddy taunted his twin. "I thought you weren't playing house servant anymore."

"Shut up," replied Harrison, moving to stand beside a substantial black marble dais at the head of the room.

"Did he get it?" I asked Zachary. "Brad, I mean."

"The knife? *Oui*," declared a melodious voice, her accent less pronounced than Philippe's. "Your conceited, onetime nobody of a rogue, Bradley Sanguini, is in possession of Jonathan Harker's kukri knife and, soon, all the powers of Dracula Prime. That brash, horrid, *American* thief stole it from me!"

"Her Royal Majesty Sabine," Harrison announced. "And in a chipper mood."

Damn, damn, damn. The newly crowned queen of the undead, and she somehow had learned what the knives could do.

Strolling around a red-padded, gold-framed throne that was much taller than she was, the regal vampire effortlessly lowered herself to perch with one slim ankle tucked behind the other. An ash blonde, with skin like a china doll and serpentine grace, she could've passed for a high-school freshman. Or at least she could've if she'd traded in her black A-line satin tulle gown for something a bit less resplendent.

"Curtsy," Freddy hissed as he executed a formal bow.

I'd never curtsied before, but I did my best, if only to lower Freddy's anxiety level. Zachary, in contrast, angled himself protectively in front of us. He didn't bow.

I would've felt a lot better if he'd brought along his flaming sword, but recalled what Freddy had said about the castle metal detectors.

Philippe positioned himself alongside the throne while Sabine regarded my GA, dipping her delicate-looking fingers into a red velvet pouch, drawing out what appeared to be soil, and letting it fall aimlessly onto the platform.

"Friend Zachary," she began in a weary tone. "You and these neophyte girls . . . You cannot save them all."

"I'm only sorry," he shot back, "that I never had a chance to save you."

Direct hit. Sabine drew her slight form taller in the chair, though her manner still seemed more resigned than imperial. "You have requested this audience. I have guests waiting. Yet I am at your disposal. What is it that you wish from me now?"

I blinked at her cooperative attitude, her deference. The man at the party had been right. The vampire queen did fear God, and by extension, his messengers.

"The legend of the knives," Zachary said. "I've heard the story from Freddy. But you're an Old Blood. What do you know about it?"

"The details have been lost," Sabine replied. "*Mais oui*, it is said that Dracula Prime was survived by his Carpathian powers, split between and contained within Harker's and Morris's knives. A bloodletting, perhaps as inconsequential as pricking one's fingertip, while reciting the appropriate incantation, has been mentioned with regard to accessing those abilities from the respective weapons."

Again, she dipped her fingers into the velvet pouch. "A full and permanent transfer of the powers, however, from the knives to an individual eternal would require a more significant spell, a more substantial sacrifice."

More falling dirt. "Without that larger ritual, a rival eternal could abscond with the knives, repeat the minor bloodletting, and spirit the Carpathian magic away."

"The incantation?" Zachary pressed. "The details of the larger ritual?"

"Unknown, or even I—no aficionado of the dark arts—might have been tempted to try them, once I'd heard there might be some truth to the story."

Philippe tapped his cane once. "You mentioned Texas earlier?"

At Zachary's nod, Philippe informed us that over the past two years the U.S. southwest eternal aristocracy had been wiped out in a series of bombing attacks. One in Tucson, one in Dallas, one in Las Vegas, and one in Salt Lake City. He added that Henry Johnson, AKA Bradley Sanguini, had been identified as a "rogue of interest" in those cases. "Harrison?" Philippe prompted.

"We sent three enforcers after him, but they have not filed reports in some days."

So Mullet Man and Mole Woman had been their goons. The guy in the park, too.

"Meanwhile, I personally began tracing the upstart's writings," Harrison added. "At the Chicago History Museum, I came across a 1943 article in which he referenced a spell book associated with the knives. It allegedly had been last in the possession of a mobster killed in the Saint Valentine's Day massacre back in '29. It was rumored that a member of Al Capone's gang had stolen the book, but no one knows for certain."

From there, Philippe explained, they began to look seriously into whether the story of the knives was fact or fiction and eventually concluded that it was true.

I probably should've taken a hint from Freddy's subordinate demeanor and continued to let Zachary do all of the talking. I didn't. Instead, I moved forward on the long, narrow crimson carpet leading to the throne. "We believe Brad is raising an army. An army of soon-to-rise neophytes whose minds he may be able to manip-ulate, even control, using the power that had been trapped in Morris's bowie knife." I paused at the edge of the black marble platform. "So. How. Do. We. Stop. Him?"

"You dare to address me in such a tone?" Sabine countered. "It is I who rule the Mantle of Dracul."

Clearly, her accommodating attitude toward Zachary didn't extend to me.

"Beware, little neophyte, I am not only an Old Blood but the current Dracula as well. *I* rule the underworld. *I* maintain order. *I* represent our interests in dealing with the lesser beings—domestic and international, natural and supernatural."

Apparently, the vampire royalty had puffed itself up by adopting "Dracula" as a title. "But, even as an Old Blood, even as queen," I argued, "you're not as strong as the count. As any Carpathian. When it comes to para-normal firepower, no eternal like us could hope to match one of them."

"Friend Zachary, I liked your last girl much better!" Sabine flung aside her bag of dirt and glanced up at Philippe. "What is this one's name again?"

"Quincie," he replied.

"Pray tell, *Quincie*, what do you, with your pre-cious baby teeth, think you can do against the many awe-inspiring powers of Dracula Prime?"

Good question. I'd sort of hoped that Zachary would deal with the big-picture stuff, and I'd just help out as needed. But Sabine was still looking at me.

Then Freddy spoke up. Standing with his hands clasped behind his back, he said, "Forgive me for speaking out of turn, Your Majesty, but my brother—in light of his recent promotion—is already rusty when it comes to proper introductions.

"This young woman of the gentry is not just 'Quincie.' Her full name is Quincie P. Morris, and it comes to her by blood."

"Non?" Sabine steepled her fingers and stared at me as if I'd suddenly become fascinating. "Gentry, you say. You are a young woman of property?"

"Um, yes."

She narrowed her eyes. "What?"

Okay. "An Italian restaurant in Austin, Texas. I have a house, too."

"Acreage?"

"Just a regular yard for the house and a parking lot for the restaurant."

The queen tilted her head. "About this restaurant. It's in your name alone?"

"Yeah, I inherited it from my parents. They're dead."

"You killed them?" she asked with too much enthusiasm.

"No," I said. "Car accident."

"Still," she replied. "Good for you."

"Sabine," Zachary said from directly behind me. "About the knives?"

She laughed, kicking her tiny feet and clapping her dirty hands. "Quincie P. Morris is a girl! And here in my very own castle. *Très bon!* This presumptuous beast Bradley, he must be stopped. Friend Zachary, I am on your side once again."

"You might ask the Wolves," Philippe said. "They maintain the resources to decipher the ancient magic, though after a long-ago series of mishaps, most of their scholars in that area confine themselves to the healing arts."

Like Miz Morales. "Because it was Wolves who created vam—eternals, right?"

"Such blasphemy!" Sabine sprang to her feet. "*Mon ami*, make her stop!"

"You want to talk to *me* about blasphemy?" Zachary replied. "Sabine, I thought we had an understanding—"

"Tonight's prey, they came freely! They did not want to live on."

"It's worse," Zachary argued, throwing up his hands.

"*Non*," she insisted, stamping her small foot. "It is not! They are past the age of consent. We did all that you asked. The executive administrative staff cremated the mounted shifter heads, the shifter-skin rugs and furniture. The dungeon will reopen soon as a full-service night spa. The prey . . . What do we call them now?"

"Free-range bleeding stock," Harrison replied in a bored voice. "We'd considered going organic, however—"

"Stop!" I yelled. "We don't have time for this! Brad's not stupid. If *we* know that the Wolves might be able to stop him, then *he* probably knows it, too."

"If only you could contact the international training pack," Philippe said. "The elder Wolves—the one or two with enough expertise in the historical supernatural to perhaps counter Bradley, they would most likely be teachers there."

Shaking her head, Sabine returned to her throne. "If all that you say is true, this Bradley will find and kill the Wolves—the old scholars, the young. He will kill them all."

Kieren.

ENEMIES CLOSER

*W*ait!" Harrison had chased after us through the parking lot to the SUV.

Zachary paused in front of his already open driver's door. "What do you want?"

"In light of the threat, Her Royal Majesty offers use of her personal jet."

"Pass," Freddy said with a wave of his hand from the other side of the car.

"It occurs to me, brother," Harrison replied, "that you underestimate—"

"The queen has enforcers, right?" I asked. Already buckled in, I'd lowered a window. "Worst-case scenario, wouldn't she send them to fight Brad's army?"

"Of course not," Harrison replied. "The enforcers would go where the power is."

"The weak always do," Freddy shot back at his twin.

"You mean they would switch sides?" I asked. "Abandon Sabine for Brad?"

Harrison's lips tightened. "We speak of powers that have become legendary, even among creatures of legend. Yes, of course we would only be delivering the queen's forces to join his. But Her Majesty cannot stand idle with so much at stake."

After a weighty silence, he declared, "All right. If you won't accept the jet, from here on, I'll be joining you as her representative."

"You've got to be kidding!" Freddy exclaimed.

Apparently uncomfortable with my sitting next to Harrison, Zachary had asked me to ride beside him up front. On the drive south, the twins bickered in back while the angel behind the wheel seethed.

Had it been my fault he was caught and brought to Sabine? Probably. I'd never so much as exchanged a word with the security guard, let alone pitched the ruse concocted to distract him from the cameras.

As we passed Navy Pier, I remembered that Vaggio was originally from Chicago. That he was buried here. By failing to stop his killer tonight, I'd let him down, too.

Then Zachary surprised me by saying, "I was proud of you. The way you held your own against Sabine."

I stared past him at the traffic and the black abyss that was Lake Michigan. "You wouldn't have been, if you'd seen me earlier in the courtyard."

When his jaw tightened to the point that I thought he might crush his teeth, I realized that Zachary had misunderstood. "I didn't hurt anyone. I didn't partake . . ." An old-fashioned word, but it seemed to fit. "Of the suicidal. But I was tempted. Brad spun my brain, and I made a total fool out of—"

"I was proud of you," Zachary said again.

DESTINIES AND DESTINATIONS

*A*fter a hot shower back at the Edison Hotel, I'd slipped on the thick white complimentary robe and curled up in a plush chair, gripping my vial of holy water.

Tonight had been a disaster. The smell of blood had saturated the air, and Bradley had managed to reach beyond mental manipulations to take over my waking behavior. Even worse, Brad now had possession of both enchanted knives and, therefore, the full range of Dracula Prime's powers at his disposal.

Once the infected rose undead, they would all be slaves to his whim.

In fact, if Lucy's sleepwalking and Mina's blood-drinking had happened as Stoker had reported, Brad might already be able to control the baby-squirrel eaters and anyone else he'd cursed, even though they were, at least for now, still human.

Poor Aimee. It was amazing how well she was holding up.

I turned the vial in my hands. Sabine and Philippe had said the training pack—Kieren's pack?—might be able to help us and might be targeted by Brad for that very reason. But none of us knew how to contact the Wolves.

Our only potential source was Miz Morales. I seriously doubted she'd tell me, though, even if I mentioned the risk to Kieren specifically. But if I called, she'd definitely order me back to Austin. Zachary, being my GA, would have to return, too, and then where would that leave us?

I fell asleep in the chair, trying to figure it all out.

The human servant from the castle, the needy, flirtatious girl with gold ribbons in her dark hair. The toga dress had been ripped open, her spine broken, her too-pale body arranged on a circle of red satin along the lakefront.

Earth, air, fire, water. I was seeing through Bradley's eyes.

Even after brushing her off, it would've been nothing for Brad to seduce the girl into leaving with him. His long fingers swirled in her raw throat, and he began painting a lizard . . . bird . . . a dragon on the skin over her heart. A target.

Her mouth opened, closed. She'd lost the ability to speak, but — God help her — she still understood what was happening.

"Don't," I whispered, but Brad wasn't paying attention.

Instead, he grabbed the bowie knife in his right hand, the kukri knife in his left, and raised them both above the symbol he'd painted on his sacrifice.

As the knives came down, I screamed. Then he yanked the blades up and away from her still-beating heart, turned them inward, and stabbed both into his own gut.

I awoke, teary and drenched in sweat, to a pounding on the door.

After checking the peephole, I let the Possum in.

"Is it true that Kieren's in danger?" Clyde asked. Then he noticed that I'd been crying. "Hey, you okay?"

"Yes. I don't know. Maybe," I replied, trying to answer both questions. "Why?"

He motioned for me to shut the door. "Because if so, the Wolf pack is based in a little German-American town called New Schwarzwald, Michigan."

"You know this how?"

"Before Kieren left, his dad ran into my mom at Travis's house. He'd gone to drop off tamales. She'd gone to drop off a casserole. Dr. Morales gave her an envelope to give to me to give to Kieren. It had a lot of cash in it and directions—"

"To the Wolf pack," I finished. "You sneaky little marsupial! You peeked!" It wasn't until then that I remembered that Clyde should've told Zachary or Freddy instead. That Brad could yank the information from my brain. "Why tell me? You know—"

"I know that the fastest way to reach Kieren is probably a phone. He was pretty pissed at me when I dropped him off outside Denton. And if anybody's going to convince him that the ultimate badass vampire is headed his way, it's going to be you."

INVASION

I'd tried calling ahead for Kieren, but when I got directory information, the only place I could think to find him was the closest high school. The receptionist had said no student by his name was enrolled.

Aimee had suggested trying the New Schwarzwald mayor's office, but Clyde reminded her that we didn't know how the pack was organized—if its members made up all the town's residents or just a percentage of the local population. We couldn't risk accidentally out-ing the Wolves to humans who might be just as deadly to them as Brad.

On the upside, if Brad had already known about the werewolf threat and the pack's location, now we had a fighting chance to head him off. Plus, the Wolf magic experts might be able to tell us how to defeat him.

"What if he's already hopped a plane to Detroit?" Zachary asked. "He could rent a car from there and—"

"The first thing Sabine's enforcers did was to insert Brad's known pseudonyms (with a sketch) at the top of every international list of wanted terrorists," Harrison assured us. "Believe me, the Eternal Air Defense System is far, far more merciless—and therefore, more effective—than Homeland Security and, most especially, the TSA."

Passing through Gary, Indiana, I learned that Harrison was a neophyte, too.

"I'm still twice your age, children." He paused. "Not that I look it."

"And you like being a vampire?" Aimee asked from the bench behind him.

Zachary adjusted the rearview mirror.

"It holds pleasures, unspeakable pleasures," Harrison replied, "and I was reared from infancy to view eternals as superior beings."

Which didn't explain why he'd chosen one road and Freddy another, and it wasn't exactly a yes, either.

I didn't remember falling back asleep. I could still feel the motion of the SUV, but I also had the sensation of moving up and then backward. I could see the Chicago skyline to one side, what looked like an inland sea to the other. "Where are we?"

"Navy Pier," Bradley answered from beside me in the gondola. "Ferris wheel."

Of course. I'd seen it from Lake Shore Drive on the way back to the hotel. An impressive metal structure, soaring, lit by thousands of sparkling lights.

"You can't keep doing this," I insisted. "Slipping in and out of my mind."

"I won't have to much longer. My mission is nearly complete. I owe you my humble thanks. I hadn't realized those mongrels might be able to undo all my hard work."

Damn. Just as I'd feared, he'd plucked the information about the Wolf pack from my brain. Before I could protest, he began laughing. "See you in Michigan, and your little dog boy, too!"

My eyes fluttered open. Leaning forward, I urged the angel, "Hurry."

Main Street Massacre

Only moments outside of New Schwarzwald, lightning cracked, thunder boomed, and rain fell in sheets across the windshield.

"Looks like weather," Zachary said, refusing to slow down.

Meanwhile, I handed out snacks. Aimee wanted to help, but if we spun out into a tree, it was more important that she was the one wearing a seat belt.

"I categorically refuse," Harrison said, taking a whiff of porcine blood.

"Drink it," Freddy ordered. "Or we'll hog-tie you for the rest of the trip."

Harrison wasn't impressed. "You know ropes can't hold me."

"We have chains in back," his twin replied.

Just before dawn, Zachary slammed on the brakes and the SUV skidded to a stop on wet pavement.

"My God," Aimee exclaimed, opening her door to spring from the car.

"Wait!" Freddy called, but Clyde had already followed her.

"Stop them!" Zachary shouted over the thunder.

I jumped out and wiped my immediately rain-soaked hair from my eyes.

We'd parked in the middle of what looked like a historic small-town main street. Dark clouds blocked the rising sun. Lightning had set a church on fire. Countless blood-stained bodies of werewolves in gray and red Wolf form littered the pavement — necks and spines at horrible angles, heads and limbs torn off and cast aside. I heard the whines and whimpers — the moans of the wounded, the dying, largely muffled by the storm.

I shouted for Aimee, Clyde. I shouted for Kieren. I damn well did not let him leave me so he could come here and be killed.

On the far other side of the fur and annihilation, I glimpsed a shadowy figure, a man, facing my direction, wrestling with a girl. He hurled Aimee—"Aimee!"— aside, and she collided with the picture window fronting a single-story white building.

I ran toward her attacker, trying to land my feet between the fallen bodies, grimacing as bone broke beneath my shoe. Though Bradley's back was turned to me, as I drew closer, I had no problem recognizing him. In the jeans and western shirt, he didn't look much different from when we'd first met. Many of the Wolves he'd just decimated could take me in a tooth-and-claw fight, which didn't say much for my odds against Brad himself. But he wanted me on this earth, with him. The fact that I didn't return the feeling gave me a tactical advantage.

I launched off the balls of my feet, and we tumbled together. Tangled in his arms and legs, I gazed into Bradley's red eyes and found no recognition. I'd have sworn he didn't know me. That he'd never seen me before.

I threw a bent elbow into his jaw, knocking his head into the pavement.

Then Brad blinked, and his burning eyes cooled to hazel.

Pushing away, I felt his terror, his confusion, his slow-building awareness.

"What is all of this? I never act this way. I kill with purpose, calculation, for personal gain or to feed. True, a threat lurks here, among the beasts, the vermin, but why didn't I risk less of myself, remove it like a scalpel?"

"Get the hell out of my head!"

"Baby, help me. You don't understand. I don't understand. Help . . ." His lips kept moving, even as his face lost consistency. Then his body dissolved, mist into the storm.

That's when I saw Kieren, standing above me, his torn black T-shirt plastered to his wide chest and shoulders, dark hair dripping, a gash above his left eye. He'd shaved his goatee, but his brows had thickened. "Kieren?"

He tossed aside a wooden stake and, falling to his knees, winced as his claws retracted. He tried to speak, but the sound was guttural.

Kieren wrapped an arm around his ribs, as if to hold in the pain, flinching when I reached for his shoulder. I noticed the raised scars crisscrossing his hands where he'd turned his claws on himself to save me. I noticed the scar at his neck where I'd sunk my teeth in. "Bradley's gone," I said. At least for now.

It had to be torture for Kieren, the anger and adrenaline—his trapped Wolf tearing at him from inside. Not useless, never that, but so much less than he should've been.

I glanced at Aimee, crawling into the covered recess in front of the door to the public library, her arm stiff at her side. My friend needed me. But Kieren was here, too, and he was hurting.

For a moment, he lowered his head. His broad shoulders shook, and his breath became raspy. Then he glanced up, pulling himself together.

"Stay here," I said. "I'll be back."

As I began to stand, he reached for my arm. "Quince—"

"I'll explain everything later. Can you stand? Can you find Clyde?"

"Clyde's here?"

"Somewhere."

Damn it, I should've never let the sophomores come on this trip. I made my way, catty-corner, across the street to Aimee. She'd been thrown into the window of the public library, cracking the old glass.

Curled on the sidewalk, she cradled her left arm. "I'd barely gotten out, I'd gotten out of the car—I thought I saw Kieren—"

"He's fine," I assured her. "I just left him."

"The vampire—Brad, right?—he grabbed me and dragged me down the street. It happened so fast." Aimee took a deep breath. "When he moved in to bite, he hissed—like a snake—and threw me away." The crosses tattooed on her neck had saved her.

"What about Clyde?" I asked, remembering that the Possum had gotten a similar tattoo. That he'd been the second one after her out of the SUV.

"I don't know," she said, tentatively wiggling her fingers. "I didn't see."

"Will you be all right here while I track him down?"

At her nod, I turned to look for Kieren and Clyde, Zachary and Freddy. Even Harrison. At first glance, I couldn't spot any of them. But the rain had slackened. The sky had begun to lighten. The smell of death still filled the air, and the grisly scene made a sharp contrast to the wholesome small-town backdrop.

Some of the wounded stirred, a few shifting back to human form. They looked more beaten somehow, maybe because of their nakedness.

Just then, I spotted Kieren standing in front of the fudge shop, and picking my way back across the street, I promised injured Wolves that help would arrive soon.

Sabine and Philippe had said the pack scholars were the ones with the greatest knowledge of magic, both healing and demonic. I only hoped that Bradley's true targets—those teachers who might be able to tell us how to defeat him—had somehow been spared. I didn't know who they were, not specifically. There was no way Bradley had gotten that information from me.

Reaching Kieren's side, I grimaced at the sight of Clyde, who'd apparently been heaved into a public bench. The Possum lay on his back on the sidewalk, his eyes closed, his face and body covered with short gray hair. His mouth hung open, revealing tiny, sharp teeth, and a broken wooden bench spindle had impaled his thigh. "Is he?"

"He's not playing dead," Kieren said, "and he's not really dead — at least not yet."

BUT FOR THE GRACE

*T*wo young male Wolves loaded Clyde onto a gurney, securing his head and neck, and I could see that his half shift to Possum form had started to recede.

"Healers in training," Kieren explained, gesturing at the medical team.

Unconscious, the Possum looked more innocent, more vulnerable, and less like a smartass.

When the Wolves began carrying Clyde off, I asked where they were taking him.

"The library," one answered. "We've opened it so we can use the community room to treat the wounded. For now, we want everybody else to stay out of the way."

That made sense, I guessed. I briefly wondered what had happened between Clyde and Kieren on their own road trip, why the Possum had said the two of them had parted on bad terms in Denton. Not that it mattered now.

"Quince," Kieren began, "what's going on?"

As more apprentice healers spread out among the wounded, I offered him a bare-bones update — about Brad, the two knives, Carpathian magic, and the ramifications for the baby-squirrel eaters.

When a passing Wolf bitch studied me a beat too long, Kieren growled in reply.

She kept moving.

I was about to ask Kieren about the town's human residents, assuming there were any, when Zachary jogged up, out of breath. "It's different," he began, "when you can smell the pain. When you're allowed to help but you still can't fix it." Different on earth than the celestial plane, he'd meant.

"Zachary is . . ." I wasn't supposed to tell the whole truth, not to Kieren, not to anybody. The GA had forgiven my slip-up with Clyde and Aimee, but he'd made me promise to "respect heaven's mysteries." Of course I couldn't very well lie in front of an angel, either, so

I settled on, "He's a new waiter at Sanguini's. And a friend."

"Quincie talks about you all the time," Zachary said, offering his hand.

It wasn't technically true. I'd always been private about my feelings, maybe more so since Kieren had left. But I had confided in Zachary, and in any case, it had been the right thing to say. Kieren clasped his hand.

I hadn't seen anything of Harrison, but Freddy headed our way with the first-aid kit from the car. Behind him, Wolves worked to douse the church fire.

I turned to discover a crossbow pointed at my nose.

"Come with us," ordered the young woman. She stood about five foot ten, tall for a Wolf, and I wondered if she was a hybrid like Kieren.

"My friend, Aimee," I began. "She's at the library. Her arm . . . She's hurt. We can't just leave her there." Even before I finished speaking, I realized how ridiculous my request had sounded, coming here and now from a suspicious stranger.

"Please, Graciella," Kieren said. "Aimee is my friend, too. She's a human and a shifter sympathizer. She's no threat."

"Friend" had been overstating it. From what Aimee had told me, she'd met Kieren on a few occasions but mostly knew him from hearing Clyde and Travis talk.

"You have prior knowledge of these people?" Graciella pressed.

"Just the teens—the girls and the young boy. But they all came together."

Apparently Harrison had stayed with the car. I hoped he wouldn't steal it.

"Interesting timing." Graciella lowered her bow. She looked like some kind of Amazon warrior. Older than us, more like Zachary's age. Rain had soaked her tight black curls, low-slung jeans, and T-shirt, and I could tell that she wasn't wearing a bra.

Clyde would've been over the moon, but to his credit, Kieren didn't seem to notice. Then again, pack Wolves saw each other naked all the time. Or at least when they shifted. I preferred not to think too much about that.

"Very well," she declared. "I'll send someone to look after . . . Aimee."

My GA motioned to Freddy, who fell in step behind us.

Making my way down the sidewalk, I took in the Sausage Haus, Zimmermann's Restaurant, the Black Forest Inn. Main Street boasted several ordinary businesses, like a pharmacy and Laundromat, along with the more Germanic flavored. Maybe one out of five shops appeared empty, and a few had been boarded up.

It was impossible to ignore the ongoing medical efforts or the lives still slipping away in the street alongside us. A naked, wiry boy with pocked skin pressed his hands against the torn shoulder of a plump, dark-haired girl, trying to stop the bleeding as they lovingly whispered to each other in the misty rain.

Kieren muttered, "Thank God Wurstfest wasn't this weekend."

For the past nearly three weeks, this had been his home. Or had it? Had he come directly from Austin to New Schwarzwald? And regardless of when he'd arrived, what had Kieren's life here been like? "Is everybody in town a Wolf?"

"Not quite," he replied. "We have a couple of Wolf-Coyote hybrids and a handful of Wolf-human hybrids. I'm not sure who's left, though."

If I had made friends in the time we'd been apart, Kieren likely had as well. Friends he'd lost this morning.

"We get our share of human tourists, too," he added. "'They come; they go. They never know.' That's the saying, anyway. But what with the economy, the auto industry, it's been slow. At the moment, there are a couple of human Wolf preservationists — allies — staying at the B and B and a family of weresloths that headed for the hills."

Glancing again at the carnage on the street, I shuddered.

Kieren snagged a full-color trifold brochure from a small plastic dispenser mounted out in front of the Chamber of Commerce. "Here," he said, "look at this instead."

I grabbed it. Photos of the annual Christmas parade were especially impressive.

"Home of Schaf College?" I asked a moment later. It was supposedly located within city limits, on the outskirts of town. "Who was Schaf?"

"It means 'sheep' in German. So the translation would be 'Sheep College.'"

I looked sideways at him. "A Wolf college in sheep's clothing?"

He shrugged. "We're on our third woolly mascot since I got here."

Had that been a joke? I suppressed a nervous laugh. It wasn't funny, not now, but he was doing his best to distract me. The least I could do was try to play along.

"Have you seen my family?" Kieren asked.

"You could say that." I wondered what he'd think about my living in his house and hoped he'd have some advice on how to win over Meghan and wanted so much to tell him about Angelina and her puppies and, *oh yeah,* that he wasn't under suspicion of murder anymore. But all of that would have to wait.

Graciella led us into a crowded *biergarten*. What with the colorful pennants strung along the heavy wood-beam ceiling, the space appeared too festive for such a somber day. On the low stage, a man lay unconscious on a long picnic table. I'd put his age at about midseventies, which was remarkable. The average life expectancy for Wolves was about fifteen years shorter than that for humans.

"Ivo," Kieren whispered at my shoulder. "He's the only surviving professor who specializes in magic. The last that I know of who might've seriously studied the Carpathians, given that they were believed to have been long extinct."

It seemed significant that Ivo was being kept here, the most protected place in town, instead of at the library "clinic" like Clyde and Aimee and so many others.

The assembled pack members—most in human form—bickered and soothed one another in English and German, Spanish and possibly Chinese, as well as a few languages I couldn't begin to identify.

"We should've exterminated the last of the demon vermin generations ago!" exclaimed a deep voice. "We must destroy the vampires—every last one."

To calm my nerves, I counted fortyish Wolves, most high-school to college age, though a few middle-aged folks had joined us, too. The way I figured it, the New Schwarzwald families ran the local businesses. And from all over the world, teen Wolves in training relocated here. They studied demonic magic or healing magic or history or forestry or who-knew-what-else, and most graduated to more traditional packs elsewhere.

Graciella took center stage, reminding me, despite the rustic setting, of Sabine on her throne. Not that either of them would appreciate the comparison.

"Kieren?" the Wolf woman prompted. "Who are these people?" Her tone bordered on confrontational, but she was giving him a chance to explain.

He stepped into an open space in front of the stage. "This is my best friend, Quincie," he said. "Her parents were my godparents. You can trust her. All our lives, she has kept the secret of my heritage."

"Then why did she lead others to you now?" Graciella prompted.

I tried not to take it personally. The pack radiated grief, anger, frustration.

Zachary and Freddy moved to stand beside me.

Still no sign of Harrison, which was probably a good thing.

"I never told Quincie the pack's location," Kieren insisted. "I didn't know it myself until I thought I'd left her for good."

"It's true," I said. "We came because your scholars have a reputation as experts in demonic sorcery. We're trying to find a way to defeat the vampire that attacked you. He's done terrible things where we're from, too." I wasn't inclined to say more.

A male Wolf leaned toward me, sniffing, and Kieren shoved him back.

"Enough!" Graciella shouted over the growls. "Enough bloodshed for one day!" Returning her attention to me, she asked, "How did you find us?"

Before I could reply, Zachary announced, "We're sorry for your losses." Sunshine broke through the clouds, streamed in through a window. His golden brown hair took on a glow. "We'll pray for your dead. We'd be honored to help in any way we can."

Wolves crowded in to get a closer look at him.

Angels were everywhere, he'd said. Now that I knew, it was hard to imagine that anyone couldn't recognize Zachary for what he was.

"When we realized the pack might be in danger," Freddy began, "Clyde revealed your location. He acted out of concern for Kieren and out of fear for all of you. He'd hoped we could warn you in time."

"Clyde is the boy," Kieren added, "the one who's hurt. He's an Opossum."

Graciella shook her head. "So you're blaming an unconscious adolescent marsupial—convenient." Shooting Kieren an exasperated look, she added, "I don't suppose you know how he found out where we were?" When no one replied, she asked us all, "Did you come for information or to give warning?"

"Both," Zachary and I answered.

"Very well." Graciella raised her voice to address the crowd. "Kieren vouches for the kids, and our visitors include"—her gaze swept Zachary, lingered a moment—"werepeople among them. Their own have suffered grievous injuries. They offer assistance, and we need assistance." Glancing my way, she added, "We will not kill you."

"Thanks," I muttered, previously unaware that that had been an option.

I'd noticed that Kieren had let the rest of the pack assume that he'd confided its location to Clyde. As much as Wolves valued their security—and today certainly served as a reminder as to why—I wondered what Kieren's penalty might be. But in any case, the issue had been tabled, at least for the moment.

"When do you think we might be able to talk to Ivo?" I asked.

If I'd sounded insensitive, Gabriella didn't seem to care. "Tomorrow at the earliest," she replied, "if he lives. Do you require lodging?"

"We'll stay at the inn," Freddy announced. "Paying customers."

"Good." Graciella nodded. "We don't take American Express."

LOVERS, ALLIES, AND ENEMIES

*T*he one road leading into and out of New Schwarz-wald had been blocked off, the wounded and dead cleared from Main Street. Outside the *biergarten,* Zachary hugged me, shook Kieren's hand again, and left to help the Wolves build a funeral pyre. Then Freddy excused himself to check on his "dear brother" and to register our party at the B and B.

"Exactly how many older men are you traveling with these days?" Kieren asked.

On our way to the library/clinic, I replied, "Just the three."

He took a moment to digest that. "What do you know about Freddy's brother?"

"Harrison? He's like me. You know . . ." As we passed the Tea Rose Quilt Shop, I glanced around to make sure no one was listening. "I don't trust him. It's complicated what with him being Freddy's twin, though Brad is a mutual enemy. We picked him up just north of Chicago, but it's not like he's been all that useful."

After a moment, I added, "Have you, um, made any friends?" It had sounded so much less needy in my head.

Kieren reached for my hand. "I missed you."

The library building was a one-story, with white walls, redbrick trim, and a low-pitched, wood-shingle roof. The front window had been cracked in that morning's battle.

I began scanning for Aimee but didn't see her anywhere.

Inside, up front, the books looked typical—fiction, nonfiction, biography, romance, sci-fi, fantasy, horror, mystery, a hearty section of YA lit. But peering into the locked cage for Special Collections, I spied the antique volumes, the leather bindings, the foreign-language titles. . . . Books reminiscent of Kieren's private library back home.

A children's alphabet book, *A Is for Apocalypse,* lay open on a round table.

Back in the community room, candles—some in human shape, some in Wolf—burned on a countertop, smelling of mint and myrrh. Some thirty wounded Wolves rested on sleeping bags and cots. Most were conscious. A few were using their cell phones.

"This can't be everyone who was hurt," Kieren said.

A nearby Wolf clarified, "There's a second clinic at City Hall."

As I looked around for Aimee and Clyde, I reminded myself that shifters healed faster than humans and that these Wolves had magic to help.

"The Possum?" Kieren asked a healer, who pointed to a walk-in supply closet.

With his head wrapped in bandages and his legs in splints, Clyde—still unconscious—looked fully human again and awfully scrawny compared with the nearby predators. His entire face had turned purplish blue, except for the raw spots on the nose and right cheek where the skin had ripped off.

"Why is he resting off by himself?" I asked.

"The student healers were worried about the effects of Wolf spells on him," Aimee explained from the doorway, her arm in a sling. "They're not sure how badly hurt he is. But he's definitely broken both lower legs."

Where the spindle had impaled it, Clyde's thigh was bandaged, too.

As Kieren took a seat on the corner of the foldout cot, I gave Aimee a quick hug and apologized for not staying by her side.

"I've just got a sprain," she assured me, "and some bruises, but they gave me these bang-up pain meds"— she yawned—"which are making me sleepy. If you two are going to be here awhile, I should run. I need to check in with my mom from, you know, 'church camp,' and then I'm going to crash." She yawned again.

Kieren said, "There's a computer in the lobby of the B and B. It's just down the street. You can't miss it."

After Aimee left, I pulled up a chair and we settled in at Clyde's bedside. I babbled to Kieren—talking around my own vampirism because of the many sharp Wolf ears—but updating him further on what had happened in Austin since he'd gone.

I mentioned in passing that his parents had moved me into his room and then dived into the great news that APD no longer suspected him in Vaggio's murder.

He let me talk and talk, uninterrupted. Then all he said was, "Y'all cleared my name the same day that I left?"

I shrugged. "It helped that we had those two very dead vampires—Uncle D and Vice Principal Harding— to point at."

Technically, they'd been just as dead when Kieren left, but after facing off against Brad, neither of us had really been thinking strategically. I'd thought he'd be more excited about the news, ask more questions. But what was he most interested in?

"You've been living in my room? You've been sleeping in my bed?"

What was I, Goldilocks? "You can have your bed back."

He reached to touch my knee. "It's not that. It's just . . . Do you ever think about me, you know?"

I knew. "All the time."

We talked the day away. I could almost imagine Clyde rolling his beady eyes at our moony behavior. But he didn't wake up.

At one point, a healer came in, gave me a quick once-over, and then cleaned and taped the gash over Kieren's eye. But mostly, it was just us and the unconscious Possum.

I didn't so much as hint at Zachary's angelic nature or go into any detail about what had happened between me and Brad in the castle courtyard at Sabine's party. But I did admit that Brad's Carpathian powers had made it possible for him to affect my mind and those of the infected. "We haven't seen any sign of it in Aimee, but the new chef, Nora, is keeping an eye on everyone at Sanguini's while we're gone."

Kieren leaned forward. "What do you mean by 'affect'?"

"He whispers into my mind. Says things only I can hear. Manipulates my dreams. At the hotel in Chicago, it was like I could see through his eyes. I'm still not sure if he was showing me what he was doing or if he accidentally let me in."

"So the connection works both ways," Kieren observed.

"I think it's easiest for him when I'm sleeping, but he's managed it when I'm awake. A couple of times—at the computer, when I was driving. Maybe I spaced out or even dozed off, just for a second." I shook my head. "But when he touched me—"

"He *touched* you?"

Damn. "He brushed his fingers against my back at the party in Chicago." At Kieren's fierce expression, I quickly clarified, "I was wearing a backless evening gown. Brad's fingertips barely grazed my shoulder blade. But, God, he'd made it so that I didn't recognize him, and for a few moments, it's like I was transported to hell itself."

Kieren ran a hand through his thick hair, clearly disturbed by the news. "But he didn't try anything like that on Main Street this morning?"

"No, it was the weirdest thing. At first he didn't seem to recognize me. Then he sounded baffled by what was happening. Not at all like his usual self."

It wasn't until after sundown that I brought up the hatred the Wolves had expressed toward vampires, toward what I was, chosen or not.

"It's not personal," Kieren assured me, rubbing the back of my neck. We'd dragged in a big cushy reading chair that barely fit through the door, and I was curled up in his lap. "They don't mean you," he added. "They don't know you."

"It *will* be me," I insisted, "'after a circle of seasons.'" It was a phrase I'd read in more than one of his books back home. "I've had moments when I was tempted to—"

"But you didn't," he insisted. "You won't. I don't care what the books say."

I could hear the certainty in his voice. But I also remembered, not so long ago, when he'd called vampires "dead people too selfish to lie down." And he'd always taken those books seriously enough before. He'd practically built his life around them.

Had my being transformed changed his mind? Or just his heart?

Meanwhile, it was difficult not to fret about Clyde's condition. I sang the Possum's praises, telling Kieren what an amazing—if occasionally annoying—friend the furry little guy had been to me and Aimee.

Graciella came in, glancing at our cozy embrace. "Still no change?"

Kieren hugged me closer as she checked Clyde's pulse. "No," he said. "Nothing."

"You may want to talk to him," she replied. "Tell him . . . tell him whatever you don't want to leave unsaid."

Kieren tensed, and I remembered that he and the Opossum had parted on bad terms. I got up reluctantly, to give the boys privacy.

Once the healer stepped out again, Kieren said, "Quince, tonight I'll have to howl and feast for the dead. But afterward, can I come to see you at the inn?"

Whatever he was asking, the answer was . . . "Absolutely."

As I strolled up to the B and B parking lot, Harrison was leaning against the black SUV and puffing on a cigar by the glow of the streetlight. "It's a no-smoking establishment," he explained, "and the mongrel *frau* innkeeper sniffed me out in my private bathroom with the window open." He paused. "What are you doing out here?"

"I haven't even been to my room yet." I updated him on Clyde's condition, adding, "I'd sort of been planning to go to the pack funeral tonight, but Kieren didn't invite me." I didn't mention that he would be by later.

"Smart puppy you've got there." Harrison took another drag. "The blood didn't tempt you this morning because of the rain. It won't tempt you on the dead because it's dried. But tonight's little 'cookout' could get messy. You know how the beasties can be."

Because vampire—eternal—social affairs were oh-so-antiseptic.

"Zachary and Freddy can represent our group. Your friend Aimee and I raided the B and B bar for some gin. I gave her a shot and sent her off to bed."

Accepting alcohol from a vampire was never a good idea. Besides, didn't Aimee already have some kind of medication in her system? "Is she—?"

"Don't fret; I didn't bite her." Harrison reached into his inner jacket pocket and withdrew another cigar. "Want one?" When I shook my head, he reached in again and this time withdrew a silver flask. "How about a shot of the good stuff?"

Human blood. I should've guessed he'd bring his own. "If Zachary finds out—"

Harrison winked at me. "Our little secret." He glanced around, making sure no one was watching, and took a swig. "Take care, Quincie. No matter how Germanically cuddly this burg may seem, if either of us reveals our true nature . . ."

"What?"

"The last time a Wolf pack got its paws on a neophyte . . ." He grimaced. "Well, I'll show you the video on YouTube sometime."

ANGELS ON ROOFTOPS

*T*he B and B looked hospitable enough, with its real antiques and plastic flowers, dark, heavy wood furniture, and the cuckoo clock behind the front counter. I could've done without the mounted deer head on the wall, but it did add to the atmosphere.

The Wolf *"frau"* innkeeper, as Harrison had called her, had left a note saying that she was off mourning a daughter and that guests could help themselves to microwave popcorn, day-old cookies, or soft drinks in the fridge. We were also welcome to borrow a variety of

DVDs—ranging from chick to horror flicks—on an honor system.

Taking advantage of the privacy, I used the complimentary guest computer in the lobby to confirm that no drained bodies had shown up in Austin lately. Then I deleted the browser history.

Homesickness came in a wave. I wondered if Mitch had returned to Nora for provisions. I wondered how Mr. Wu and Mrs. Levy liked washing dishes. I wished I'd left the Moraleses a note, though I still had no idea what it would have said.

I wondered if the infected had shown any warning signs.

I'd been gone only a few days, and in that time, I'd traveled to Chicago, crashed a royal vampire gala, drunk from Brad, both offended and impressed the queen of the damned, been "hit on" by a human servant who later became a ritual sacrifice, traveled to New Schwarzwald, stumbled into a preternatural killing spree, and knocked Brad onto his ass. Now, in the forest not far away, a community of mostly teen Wolves were honoring their dead by chowing down on an elk or twenty.

The best part? Seeing Kieren again.

Upstairs, my room at the inn—with its oak sleigh bed, eyelet curtains, and private full bath—felt cozier than the suite at the Edison Hotel back in Chicago. It was the bath, though, that caught my imagination, specifically the two-person Jacuzzi tub lined with unlit eucalyptus-scented votive candles and porcelain bud vases filled with baby-pink sweetheart roses. What would Kieren think of that?

Later, Zachary—carrying my sports bottle and a roasted turkey leg—passed on a message that Kieren would be by in an hour or so and invited me, in the meantime, up to the roof to see the funeral pyre down the hill. "As long as we're in New Schwarzwald," the angel had suggested, "let's both take the stairs."

No wall-crawling. No wings.

I slung a crocheted blanket from the foot of the bed over my shoulder and followed. My GA mentioned that he'd last seen Kieren having a heart-to-heart talk with Freddy, which surprised me. Then I realized that they had something in common—a loved one who'd recently turned from human to neophyte.

Stepping onto the gently sloped roof, Zachary said, "I'm not sure it's my place to tell you this, but I learned today that Kieren was turned down for admission to the Wolves' college. He can reapply for the summer semester, but it doesn't look good."

"How is that possible?" I asked. "Kieren is a genius. Back home, if he hadn't dropped out of high school, he would've graduated valedictorian."

"It cuts against him, being not only a hybrid but also one raised by a mother who long ago severed ties with the international pack network. Especially since he's never achieved full Wolf form, the consensus seems to be that—however brainy or knowledgeable—he's not tough enough to rise through the ranks."

It was so unfair. Kieren couldn't live in the human world because he couldn't master his inner Wolf, and he couldn't succeed in the Wolf world for the same reason.

"By the way," Zachary said, glancing up at sharp, bright stars, "the pack leadership—or what's left of it— thinks we're both shifters."

"What? Me, too?"

The angel nodded. "Because of your relationship to Kieren. Because their healers have verified that Clyde is a Possum. Because of my appetite. But also because of your display of speed on Main Street this morning. Quincie—"

"I know," I said. "I have to be extra careful around the Wolves. Harrison already hit me with the scary bed-time story."

"It's not just that," the angel replied. "Whenever you tap into the demonic . . ."

"What?" Taking careful steps, I added, "What's the big deal?"

"It further jeopardizes your soul."

For a while, Zachary and I both went quiet. I gave him the blanket, and he gave me the sports bottle filled with blood. We perched, side by side on the edge of the roof, peering through the Michigan woods at the immense funeral pyre, listening to the mournful music of the Wolves. Everywhere that Brad went, grief and chaos followed.

I took a long drag of animal — deer? elk? — blood (it tasted gamy). "Does it matter how a neophyte is destroyed?"

"You've been reading Wolf lore," Zachary observed, pulling the blanket around his shoulders.

"And Stoker's novel," I reminded him. I recalled Arthur staking Lucy. How she was decapitated and her mouth stuffed with garlic. How, later in the story, Mina had begged Jonathan and the rest to, if necessary, do the same to her. Kieren's notes had mentioned the same ritual. "Does it? Matter, I mean. So far as the soul is concerned?"

"I'm not disputing the Wolves' beliefs," Zachary replied. "But giving up one's soul to the Big Boss falls under the powers of the divine. Not the supernatural and especially not the demonic."

I was sure that my GA knew what he was talking about, but it still seemed that if a price of becoming an undead immortal was the loss of the soul, the demonic had something to do with it. "I just don't get it," I began again. "Why would God send me an angel and then reject me because of what I'm becoming through no fault of my own? That doesn't sound like—"

"In my experience," Zachary said, "when the Big Boss green-lights something that seems unfair, it's to protect us from a worse potential future. One we can't foresee."

Actually, I could foresee it in high-def. Better that I—like his Miranda—be destroyed than lose my soul and claim victims for centuries to come.

Hard to argue, but where was the justice in that?

Fine. Maybe I had it coming for having doubted Kieren's innocence, for letting myself be wooed by Brad. For having been too much of a big dummy, in my blood-wine stupor, to see what was happening. But what about Aimee? All she did was eat a tainted dessert.

"It's not about punishment," the angel added. "Dying with your soul, it's a blessing. A second chance at redemption. A second chance at true eternal life."

I thought about what Kieren had said at the library about how the old books could be wrong. Had it just been the love talking? "With Miranda, did you always feel like it was best—"

"No," my GA replied. "There were moments when I longed to rationalize the whole thing away. To pretend we were the exception. That it would be different with us."

And it hadn't been. I briefly considered asking how evil she'd become by the end. But I could tell it was a painful subject for Zachary, and I had a feeling that it was a very, very long story.

We sat companionably and stared out at the flame below and the stars above. Zachary finished off the turkey leg, and I finished off the whole bottle of blood.

"Do you spend a lot of your time on rooftops?" I asked.

"I can't fly around all the time. Too showy. But I like being up high."

I wasn't the only one who was homesick.

Endless Love

After a Jacuzzi bath, I slipped on an oversize Fat Lorenzo's T to watch *Ladyhawke* and then sang along in a soft voice with *Lady and the Tramp*.

There had been noticeable wolf, canine, and shifter representation in the B and B movie library, though too many in which the four-footed died at the end.

On the registration desk counter, I'd also noticed a stack of brochures for a nonprofit organization advocating the protection of Michigan gray wolves. If someone didn't know they were staying in a pack-run B and B, they'd probably just assume that the owners were environmentalists.

Much more than an hour had passed, but Kieren had told Zachary that he was still coming to see me, and I had faith in that.

At half past midnight, I pushed aside thoughts of Harrison's YouTube horror stories and unlocked the door of the München Room. Then I climbed into a queen-size bed so tall it had its own step stool, resting my body on the double wedding-ring quilt and my head on the eyelet-fabric pillows. I'd wake up when Kieren knocked.

"It's me," a familiar voice whispered. "Sorry I'm late."

I felt the bed dip. A muscular, warm arm pulled me closer to a muscular, warm body. Kieren. He'd taken a shower. His hair was still damp. But I could still detect the scent of smoke and pine. It wasn't like him, just crawling beside me onto the quilt like that. As if it were something he'd done before.

The cut over his brow had scabbed over, but now the eye beneath it was swollen. "What happened?"

"Long night," he replied like it was no big deal. "Not everybody is as understanding as Graciella about y'all showing up at about the same time as Brad."

I hadn't come here to ruin Kieren's new life. "We

have to try to talk to Ivo, but if that doesn't look like it's going to happen, we'll hit the road. Depending on Clyde's condition, you know, whether he can travel, if it makes sense to move him."

If he wasn't already dead.

"I'm glad you told me what a hero he's been," Kieren said.

Had I said *hero*? Maybe not, but it fit. I'd never forget the sight of Clyde — *Clyde* — this morning, jumping out of the SUV right after Aimee. He'd honored Travis's memory and his promise to Kieren by being there for both of us.

I closed my eyes. "He's my friend, too."

Kieren kissed one eyelid and then the other. "I love you, Quince."

Just like that. I. Love. You. Quince.

I rested my hand on Kieren's chest, and he flinched. "What?"

He reluctantly raised his black T-shirt to reveal a dark purple bruise running clear across his rib cage. "There used to be a gazebo in the town park," he explained. "Brad threw me into it this morning. We fed the scrap to the funeral pyre."

With those injuries, Kieren had held me against his chest at the library and then been forced to defend himself tonight. "How bad is it?"

"I asked one of the healers to take a look after you left the clinic. The ribs may be bruised or cracked. Don't worry, though. I heal fast, shifter fast, and I did manage to lie still on a cot while Graciella chanted in Latin and waved some rosemary over me."

"Did Brad recognize you?" I began again. "You know, this morning."

"Now that you mention it," Kieren replied, "I've been thinking. When I first saw him, I thought that he'd come after me."

Not surprising, given their history. Brad had gone to a lot of trouble framing Kieren for Vaggio's murder, in large part to diminish the young Wolf in my eyes.

"But then he tossed me aside, just like anyone else."

"Something's wrong with him," I whispered. "I wonder whether it's something we can exploit to our advantage."

"Exploit to our advantage?" Kieren slowly blinked at me. "You used to have business strategies, not battle strategies."

Neither of which sounded especially feminine. "I don't mean to —"

"Please don't stop on my account." He brushed a curl from my forehead. "It's very sexy. Very animal, as the Wolves around here say."

"Be that as it may," I replied, blushing, "I don't want

to waste tonight talking about Brad." I reached to touch Kieren's shoulder, and he winced again. "Oh, I—"

"How about I take the lead?" he suggested. "It's my turn and then some."

"About damn time," I replied, and we both grinned.

There were no Jacuzzi bubble baths or burning eucalyptus candles or, for a long while after that, words. There didn't need to be. It was a celebration of what should've been. We didn't need to do anything in particular, let alone everything.

Just kissing, *kissing*, was so new to us. He tasted sweet and bitter. Like orange juice and beer. My touches were tentative, aware of his injuries. His were more assertive, mindful of me. We whispered things we'd never said before.

We didn't hurry, and then we did. When I reached to guide his hand, he threw his arm across his face, rolled onto his back, and asked if we could just talk awhile.

I felt a flutter of rejection before realizing Kieren was simply trying to rein himself (or maybe his Wolf) in a little. If he wanted to talk, we could talk. "Clyde spent most of the trip to Chicago with a cricket leg stuck between his two front teeth. He wouldn't take it out, even after Aimee offered him two bucks."

Kieren glanced over. "Then what happened?"

"Freddy offered him five."

I'd missed his laugh.

After a while, I began tracing circles on Kieren's forearm and he kissed me again.

I arched against him, resenting the cotton between us, until he brushed the tiny twin scars beneath my breast.

I jerked back, sat straight up on the bed. "What if . . . what if Brad's watching us?"

Kieren blew out a long breath. "Is there anything we can do about it?"

"I don't think so."

He frowned. "Do you want to stop? Because we don't have to —"

"Hell, no. I really don't want to stop."

Kieren opened his arms. "Then let the jealous SOB look."

He kissed my smile, my earlobe, my fingertips . . .

Hours passed, the sun rose, and we burned hotter.

Again, kissing, just *kissing,* was so new to us. So heavenly.

"DENN DIE TODTEN REITEN SCHNELL"

*B*y early the next afternoon, Ivo had miraculously recovered enough to summon us to the *biergarten*. He offered everyone a Bavarian lager.

"No, thank you," I said. "I never drink . . . beer."

While Zachary, Freddy, and I joined Ivo at the table, Kieren kept his distance. He made himself comfortable on the concrete steps leading to the adjacent kitchen.

When I glanced over, he offered me a slight smile.

Because we "visitors" were presumed to be human or non-Wolf shifter, it was considered acceptable for us to deal more directly with the professor than Kieren could, as a lower-ranked Wolf. The whole thing made me appreciate Mrs. Levy and Mr. Wu.

Ivo speared a chicken-apple sausage from a platter on the table. He reached for the horseradish and hollered to the kitchen for sauerkraut. "You tell me what you know."

It was mostly Freddy, with Zachary's help, who explained about Bradley, the knives, and Dracula Prime's powers — minimizing my role in the story.

Leaving out the baby-squirrel eaters altogether.

While the others talked and I took notes in Frank, I could feel Kieren staring at me. Harrison had questioned my coming. But I was our link to Kieren, and Kieren to the Wolves, and the Wolves, hopefully, to — if not a solution, at least a way to fight back.

"It is as I feared," Ivo declared. "You say your Bradley extracted the abilities from Morris's knife, likely in Texas, and then those from Harker's knife in Chicago.

"I am sorry to tell you . . . at the lakefront, when he completed the blood rite, he did not only permanently transfer the knives' combined powers to himself. He also unleashed something unexpected and far worse."

Not what we'd been hoping to hear.

"The Wolf pack was attacked *not only* by your Bradley, using the Carpathian might of the Abomination," Ivo explained, "but also by the *essence* of the Abomination himself."

I scribbled that in my planner. "Essence?"

"The personality," explained Freddy, adjusting his glasses. "The will."

Zachary set down his stein. "It's what continues to animate the undead. What, after a soul has been eaten away, can still be banished to hell."

That essence. "So you're saying that, inside the knives, Dracula could think?"

"No!" Ivo barked, loud for an old Wolf on the mend. "I am saying that the Abomination's essence could have remained intact, if long ago he had been felled by one weapon. However, in the two-fronted attack by Morris and Harker, his consciousness—like his powers—was split between the weapons and thereby rendered dormant.

"I am saying that, with your Bradley's blood-sacrifice spell, he not only unleashed all of the Abomination's supernatural skills into his own form. He also reunited and took in the actual essence of the Abomination.

"I am saying that the Abomination *thrives again* within your Bradley."

Damn it. "He's not *my*—"

"Drac is back?" Zachary and Freddy exclaimed.

"Brad must be losing ground already," Kieren observed. "That explains why he didn't recognize me yesterday or, at first, even Quincie."

"Ultimately," Ivo said, "there is no halfway. The count will triumph in any contest of wills, utterly vanquishing the foolish younger Nosferatu who resurrected him and fully adopting the body for his own use."

It took a moment for that to sink in. "No more Brad?" Was *that* why I hadn't heard from him—no thought whispers, no dream visits, no delusions—since the showdown on Main Street?

"As you knew him, no," Ivo confirmed, "though the struggle may take some time. I suspect that, after so long dormant, the Abomination will be disoriented, confused by changing times and by the mental influence of your Bradley, as long as he lasts."

This time I restrained myself from arguing that Brad wasn't mine.

It was ironic. My soul was being eaten away by the vampirism that Brad had cursed me with while his essence was being overtaken by an even stronger variety.

Bradley was smart, ambitious, and successful—what with his mass-infection scheme, acquiring the Carpathian magic, and crippling the Wolves.

But he hadn't counted on the count. Dracula Prime was more monster than . . . what the hell . . . *my* Bradley could chew.

"In life," Ivo continued, "the Abomination was a soldier, a statesman, an alchemist. Who knows how much of that existence he remembers now."

I recalled Van Helsing saying something along those lines.

"But in death, *in death,* his power is godlike. We speak of affecting the forces of nature, of affecting animal, human, and inhuman minds.

"The Abomination is not like any other Nosferatu, not even like other Carpathians. He sets his sights beyond his own borders. And yet, when cornered, he flees. He is patient, immortal. He can afford to wait. It makes catching him more difficult."

The conversation cycled for a while.

Finally, we stood to leave, thanking Ivo for his information and hospitality.

"Be swift," the professor urged. "'For the dead travel fast.'"

"You May All Go to Hell, and I Will Go" to the University of Texas

*O*utside the *biergarten,* as Freddy and Zachary went ahead to the library to check on the Possum, I lingered on the sidewalk with my Wolf man.

"I should see about Clyde, too," I said.

Kieren gave me a quick peck on the cheek. "And I have to go back and talk to Ivo. I'll meet you at the library, you know . . ." To say good-bye.

It didn't make it any easier that this time he was the one staying behind.

* * *

"Your friend Clyde has slipped into a coma," Graciella announced at the makeshift clinic. "Our professor of healing is dead. As students, we don't have the level of expertise necessary to treat him. We have called for assistance and supplies from the nearest affiliated pack, but it will be another two days before they arrive."

I fisted my scarred hand. "I know someone who may be able to help."

Meara. I had to get the Possum home to Austin. Now.

Aimee sported her sling and a royal-blue, long-sleeved shirt with a short vertical collar, purchased that morning at a local shop. Not her usual style, and she'd blown off the heavy eyeliner today too. The way I figured it, Aimee felt self-conscious about the fang marks on her neck, even if the crosses tattoo had prevented Bradley from really sinking his teeth in. Then again, it was cloudy, chilly. Maybe she was just cold.

I joined her on the bench in front of the library while Freddy and Zachary loaded Clyde into the back of the SUV.

"Where's Kieren?" Aimee asked. "We're about ready to go."

The plan was to wait in the car until Kieren came out of the *biergarten*. As the SUV slowly rolled past the Sausage

Haus, Harrison mentioned something about the private jet—Sabine's—that would meet us in Detroit.

"Excuse me," said Aimee from beside me. "I've never been on a plane before, and you want me to take one owned and operated by the forces of darkness?"

"For Clyde," I reminded her. "We don't have a choice."

Harrison, on my right, ignored us. He told Zachary, "If you want to fly down with Freddy and the kids, I can drive the car to Austin."

Zachary glanced over his shoulder. "It's not that I don't trust you—"

"You don't trust me."

"True," the angel agreed. "But it's not that. It's—whoa! Holy crap!" He swerved the SUV hard to the right, hitting the brakes.

"Everyone okay?" Freddy called from the front.

Through a window, I saw Kieren stagger to his feet. The car had barely missed him. Then a Wolf jogged up and kicked him in the gut.

I pushed Harrison aside, opened the door, and leaped out.

"Stupid!" one of a dozen or so Wolves shouted at Kieren.

Though they had been spared Brad-Dracula's worst, the group still looked scabbed and beaten. Two limped.

The nearest bitch had a patch over her right eye. No one had fully shifted yet, but their beards—both boys' and girls'—had thickened. Their eyebrows had become bushier, and their claws long and sharp.

"I told you," Kieren said as I stopped only steps behind him, "I take full responsibility for Quincie and the rest."

"Selfish!" yelled another. "Traitor!"

"But I have *no* idea," he went on, "how the vampire found us."

I'd never said in so many words that Bradley had extracted the pack's location from my mind, but I was sure Kieren had already figured that out.

"Leave him alone!" I shouted.

Zachary and Freddy—yelling at Aimee to stay in the car—moved to flank me, Harrison right after them.

"Vampire!" exclaimed the bitch with the eye patch.

Baffled, I checked my incisors with my tongue. They weren't especially pointy. Then I glanced back at Harrison. His control had slipped.

"Traitor!" Wolves pointed at Kieren. "Traitor!"

Now they'd *never* believe that he hadn't led Brad-Dracula here. I didn't want to do it, but the situation had gone nuclear. I showed my fangs, too.

"Traitor!" the shifters chanted at Kieren. "Traitor, traitor, traitor!"

It was thirteen against five, the odds in their favor. Growls deepened, grew fiercer, and I braced for an attack.

From behind me, the SUV's engine revved. Aimee leaned out of the open driver's window. "Back off, you losers! Back *way* off!"

Then, from the sidewalk in front of the *biergarten,* Ivo barked at his Wolves to stand down. He ambled over, with the aid of crutches, to what had almost been the middle of a bloody fray.

"Kieren," the professor began, "as you know, there are those who have questioned your fitness for pack life, for advanced studies. They pointed to your upbringing, to your hybrid DNA.

"Jealousy, directed at a newcomer whose intellect made them look like mere animals by comparison." A chastised male began to whine, and Ivo conked him on the head with a crutch. "I say a Wolf is as strong as his loyalties, even more so when they are tested to extremes.

"I won't pretend to understand why you would fight alongside Satan's minions or take one as your mate."

His words shocked my teeth back to normal. Zachary had to be horrified.

"Yet as it was foretold, the End Days are coming. We face an era of great change, fear, and uncertainty, but at the same time, an era of great heroism. Should you succeed in defeating the Abomination, young one, you shall be welcomed back to the training pack as a member in full standing. You shall be admitted to study demonic history and sorcery by my side. You shall be welcomed back with feast and song and remembered in legend until the last Wolf draws his last breath."

Very poetic, but what? Was Kieren leaving with us to chase down Bradley? Was that what he and Ivo had been talking about in the *biergarten*?

"You will be celebrated . . ." Ivo glared at me. "No matter the mistakes you have made. We understand too well the seductive power of evil."

Ouch. Still, the professor had just offered everything that Miz Morales had ever dreamed of for her son, everything that Kieren worked his whole life to earn.

So long as we succeeded in defeating the Abomination.

Kieren raised his gaze to challenge Ivo's and reached for my hand. "Quincie has *never* been a mistake."

dolce

DRACUL ONE

*T*he SUV had been crowded before, but I didn't mind sitting on Kieren's lap. I curled my fingers in his hair, feeling guilty because, inside, I was celebrating.

I understood that Kieren had seen the pack as the answer to mastering his shift. I understood that—like me—he'd have to struggle not to hurt anyone. I knew what a burden that could be, and it made more sense to me now why he'd felt he had to leave in the first place. But despite all of that, the ongoing threat, Clyde's dire condition, and the fact that the infected—including Aimee—were facing impending undeath . . .

No matter that none of it could end well, in that moment, my only thought was, *Kieren is coming home. With me.*

I glanced at Aimee in the back row with Clyde's legs in her lap. She opened my copy of *Dracula* and offered me a little wave that said she was happy that Kieren and I had been reunited for good, even if he was in a big, bad mood.

I appreciated the support. I'd needed more girl-friends near my own age.

Since I'd had to get along without Kieren, I'd connected with new people . . . Mrs. Levy and Mr. Wu . . . Clyde and Aimee . . . Nora, Freddy, and Zachary. And I'd nearly cemented myself in the Morales family.

Harrison, I could take or leave. Because of course the person that I liked least was the other neophyte. It still mystified me why Zachary had let him come along. Maybe, though, it was because he had access to things like on-call private jets.

Over an hour later, we arrived at Detroit Metro Airport. Alongside a small business jet that Harrison called Dracul One, Zachary pitched the car keys to him.

"You're sure?" the vampire asked. "I'd understand if you'd rather that Freddy—"

"Nice of you to say so," my GA replied. "But you were her friend, too."

Zachary's great love, Miranda, I realized. The SUV had belonged to her.

"How 'bout I ride with you?" Freddy asked his twin.

Harrison paused. "I was hoping to stop by the castle. There's something I'd like to pick up along the way."

"No problem," was the reply.

The plane's interior resembled a long, narrow luxury-hotel suite. Custom cabinetry, black leather chairs, ottomans, and sofas. Plush black carpet with a red border, two bathrooms with black marble sinks, a shower. There was even a new-car smell.

On a side table, I noticed a glam shot of Sabine on the cover of *Eternal Elegance* magazine. Beside it, a silver decanter held a warmed bottle of blood-infused Cabernet.

Aimee, still carrying Stoker's *Dracula,* observed, "Evil travels in style."

Zachary and Kieren hauled Clyde up the stairs and through the length of the jet to a bedroom in the back. Aimee followed, saying she'd watch over him.

The angel grabbed a cup of coffee from the galley and then slid into the desk chair of the small executive office. "I'll give Nora a call, see how it's going at Sanguini's, and ask her to contact Kieren's parents. That'll give them time to process what she has to say before we touch down." Damage control.

Up front, Kieren sank into the leather sofa in the lounge area, but I lingered outside the office doorway. "About Freddy, you know, traveling with Harrison . . ."

Zachary looked out a side window at the twins walking toward the hangar. "Don't let their bickering fool you. They're more devoted to each other than either would admit, and Freddy is much tougher than he seems."

"Still, Sabine's castle? Where humans equal appetizers?"

"Freddy has been there hundreds of times before," Zachary replied. "Remember, he and Harrison were raised by servants of the vamp aristocracy. As an adult, Freddy spent much of his career interacting with the undead hierarchy, royalty included, as an event coordinator. Plus, Harrison is a neophyte."

Leaning against the doorway, I said, "So he still has a soul."

Zachary pulled his cell phone out of his jeans pocket. "That's right."

"But no GA," I whispered, shooting a look down the aisle at Kieren.

"That's right, too."

I moved to stand across from the desk. "It's not right. It's not fair. Don't get me wrong; I'm not Harrison's biggest fan. But he needs help, too."

"Which," Zachary said, "is why Freddy wanted to spend some time with him."

Kieren and I hadn't talked much on the way to the airport—too crowded. But I knew him well enough to tell he had mixed feelings about leaving the Wolf pack. And I suspected he wasn't looking forward to dealing with his mama's disappointment, either.

I understood that Miz Morales was concerned about Kieren's inability to fully shift and the dangers that came with that, but the pack hadn't been able to help him. And while I didn't know the whole story, it struck me as deeply hypocritical that Meara seemed to want her children to take exclusively after their Wolf heritage, especially since she herself had given up pack life over twenty years earlier.

"How're you doing?" I asked.

Kieren held up the copy of *Eternal Elegance* magazine. "Scary."

With a grin, I reached into my backpack and presented him with the U.T. admission letter that I'd found when I cleaned out his school locker. "Check this out."

Kieren briefly brightened, then sobered again. "Quince, I'm still not safe to be—"

"How about we try some optimism?" I suggested. "We're together again. So what if everything's not perfect? Let's take it one disaster at a time."

He still looked doubtful. "Some things never change. My mom, for instance."

"Oh, yeah?" I booted my cell and showed him a pic of his folks decked out as Gomez and Morticia.

"Quincie!" Zachary called. "Phone!"

I hurried to join my GA in the small office toward the back of the plane.

"Can't talk long, hon," Nora cheerfully reported on the other end of the call. "Sergio's waiting to go over some changes in the meat order. How 'bout you swing by tomorrow, and we'll get caught up?"

It didn't surprise me that they'd both gone in on a Sunday. With Sergio hovering, though, she couldn't speak freely. Especially since he was among the infected. I was sure Zachary would fill me in on whatever he'd gleaned from the call, but I also wanted to hear the latest news from the chef herself.

"On a scale of one to five," I began, "one being a picnic basket of bunnies and cream puffs and five being 'holy crap,' how're we doing?"

"Between three and four," she replied. "I'd say I should have some time to chat then. But you feel free to stop by anytime. After all, you're the boss."

Translation: some funkiness had ensued at Sanguini's, but nothing that couldn't wait till morning. I hoped.

THE ARCHANGEL MICHAEL

The Sword of Heaven
The Bringer of Souls

To: Zachary
From: Michael
Date: Sunday, October 6

Be advised that this office has received 105 Guardian Angel reports of the vampire Henry Johnson (also known as "Bradley Sanguini") exhibiting Level 13 demonic skills likely acquired during study at the Scholomance.

Several of the reports identify you at the scene of yesterday's sighting on Main Street in New Schwarzwald, Michigan.

Consequently, you should plan to meet me at 9:30 P.M. local time in the bar of the Driskill Hotel on Brazos Street in downtown Austin so that we may discuss this emergency.

See attached Yahoo! map.

UNRESOLVED

At Zachary's suggestion, I'd hung back in the plane and let Kieren go down first to meet his parents, so all I knew about their reunion was that, afterward, he was quieter.

Later, back at the Morales house, Roberto had called Clyde's parents while Meara examined the Possum, who'd been stationed on the fold-out sofa in their home office.

I'd expected yelling, grounding, that the Moraleses would confiscate the keys to Kieren's truck and The Banana and ban me from Sanguini's until I turned twenty-one.

At least for the moment, though, they'd seemed too relieved to see us home alive and too freaked out about Clyde's coma to bother.

"It's not good," Miz Morales told us, "but you were smart to bring him to me. I have a call in to Detective Zaleski. He should be able to obtain a few spell ingredients."

Unlike the students at the Wolf pack, Meara didn't turn to healing magic lightly.

Good magic. Evil magic. The cost of magic. I was starting to appreciate why Sabine avoided it to the extent possible.

"How can we help?" Kieren asked.

His mama poked him in the injured ribs, making both of us wince. "Stay out of trouble." She frowned at her son. "I want to hear everything that happened— later."

I briefly considered cutting out of the house for a few minutes, giving the Moraleses their privacy and swinging by Sanguini's for fresh porcine blood. But Roberto had mentioned ordering pizza, and it was time to play human girl again.

That's when Meghan opened the front door, having just been dropped off by a friend's parent. She caught Kieren's scent and, yelping, thundered up the stairs.

We intercepted her halfway on the landing.

"Kieren!" she shouted, clamping onto his leg.

"Kieren, Kieren, Kieren!"

I understood exactly how she felt.

I begged off the pepperoni pizza, explaining that I didn't have the energy to eat, and trudged upstairs to Kieren's room to turn in for the night. He'd insisted that I take the water bed, claiming that it was easier on his ribs to sleep on a more solid surface.

I'd wanted to say . . . I wasn't sure what. But Dr. Morales was there, asking a thousand questions about the Wolf pack and Dracul One, and just being a dad.

On my way, I ducked into Meghan's room to turn on her pink Barbie night-light. "You should be asleep," I said, though I couldn't blame her for being excited.

"He's home," she whispered, brown eyes bright above the waffle-weave blanket.

"Yeah." I almost kissed her good night. But I knew she still didn't trust me. And I didn't totally trust myself, either. "Try to sleep. He'll still be home tomorrow."

Lying on the water bed, I stared at the ceiling and thought about Meghan. About how vulnerable she was with me staying only steps down the hall. I couldn't keep trying to fool myself that carrying around holy water or maintaining an animal-blood diet would be enough to defang me.

That night in the castle courtyard, I'd drunk from Bradley, greedy and grateful. I'd relished it, and I couldn't blame that on being newly risen. He'd been spinning my mind. But the blood had still called.

Afterward in the throne room, it had seemed so clear. I couldn't go on this way much longer. But now that I'd been reunited with Kieren, I couldn't imagine giving him up again.

Miranda had been a teenage girl, just like I was. She'd had her humanity ripped away and known what it was to love. She'd not only been immersed in the demonic world; she'd briefly ruled it. But ultimately, she'd made the right choice, the brave choice. I'd try to help rid the world of Brad-Dracula. But then what would I do?

MORTIFIED

*W*hen I heard the knock, I hoped it was Kieren, but Miz Morales walked in instead. "Clyde!" I exclaimed as I sat up in bed, sloshing a bit. "Is he—?"

"Still stable," she said. "His parents are a wreck, though. They're with him now. Don't worry, Quincie. I'll find a way to save him. Somehow."

I wished she sounded more confident.

"I know you will." I wished I sounded more confident, too.

As Miz Morales pulled up the desk chair, I readied myself to hear my punishment.

Instead, she said, "I understand why you did what you did, running off with your friends like that. I know it wasn't your fault, the massacre at the training pack."

So Kieren had told her at least that much.

"I understand," Meara went on, folding her hands in her lap, "that you feel responsible for the vampire Brad because of his history with your uncle and Sanguini's. I also understand that you didn't tell me what was happening because I would've forbade you to leave."

Boy, we were just bursting with understanding.

"You're a brave girl, and no one would call you irresponsible, least of all me. But Roberto and I, we can't help noticing that you've been begging off meals, complaining of stomach trouble, acting a bit strangely. At times, it's like you're trying to avoid us. Even Meghan has noticed it. She keeps saying that you're 'weird' now."

Uh-oh. They *knew*.

"Is there anything you want to tell me, Quincie?"

This was it. They'd stake me, cut off my head, and stuff my mouth with garlic.

"What do you mean?" I wasn't ready to face my end, not yet.

Miz Morales scratched behind her ear. "Well, I'm a Wolf, a full Wolf, with a Wolf's senses. You're living with me. I'm your guardian now, and I've known you since long before you hit adolescence."

Had Kieren told her? No, why would he? I began toying with his crucifix.

"When's the last time you got your period?" his mama asked.

Before I'd died. I no longer needed a menstrual cycle anymore. Dead things couldn't reproduce. Was Miz Morales waiting for me to admit it?

Clasping her hands again, she forged on. "I know how close you and Kieren are. And I respect that your feelings for each other are more than puppy love." She offered a reassuring smile. "If you two are facing the possibility of becoming parents, please don't worry about confiding in me and Roberto. We love you both very much, and you have our one-hundred-percent support."

Oh, my God. She didn't think I was undead. She thought I was pregnant!

Relieved, embarrassed, mortified, I burst out laughing.

ALL THE WORLD'S A STAGE

I couldn't tell if Bradley had invaded my mind or if I'd entered, unnoticed, into his. Given what Ivo had said, I'd begun to hope that he'd abandoned me and turned his full mental forces to the inner battle between him and Dracula Prime.

I didn't know where Brad was, but I could feel his presence. Watching.

A clump of teenagers wandered up a gravel road. A private driveway?

The fog was thick. Two of the girls clung to each other, wide-eyed like they expected a boogeyman to leap out. Their friends marched forward. The vivacious blonde up front skipped. They looked more city than suburbs, more style than cash.

Muted blue and purple lights illuminated a trio of cheesy coffins arranged against the backdrop of a decrepit altar and what appeared to be dry-ice vapor.

The scene resembled something out of a Halloween haunted house.

"What a joke!" complained a guy in a Spurs shirt. "I want my money back."

The girl in front let slip a snorting giggle. "You didn't pay no money."

Then the lids of the coffins rose, and three bewitching female vampires emerged. One cradled a sleeping boy, a toddler, with a swath of dark hair.

"Run!" I shouted, but they couldn't hear me. I wasn't there. Like with the blood rite with the knives, I was seeing what Brad saw.

The teens jeered and laughed at the approaching fiends. Under other circumstances, some of their comments might've been funny. At least one was crude.

Then the undead woman tossed the little boy like a sack of burlap. He landed at the feet of the blonde in the lead, the one who'd been skipping. I could see the child's throat, torn open. I watched a blood-drenched beetle crawl out of the seeping wound.

MOONLIGHT AND MAGNETISM

At about half past 2 A.M., the bedroom door opened a crack.

Kieren held a finger to his lips, urging me to keep quiet. He set his running shoes on the carpet and slowly shut the door. Then, carrying a black vinyl tote, he cruised over with a note. *Get dressed. Going out.* Sneaking out sounded more like it.

Minutes later, we strolled in the moonlight toward the neighborhood park. When I felt the first sprinkles hit my nose, I scanned the clouds.

"Relax," Kieren said. "I caught the news earlier. Thirty-eight percent chance of light showers. It's natural weather. The kind of rain—"

"That only makes it more humid." Nothing Brad-Dracula had done, and nowhere near heavy enough to impact the drought.

As Kieren and I paid our respects at the community shrine—homemade cards and signs (WE LOVE YOU, TRAVIS!!!), burned-out candles and 'dillo plush toys—the rain fell harder, and I knew Kieren had to be thinking of Clyde, too.

At the open-air shelter, Kieren unzipped his gym tote, took out a carefully rolled, forest-green tablecloth, and unfurled it over the picnic table. Then he plugged an electrical cord into the outlet, making the outdoor room come alive with green holiday lights. So far as I knew, Kieren had *no* dating history.

"How did you—?"

"I may be a manly Wolf man, but I'm also the son of a wedding planner. I spent most of my childhood being bored by women plotting special occasions."

I didn't have much—or really any—experience with guys, but I knew there were a lot who would've staged a date like this to angle for a night like the one we'd had in Michigan. Brad, for example. Everything that he had said and done with me had ultimately been about taking advantage. Even the seemingly good times, cooking in the kitchen, shopping for his toasting ensemble — all of those memories were tainted now.

Kieren gestured at the carefully crafted, hyperromantic backdrop. "Too cheesy?"

Maybe a *tad* cheesy. "It's perfect."

I reached into the tote and withdrew a couple of wineglasses, a bottle of porcine blood, and a bottle of sparkling water.

Then Kieren and I settled cross-legged, facing each other, on top of the picnic table. He filled and raised his glass. "To second chances."

I paused. "You're happy to be home."

"Yeah, home with you."

I sipped without clinking. "You know, I'm different now."

Kieren took my glass from me and set it beside his. Then he slid his hands under my thighs and pulled me closer, until our noses touched. "That night at Sanguini's, it was the first time you'd fed as a vampire. By all rights, you should've sucked me dry."

"I almost—"

"Quince, *all* neophytes kill their first victims — period. I'm talking every last one. They can't help themselves. Self-restraint is beyond them. That's why Bradley made the bet. He agreed to leave town only if you didn't kill me because he knew he couldn't lose."

Kieren had too much faith in me. "You thought that and still let me bite you?"

"I knew you." He brushed my curls from my forehead. "I know you." He traced a star, then a heart, connecting freckles on my face, outlining patterns only he could see.

The Hunted

*T*he next morning in the Moraleses' kitchen, Meara pitched me a blueberry muffin and asked if I could stay out that night. "Can you bunk at Aimee's? We're going to try to bring Clyde out of the coma. I've already arranged for Meghan to go home after preschool with her little friend Didi.

"I haven't talked to Kieren yet," Meara added, unusually babbly, clearly nervous about the whole thing, "but we're taking the shepherds to that new dog hotel on Lamar."

"I'll be fine," I assured her. "I still have my bedroom at my house."

"Are you sure?" she asked, clearly feeling motherly guilt over kicking me out of the house after whatever had just happened up north. And still embarrassed about our "misunderstanding," though I'd promised to go to a gynecologist, just to make sure everything was okay, if my "system" didn't get back on track.

"Nora will be there," I said, and that did the trick. I had no idea what had transpired in my absence between my chef and my guardians, but I wasn't inclined to argue with the results.

On the way out, I turned back to Meara, who was leaning against the kitchen counter, blowing on her coffee. She looked less immaculate and more tired than usual. But she still had a predator's posture and projected strength.

"You should tell him," I said.

She set down her mug. "Tell who what?"

"Tell Kieren that you're proud of him."

"He knows—"

"He knows that you love him," I said. "That's not enough."

At Sanguini's, Nora welcomed me on the back steps with a sports bottle of porcine blood. The battle-axe that Kieren had used to behead Vice Principal Harding was propped against the brick wall.

Nora reported that Mitch hadn't stopped by since we'd left town. That Mr. Wu had broken two wineglasses. That Sergio had hired new "backup" dishwashers, though Clyde's job "would be waiting for him." And Mercedes had been a smash hit as the first female Chef Sanguini, though offstage she seemed "out of sorts."

"Oh," Nora added. "I almost forgot. Last night Sergio snapped at Jamal for dropping a tray of javelina chops. I mean, literally snapped his teeth. A couple of hours later, he apologized, saying that he hasn't been himself lately."

I recalled my own mood swings just before my transformation.

Cruising into my own house, carrying the battle-axe, I noticed that the kitchen had been well stocked for mortal living. Bottles of water and cans of Dr Pepper had been stacked on top of the refrigerator, a package of whole-wheat tortillas topped the bread box, and a set of new clear glass canisters had been filled with white rice, brown rice, linguini, bow-tie pasta, black beans, red beans, lima beans, and jelly beans.

Ropes of garlic and red chili peppers hung over the sink. Baskets of ferns and a small Ficus tree decorated the breakfast nook. On the shelves, mixed among cook-books and titles from Daddy's vast archaeological col-lection, I spotted a bounty of new additions. Holy texts and nonfiction about Christianity, Protestantism, Catholi-cism, Mormonism, Judaism, Islam, Buddhism, Hinduism, Wicca, Sikhism, Taoism, voodoo, and humanism, among others, as well as volumes on agnosticism, atheism, inter-faith relationships, religion and politics . . .

Moving on, I could smell leftover shrimp lo mien and chicken fried rice from the takeout boxes on the dining-room table. I noticed that Kieren had brought over a dozen old books from his own newly reclaimed Wolf studies library.

It came as a surprise to find him and Zachary watch-ing TV.

While Aimee had stayed in the back of the jet with Clyde, the three of us had spent most of the flight from Detroit trying to brainstorm a game plan. Nobody had admitted defeat — at least not out loud. But time and ideas were in short supply.

At first, I'd been concerned about how the angel and Wolf would get along. Kieren had been so posses-sive from the moment Brad had appeared on the scene, and it's not like I could explain why Zachary and I had become so tight so fast. But from the get-go, the angel had treated him like an equal, treated us like a couple, and Kieren seemed to appreciate that.

Both guys glanced at me, and Kieren raised the volume with the remote.

On-screen, a San Antonio police spokeswoman said, "We can't confirm any connection between the missing local teens and the recent rash of disappearances in central and south Austin; however, we're pursuing every reasonable line of inquiry."

I held the axe out to Kieren. "You may need this."

By midafternoon, we still had no leads on Brad-Dracula's specific location. I'd tried to call Chat Lunatique, where he'd claimed to work before moving to town, but the line was "disconnected or no longer in service."

I made a note in Frank. "It would help if we had some idea of how many henchmen Brad has." I paused. "Henchpeople?"

"Try *minions*," Kieren suggested from across the table. "It's gender neutral."

He looked so adorably studious.

"Anyway, we've got the three of us," I said, "Aimee, who's been injured—"

"My ribs are better now," Kieren insisted a little too forcefully. "I'm fine."

Zachary stood to stretch. "The twins will get in later tonight."

"Do you think Harrison will fight on our side?" I asked.

"Don't know," the angel answered. "Sabine trusts Harrison—as much as she trusts any underling— because he's a neophyte. There's a fair amount of soul still left in him, and he's with us.

"But unlike you, Quincie, he chose to become a vampire. He's spent his whole existence seeking unholy power, and this is the *enchilada grande* of unholy power."

"What about other shifters?" I wanted to know. "Forget the Wolves. What about the Bears, the Cats; hell, even the Opossums, Armadillos, and Deer . . ."

Kieren turned yet another yellowed page in yet another leather-bound book. "They'd be just as likely to behead you, Quince. We can't risk it."

After school got out, Aimee arrived with Stoker's novel. "What about hypnosis? I'm not through the whole book yet, but it worked for Mina and Van Helsing, right?"

"Right," I said, catching on. It was something that Zachary, Freddy, and I had talked about in passing. The trip north had basically been a race against Brad, first to the castle for Harker's knife, then to the Wolf pack to give warning and get information. But now that he'd beaten us twice, we mostly just wanted to annihilate him.

At least that way, Brad wouldn't be able to command the infected, before or after undeath. Aimee and the others had maybe three days, maybe fewer.

"If they could find Dracula that way," she argued, "why can't we?"

"You want us to hypnotize Quincie?" Zachary asked, reaching for the novel.

"At sunset." Aimee wrinkled her nose at the leftover Chinese food. "Quincie and me both. I haven't gotten any mind messages myself yet, but I—"

"Mitch has," I said, surer with each word. "Bradley has been using him to spy on us and God-only-knows-what-else."

Zachary nodded. "How did Van Helsing's heroes defeat the count last time?"

"They spent a lot of time chasing after him," I replied. "Like we are. Reacting to his late-night visits, fighting to catch up, trying to head off his escape . . . Once they finally cornered him, though, Dracula didn't put up much of a fight. It was the gypsies who—"

"But it's not all about him," Aimee said, clearing empty cartons from the table.

"Dracula is patient, but Brad isn't," I said, remembering the conversation with Ivo in the *biergarten*. "Dracula doesn't know the modern world, but Brad does."

Kieren set aside another weighty tome. "Whoever the hell he is, if we manage to find him again, I somehow doubt he'll give up easily."

LOCKOUT

I stretched out on my calico-print bed-spread, underneath the canopy.

Seated in the rattan chair to my left, Zachary said, "Try to imagine somewhere calm. Soothing. Where you feel happy."

"But only if you want to," Kieren interrupted from my other side.

"We've been over this," I countered. He'd argued that I might be hurt, and I'd insisted that locating Brad-Dracula was worth taking the chance.

"It's still risky," the Wolf insisted.

"And it's still my decision."

After a cautious pause, Zachary began again. "Let's start over. Quincie, try to imagine—"

"Somewhere I feel happy." I used to feel happy at Sanguini's, but now I couldn't help worrying about the infected. I used to feel happy at the Moraleses', but now I had to hide who I was. Kieren—wherever he was, that was my happy place. And he was here.

"Breathe deeply . . ."

I didn't have to breathe, but I could. I imagined myself with Kieren under the picnic shelter at the park, the twinkling green lights, the whisper-soft rain . . .

"Relax your toes," Zachary continued, "the balls of your feet . . . the heels . . . feel your calves loosening up . . . your thighs . . ."

Kieren cleared his throat, and Zachary stopped listing body parts.

"With every breath, you're letting go. Giving up control. Letting in—"

"Sorry, guys," I said, sitting up. "You might have better luck with Aimee." It was ridiculously indulgent to be so self-conscious, but I couldn't help it.

"We could contact a pro hypnotist," Kieren suggested, "and try again at dawn."

"Hang on," I said, crossing my legs in a meditative pose. "Let me see if I can connect on my own." I'd never been the tranquil type. This time I didn't bother breathing. I didn't go to a calm, soothing, happy place.

I went to a dangerous one instead. A kaleidoscope of images flooded my memory—Brad in his 'kicker duds, cooking at the restaurant, modeling red satin and black leather, pouring my blood wine. My undeath in his basement, the dining-room wager, and then, at Sabine's gala, the way I lapped blood from his pale, hairless chest.

"Bradley. It's me. Back in Michigan, you asked for my help. You said you didn't understand what was happening. I can help you understand. I can help.

He's your enemy and mine. Brad . . ."

An invisible force slammed my body into the headboard. I coughed, choked, as a mouthful of blood sprayed from my lips.

Wiping my face, I glanced first at Zachary, then Kieren, who were holding on to me, aghast, from either side. "I feel pretty," I said.

The guys insisted that Aimee wait for me in the bathroom while I took a shower, in case I started spewing blood again or my head spun all the way around.

She'd seemed disappointed when Zachary declared that hypnotizing her next was out of the question. At least until she got a look at me. "Why would Bradley do that?"

"I don't think it was him." I lathered up the lemongrass bodywash I'd found on the edge of the tub.

"In life, the count would abandon his soldiers, and in undeath his . . ."

"Spawn?"

I peeked out from behind the shower curtain. "Can we please not call me that?"

Seated cross-legged on the toilet-seat lid, she replied, "Hey, I'm spawn, too."

"Anyway," I replied, "he'd do it to protect himself. Cut his losses. Cut me off."

"Sure, but from what Travis told me, Bradley was way more into you than the count was into Lucy or Mina. Do you think Brad's still in there, or that it's all about the Carpathian now?"

We couldn't know for sure.

It's Elementary...

In Sanguini's private dining room, an hour into the second wave of seatings, Kieren had his nose buried in yet another leather-bound book.

Earlier, he'd assured me that Detective Zaleski had arranged for a couple of on-site shifter EMTs in case something went wrong at his house tonight. But otherwise, my Wolf man had said nada all day about Clyde's coma and his parents and the spell.

Then again, we had our own battle to fight.

I'd brought him a carnivore taster. "How goes it?"

"We've got a lot of pieces of the puzzle," Kieren replied. "I just don't know to put them together yet. We need a break, a sign. And now."

Harrison, who'd apparently just pulled into town, strolled in through the crimson velvet curtains. "Perhaps I can help." He gestured at my laptop. "May I?"

At my nod, Kieren moved to the next chair and took a bite of the prosciutto.

"How was your road trip with Freddy?" I asked Harrison, proud of myself for not instead asking whether his twin had made it down alive.

"Wretched traffic on I-35," he replied. "But we did manage to stop at a honky-tonk featuring a framed guitar that had been autographed by Willie Nelson. Freddy's in the kitchen right now, telling Nora and Zachary all about it."

I almost warned Harrison to watch his tone, talking snide about Willie in this town, but then I remembered that I didn't like the neophyte that much.

He logged on to a website called Eternal News Network or ENN.

Standing behind him, I skimmed headlines about Sabine ("Hail to the Queen") and her fashion decrees (mermaid skirts were out) and spotted a photo of a castle like the one in Whitby Estates that was under construction in San Miguel.

"There!" Harrison clicked a flashing ad for custom soil from around the world. It proclaimed: *We ship anywhere!*

"What?" Kieren asked, downing a piece of venison blood sausage.

Harrison clicked to a contact page and glanced back at me. "You'll recall that Sabine carries soil from Paris in a velvet pouch tied at her waist?"

"You mean the dirt she kept tossing around her throne?"

"A nervous habit," he explained. "A handful of Old Bloods carry such pouches as fashion accessories, nods to the history. It's rumored that Sabine flings a handful of soil onto her silk sheets at night. A mere affectation. But for the count, Carpathian earth—"

"It's key," I said, remembering that he'd had fifty boxes shipped to England, traveled with them, taken refuge in them. Van Helsing's men had chased all over, purifying the boxes with holy wafers before Dracula shipped himself home in the last. "But since when is Vlad tech-friendly?"

Harrison keyed *drac3* into a form. "Vlad Tepes was most certainly not the human aristocrat who became Dracula Prime, though he nevertheless has something of a cult following among eternals."

To his credit, Kieren tried to answer my actual question. "Brad probably realized that the Carpathian powers would come with their limits, like the need for homeland soil, and put in the order himself. I'm not sure if he'd theoretically want it shipped from the count's lands in Eastern Europe or from his own hometown. . . ."

"Kansas City," I said, feeling optimistic. "If it were me, I'd order both to be safe."

"Both!" Harrison exclaimed. "Here we go. I've got the delivery address outside San Antonio."

"You *found* him?" Kieren exclaimed, leaning over to look.

As he and Harrison did more research on Brad-Dracula's lair, I took a moment to digest the news. With any luck, this time *we'd* be the ones with surprise on our side.

"We should wait until daylight," I said, pushing up to sit on the table. "He's—"

"According to the proprietor," Harrison interrupted, "twenty boxes should arrive at this address tonight. If we don't move fast —"

"Tonight?" Kieren exclaimed. "Make him cancel it!"

"He's trying, but his driver is one hundred and thirty-two years old and always forgets to turn on his cell phone."

Our deadline had just been moved up. Before we could act on it, though, Aimee burst through the drapes, waving Stoker's novel. "Is this book all true?"

Harrison reached to take it from her. "Yes, no, sort of. Even if you accept it as gospel (and you shouldn't),

403 ❧

the text itself is inconsistent. Besides, Van Helsing is a terribly vague fellow for someone so fond of hearing himself blather on. Why?"

Aimee raised her upper lip, showing that her gums had begun to retract around the incisors. "Like Lucy." Then she lowered her collar to reveal a swollen, angry burn mark circling her neck where the tattoo of crosses had been. "Like Mina."

"When did this happen?" I hopped off the table for a closer look. "I mean, when did you first notice—"

"Michigan," she admitted. "The pain woke me up at the inn."

"Why didn't you tell anyone?" Kieren wanted to know.

I moved to rest a hand on his shoulder, remembering the shame Mina had felt when Van Helsing had inadvertently singed her forehead with a holy wafer. "What were you saying, Aimee, about the novel?"

"Why didn't y'all *tell* me that destroying the count saved Mina?" she asked.

"By destroy—" Harrison began at the same time Kieren said, "Harker—"

They glared at each other, and then Harrison said, "All right, boy, you unravel the vast mysteries of the demonic."

Kieren folded his hands on a closed book, every inch the future valedictorian of this year's senior class at Waterloo High. "Here's what we know: Harker and

Morris destroyed Dracula Prime's body but not the count himself.

"Using sorcery, the über-vampire arranged it so that his essence, including his powers, could take refuge in any weapon that felled him, at least until he could find another host. Or maybe he couldn't free himself but left a restoration spell in the hands of his most loyal followers, trusting that they would bring him back.

"Regardless, the count hadn't expected a nearly simultaneous attack with two weapons—Morris's and Harker's—or to be split between them, leaving his will dormant.

"The upshot was that with Dracula temporarily out of the game, his Carpathian powers also seemed to have vanished from the world—at least until Brad, using spells of his own, began accessing those abilities from Morris's knife.

"Then Brad went after and obtained Harker's knife, too.

"Problem was," Kieren continued, "Brad hadn't realized the Carpathian *capabilities* still came attached to their original *owner.* When he reunited the knives in the blood rite at the lake, his goal was to make the transfer of powers permanent. But—surprise—the count's essence also became whole again.

"Like Ivo said, the newly resurrected will of Dracula, though disoriented and confused, was eager to claim a new body. And guess who had accidentally invited him in? Brad and the count have already begun to merge — in terms of their abilities, the respective sorcery that animated them, and the individual monsters themselves."

Damn. Smart *was* sexy.

Harrison, less impressed, yawned. "Didn't we already know all that?"

"I didn't," Aimee said, adjusting her sling.

"We didn't know how far along the merger was," Kieren said. "But now, given what's happened to Aimee, we're out of the gray area." He shook his head, seemingly astounded by what he was about to say. "I have good news and bad news."

"The bad news?" Harrison asked.

"When Bradley's victims begin to die toward the end of the week, they'll rise as the much-scarier Carpathian variety of vampires."

As terrifying as it sounded, that tracked. Like Mina, Aimee suffered from a horrible burn triggered by a holy symbol. But at that very moment, a decidedly non-scalding crucifix was resting against my decidedly non-Carpathian skin.

And what was it Nora had said about Sergio snapping at Jamal? Like Lucy had lunged for Arthur on her deathbed. In my last days of humanity, I'd been emotionally erratic. But it wasn't until after I'd died that I'd been tempted to take a bite out of anyone.

What was happening to the infected was worse than what had happened to me.

"Unlike most vampires," Kieren added, "who build strength and skills from the time they're neophytes to the time they're Old Bloods, Carpathians rise fully juiced but without so much as a remaining drop of soul to temper them."

"No soul?" Aimee and I repeated at the same time.

"It doesn't gradually fade like the souls of other vampires," he explained. "It's just gone. Immediately. We're talking about a much bigger, much badder magic."

So there's a bigger, badder price . . . for the baby-squirrel eaters, for everyone.

"Why isn't Quincie a Carpathian?" Aimee asked, taking a seat. "Brad made her."

"When one eternal blesses another," Harrison began, "the magic flows from the parent to the . . ."

I rejoined them around the table. "We've just decided to go with *spawn*."

Kieren reached for my hand. "During the month-long infection period, a connection exists between vampires and those they've cursed with their blood."

The invisible, preternatural umbilical cord. I remembered Freddy mentioning it.

"In Quincie's case," Kieren continued, "Brad had acquired some of the count's powers—those in the Morris knife—during her transformation period. The psychic skills at least. But she still became the relatively weaker kind of vampire that he was originally. However, with the newly infected, the essence of Dracula must have slowly overtaken the connection between them and Brad, altering the transformation magic in some critical way so that they are becoming Carpathians instead."

"Or," Harrison put in, "it's equally likely that the power to create new Carpathians had simply been one of the powers embedded in Harker's knife and came into play—through the same connection—only after the blood-sacrifice ritual."

Kieren nodded. "What matters is that the game has changed."

"For Quincie, what's done is done," Harrison added. "But looking ahead, we must face the reality that our opponent is on the verge of raising an almighty army of Carpathian hellions."

I desperately wanted to know, "And the good news?"

Aimee answered, "Now that Carpathian magic is affecting my transformation, it may mean that the rules of Stoker's novel apply. And according to the book—"

"If we can take out the count," I exclaimed, moving to hug her, "you'll be saved!"

"They all will." Kieren broke into a huge grin. "All of those that he infected—"

"Or at least the ones who aren't already elevated," Harrison muttered.

Already undead, he meant. Like me.

"Everyone," Kieren went on, "who tasted the chilled baby squirrels will live on as human beings." He paused. "Possibly."

"But there's nothing we can do to help Quincie?" Aimee pressed.

Or Mitch, I realized.

Harrison stood and put a firm arm around my shoulder. "Really, children, there are far worse fates than ending up like me."

What was it that Mina had said about euthanasia?

TAKE BACK THE NIGHTMARE

*W*e're going to annihilate Drac Prime for good," declared Zachary as we burst out of Sanguini's back door and into the parking lot with Kieren, the twins, and Aimee. "My sword is a holy weapon. He can't hide out in it like he did with the knives. I'll handle the strike. Everyone else stay clear."

"Stay clear?" Harrison echoed. "I'm happy to wait here at the restaurant."

"I'm sure your queen would be wowed by your bravery," I said.

"Her Majesty is—"

"Can it, you two," the angel scolded, opening the driver's door to the Impaler. "I'm serious. Touch the sword, and the metal will begin burning your skin almost instantly. You'll have a second—maybe two. Then you'll be obliterated."

As we piled into the SUV, he explained, "There's nothing the rest of us will be able to do. A holy fire doesn't stop burning until it's totally destroyed the demonic. Then we'd have one fewer supernatural soldier on our side." Turning in his seat, he said to Kieren, "If something happens to me, you take the weapon."

"Your sword was blessed?" Kieren asked, and I realized he was the only one who didn't know what Zachary really was.

At my GA's nod, I followed up. "You're sure the sword won't hurt him? Because he's alive, or because he's half Wolf?"

The angel started the engine. "It won't hurt him because he's wholly souled."

As opposed to me and Harrison. I remembered how the weapon had smote Sabine's enforcers, and *smote* wasn't a word I thought of often.

I realized, too, that, however much Zachary hoped I'd seek redemption and surrender my vampiric existence for "true eternal life," he wasn't expecting *this* to be the night I died for good. Ditto for my fellow neophyte.

"What are you doing?" Kieren demanded. While everybody else waited in the Impaler, he'd followed me inside my house, up one staircase and then another.

"I told you to stay in the car!" I exclaimed.

Half of the stale, musty, low-pitched attic had doubled as Daddy's retreat. Dust covered his papers and journals, the tiny handmade clay pots, rough-hewn dolls, and other treasures. Of late, alongside a wedge-spaced window, Zachary had set up a futon and lamp but appeared to be far from having really settled in.

The rest of the space still served as makeshift storage for family pieces that didn't fit into the décor—my great-grandmother's rocking chair, a stack of quilts, a large, antique wardrobe. . . . I opened it and drew out Mama's wedding dress. A long, bone-white gown with a bloodred sash and red ribbon shoulder straps. The color had matched her rose bouquet and the bridesmaids' gowns. I'd seen the pictures.

"What are you planning to do with that?" asked Kieren from behind me.

This wasn't a conversation I wanted to have. I'd already told him that Bradley had taken me prisoner on the night I'd died. But I'd spared him the details of the ordeal. Like the red calla lilies and the gauzy, long white nightgown. This was what Bradley wanted me to be. Virginal, vulnerable, corruptible, and most of all, his. "I'm going to put it —"

"For him?" Kieren pressed. "No. *No*, forget it. Let's just go."

I reached into the bottom of the wardrobe for my mother's white ballet-style shoes and turned to face my Wolf man. "Look, I've tried flat-out tackling the opposition, and it's gotten me nowhere. It's time to be more subtle. I can create the distraction we need."

At that, Kieren rocked back on his boot heels. Then he composed himself and moved to rest his hands on my shoulders. "Quince, I know we're running out of time, and to be honest, I can't think of a better idea. But that's not a good enough reason for whatever you —"

"I'm our best hope of —"

"I know what you're thinking. I know what the books say, and I know what your buddy Zachary has been preaching. But you have to promise me that this is no suicide mission, that if something goes wrong, you won't —"

"I'm already dead, so technically —"

"You know what I mean." He looked up through the skylight at the sliver of moonlight, as if for strength, and then into my eyes again. "I promise you that you're one hundred percent vintage Quince. You've had a hellacious couple of months. You've taken losses that would've crippled anyone else. But, so help me God, you're still Quincie P. Morris."

I could tell Kieren had practiced that, and it broke my heart a little. Still holding the hanger in one hand and shoes in the other, I whispered, "I love you, too."

But no promises.

STORMING THE COMPOUND

*A*t nearly midnight, I crept through the dense fog alongside the long, private gravel drive. I pointed at the second sign we'd seen that read HIGHWAY TO HELL over an arrow pointing the way. "What do y'all make of that?"

"Bait," Harrison whispered. "A lure for impulse thrill-seekers, easy prey. He's probably keeping a stable of human bleeding stock."

Zachary, in the lead, said, "If that's true, we'll have to get them out."

"I'll do it," Harrison offered. "Yes, I'll free the prey. You fight the Carpathian."

I couldn't help thinking of the old saying about the werefox and the henhouse.

"I'll help you," Kieren put in, probably thinking the same thing.

I suspected that he would've rather stayed by my side, but our whole plan depended on the appearance of my approaching Brad-Dracula on my own.

Which didn't mean Kieren wasn't armed. He had brought the battle-axe that he'd used against the vice principal. Harrison wielded a far fancier, bejeweled axe that he'd brought down from Chicago (Miranda's, he'd said), and Zachary had his holy sword, which at the moment was not on fire.

My only weapon? Mama's wedding gown. Not that it mattered, but the hem needed to be let down. I hadn't realized it before, but over the last few years, I'd grown taller than my mother.

Kieren cocked his head, listening. "Get back!"

We drew away from the road, crouching behind dry scrub along the drive.

A minute later, an unmarked white delivery truck passed by.

"That's it!" I exclaimed. "The count hasn't left yet."

As the truck rounded the bend, a howl rose into the night, only to be joined by another, another, another . . . Bradley had made a lot of friends. Minions. Spawn.

"Sentries," Harrison hissed. "I warned you."

"Any chance that they're real wolves or werewolves?" I asked.

Kieren slowly shook his head. "No, I can smell the difference."

They could even be Carpathians, I realized, if they'd died not long after being infected. We didn't have a fall-back strategy for that.

Aimee and Freddy had agreed to wait in the Impaler, which was parked down the hill. They weren't defense-less. In Chicago, Freddy had picked up a couple of motorized, double-barreled holy-water rifles. But espe-cially after what had happened to Clyde, I fretted that if we didn't return to the SUV soon, our human friends would come after us.

"There!" Kieren whispered, pointing through the trees.

At first, with the leaves, the fog, I couldn't see. Then a breeze wafted by. The drive wrapped around the front of a two-story Victorian, pale yellow with dark trim. The porch light had been turned on, but I couldn't see any lights in the windows.

From the online aerial view, we knew that the house stood at the front of a quad, its rear opposite what

looked like a barn, with two rectangular buildings—
barracks?—arranged parallel to either side. Sort of like
the castle courtyard.

"Quincie," Zachary cautioned, "don't let Brad lure
you in too close. Remember, if *any* vamp has even the
slightest contact with my sword—"

"Got it," Harrison and I replied at the same time.

"Don't forget," my GA added, "other vamps we run
into may be typical neophytes like you two. Salvageable
souls. We're not on a killing spree. We go in. Destroy
Drac. Get out."

Harrison coughed. "You don't suppose it will be that
easy?"

TREACHERY

*B*rad-Dracula had probably gone around back to meet the truck, so I left my angel, my true love, and Harrison behind as I started off to do the same.

"Quince, hang on," Kieren called in a low voice, jogging to my side.

"We've been over this," I whispered. "I have to go now."

Ignoring me, he crouched to grab the hem of Mama's wedding dress. Before I could wrench it away, Kieren purposefully turned his other hand palm up and extended the nail of his index finger—like a switchblade—into a curved Wolf claw.

"How did you do that?" I asked.

"Ivo showed me. That's as far as I've been able to get and stay in total control."

Still, it was a significant step forward.

Kieren used his claw to rip a slit up one skirt seam, stopping midthigh. "In case you need to run." Then he gestured for me to turn, and when I did, he ripped open the seam on the other side. "Or kick."

As Kieren jogged away, I squared my shoulders, raised my chin, and, despite everything, reminded myself that if I ever had a chance to wear Mama's wedding dress again, to wear it for real, Miz Morales could set me up with the best seamstress in Austin.

As if I were an expected guest, I strolled around the back of the Victorian. The drive split into a V—one side leading into a spacious quad and the other along the far side of a barracks toward the woods beyond. A third HIGH-WAY TO HELL sign with an arrow guided any would-be victims toward the back of the property, where the faux altar and real coffins from my nightmare awaited.

Eight-foot-tall torches lit the compound quad. The delivery truck had been parked alongside the barn. Lush green grass blanketed the courtyard. Apparently, evil things didn't believe in drought watering restrictions.

In the smoky fog, it took me a moment to make him out. Bradley's fair hair had gone totally white. He'd grown a beard to go along with the mustache. A glass of blood or maybe blood wine rested between his long fingers. He wore the elegant dark gray suit, the one he'd used for toasting at Sanguini's, the one that made him look like Fred Astaire.

Glancing from his wristwatches to me, he said, "Good evening, baby."

"Howdy, Brad." My voice had wavered. Wearing Mama's dress had been a mistake. It took him back to his fantasy, but it took me back to that night, too. I remembered shredding the white nightgown, butchering the iron twin bed frame. Now, here I was, like this, taking another step toward him. Freely and of my own will.

On one hand, I was relieved not to be dealing with the count.

On the other, I couldn't help remembering Freddy's warning about Sabine. The devil you know is still a devil.

"It was Uncle Davidson, wasn't it?" Let Brad think I'd come, at least in part, for answers. "He gave you Quincey Morris's bowie knife."

"It went first to your father," Brad replied, taking the bait. "After he died, your uncle stumbled onto the family history. I contacted him, pretending to be an antiques dealer. But he realized what I was. He delivered the knife in exchange for immortality."

I remembered Uncle D, facedown in his bed with a stake through his heart. How was that immortality? "And then he delivered me to you."

"It wasn't like that," Brad assured me. "I saw you one day, laughing with Vaggio at Fat Lorenzo's. I began watching you at home . . . school . . . the restaurant." He smiled, wistful, and took a sip. "You had such zest, passion, sensuality. You gobbled up life."

A fitting expression from the former vampire chef. I'd once thought of him as the eternal who missed humanity so much that he fed it.

Moving closer, I began again, "At the Wolf pack, you asked for my help—"

"Did I?" He looked confused. "I lost myself for a while there."

Didn't he understand what was happening? "You're losing yourself now."

His head turned as warning howls rose into the night air.

Damn, the wolf-form sentries had found Zachary.

"What's this?" Bradley asked, slamming his wineglass to the driveway, shattering it. "Friends of yours? Well, baby, I have friends of my own."

A vacant-looking crowd of young people flowed out of the barn, shuffling our way. It was hard to count through the fog, but I put the number at roughly fifty.

"My personal blood supply," he added, "but they're more than that. I've blessed them. They're my children now, and they—like you—will obey me."

So this was thrall from the outside, looking in. "They're still human."

"Not for long," Brad reminded me.

I couldn't help thinking of Aimee, still waiting with Freddy in the SUV.

The zombie-like prisoners parted to reveal Kieren—kicking, yelling, trying to wrench free from two female vampires. I recognized them from my nightmare. They'd been the ones who had killed that little boy.

Behind them, another female, carrying Kieren's axe, marched in step with Harrison, who still had possession of his own bejeweled weapon.

Harrison, who'd followed the power and changed sides.

ETERNAL EMBRACE

*T*he dog-faced boy!" Bradley exclaimed, sounding equally betrayed. "I thought I'd killed him in Michigan. I thought . . . Did I see him there?" He paused. "Didn't I?"

I could feel Brad's rising anger and confusion. Once again, I felt what he felt. He hadn't trusted my apparent surrender, but Kieren's appearance had turned the ruse into an insult. I felt Brad's obsessive desire, the way he wanted it to be between us—at times raunchy and rutting, at times romantic and refined.

I saw myself as he viewed me: a trophy, a temptation, a distraction that he'd cursed again and again, even as he'd committed himself to winning my love.

Worse, underneath it all lurked an unexpected sincerity, an appreciation of the kitchen banter we'd shared, a respect for my work ethic, an understanding of the losses I'd endured. An understanding of what loss meant.

If only it weren't for his rival—a mere boy, less than even human. A lowly beast. After the glory that Brad had offered, why else would I continue to refuse him—if not for another man? How could I make such a foolish mistake? Before I had a chance to fight it, I sympathized.

"This time," he promised, "I'll cut out his mongrel heart and squeeze its last drop of blood into my own jaws."

Like he had in the castle courtyard, Bradley reached for me, only this time, he forced my lips to his, his tongue into my mouth, and his desire deeper into my mind. Then Brad's hands cupped my hips as he lifted my body, and I instinctively wrapped my legs around his waist, not caring that we had an audience. Not caring that Kieren could see.

Yanking aside a red ribbon strap, Brad briefly tore his lips from mine, only to slice his fangs into my bare shoulder. I felt twin streams of blood trickling and his tongue lapping and his teeth kneading the wounds. The punctures radiated pleasure, and pressing a hand to the back of his neck, I urged him on. It hadn't been anything like this in the basement or the queen's courtyard, and I knew he owned me now.

After I wasn't sure how long, through the bloody velvet bliss, I heard a distant rumbling growl, and then a woman's frantic voice called, "Master!"

We didn't care. No one else mattered. I was beyond wanting anything but more.

Then, without warning, Bradley raised his blood-stained face. "Who are you?" he demanded in an accented voice — Romanian? Hungarian? — that didn't belong to him.

Who Needs Gypsies?

*H*e threw me to the grass. "How dare you presume to touch me?"

Yanked from Brad's thrall, I stared up at the famed Count Dracula.

"You are not mine," he said, sneering, and the feeling was mutual.

Reaching for my still-bleeding shoulder, I began to tremble. My head throbbed worse than from any blood-wine hangover. I climbed, swaying, to my feet.

Then the growling I'd heard earlier turned ferocious, and a woman's severed head rolled by, trailing blood and bloody tissue. She'd been one of the vampires who'd captured Kieren.

Harrison! He'd faked them out. He hadn't betrayed us after all. And if his victim had been a neophyte, a salvageable soul, he didn't give a damn.

I searched the fog for Kieren and heard him whimper. He was shape-shifting. Even in the low moonlight, he'd nearly reached midtransformation, farther than he'd ever gone before. His ears had turned wolfish, and his T-shirt and cargo shorts tore as bones, ligaments, muscles strained and rearranged. Dracula called to the undead and infected alike. "Tear them to pieces!"

As Harrison swung his axe again, the enthralled mob rushed me.

"Zachary?" I called. Where was he?

A bat careened over my head, tangling itself in my hair, raking my forehead with tiny claws, escaping before I could snatch it. Dracula, he was getting away!

We'd failed. Not only that, but Brad had failed, too, and a far more hideous monster would profit from his demise. Until that moment, I'd refused to believe the worst would come. I thought of Aimee, Sergio, Yani, Mercedes, the mayor, and the rest—their lives and souls soon gone. The loud little boy who'd come to Sanguini's on his fifth birthday and would be a demon before his sixth. The human world, the shifters, the underworld, *all* would suffer, and my best excuse for continuing my tainted existence was gone.

I let my head fall, let the mob have me. A fist smacked into my jaw, another into my stomach. A hand grabbed my hair, yanking my head back, exposing my neck.

I heard my grass-stained, virginal white dress—my mama's dress—tear.

I stared up into fog, silently begging for forgiveness and for Kieren's life. What I wouldn't have given to see the heavens, the moon and stars. What I wouldn't have given to belong to heaven's light. Blows rained down, and I welcomed the pain.

Then the fog drifted, and I saw Zachary—in midair, his wings brilliant white—eclipsing the narrow moon. A boot slammed into my kneecap, but I couldn't bring myself to look away. Blood dripped from scratches on the angel's cheeks, from his fingertips. The sentries had savaged him with their teeth and claws. Now, high above, the holy weapon shook in his hands.

A fist came at my eye, and I blocked it. Shoved away the woman yanking my hair, ignored the pain as she ripped some out. Broke free. "Zachary!"

The Dracula bat reeled at the sight of him, tumbling from the sky—a spiral of shadows—and crashed in Brad's human form on the bright green grass. He moaned, still conscious. A monster at midnight.

A moment later, Zachary lost hold of his sword and, as it fell, he too careened downward. The horde would be on him next, tearing apart his wings.

From my right, a vacant bruiser of a guy charged me — out of his mind, a helpless pawn, his only thought to kill. He'd somehow gotten ahold of Kieren's axe.

Then, through the fray, a wolf-form sentry leaped between me and the new threat. I didn't understand why, not until he glanced back, his eyes yellow, intelligent, familiar.

Kieren, coming to my defense. Kieren, who'd finally fully shifted into a magnificent black werewolf. Just in time to die.

COUNT AND RE-COUNT

A split second before Kieren sprang into his own axe blade, the big guy lowered, then dropped it. He looked mystified at the blood on his hands.

Someone screamed. The pretty young blonde who'd skipped up the highway to hell. She pointed to yet another decapitated vampire head, the second I'd counted so far.

The infected backed off, unclenching their fists, returning to their senses.

Backing toward his brother, Harrison brought his axe blade straight through yet another undead woman, splitting her in two at the waist before slicing off her head.

Just then I heard Aimee's and Freddy's voices, calling to Zachary, who lay dazed on the ground. I'd known they wouldn't stay in the SUV! They assumed positions on either side of the angel, protecting his fallen form with their holy-water rifles.

Meanwhile, Zachary fought to prop himself on one elbow, and I briefly tracked his gaze to the gleaming sword lying just inches from my feet.

"Baby . . ." Bradley stood to face me. The count had receded again. It wasn't just the voice, the U.S. Midwestern versus Eastern European accent. It was in the way he held himself, the particular flavor of evil shining in his red eyes. "I know we have some issues to work out. But please tell me what's happening." He'd said it like I was his longtime girlfriend and we'd had a minor spat.

"It's the knives," I explained as Kieren took a few steps back and forth, snarling. "Harker's and Morris's. You didn't just bring back the full power of Dracula Prime. You brought back the count himself."

Brad's smug expression disappeared.

"He's tearing you apart from inside," I added, "taking over your mind and body."

Brad began pacing. "At the Wolf pack in Michigan," he muttered, "that wasn't me. That was him . . . that day and others . . . that night and others. Not me, him!"

"Quincie!" Harrison tossed me the ornate axe. "Finish it!"

A Last Whisper

I caught the handle of what had been Miranda's regal battle-axe, grateful for my supernatural reflexes. Only problem? If I decapitated Bradley with it, the count might be able to take refuge in that new weapon, biding his time until yet another opportunity arose for him to return. Damn. What had he paid Lucifer to learn that trick?

"Quincie, now!" shouted Aimee. "Now!"

Bradley paused, shaking his crowded head. "I'd thought I was losing my mind, and I see that I was right. No, I'm not losing it; he's taking it. I can feel him inside, rooting around, angling for an opportunity. But I can fight him, annihilate him. Find another, stronger spell. Kick his incorporeal ass before he owns my real one. I'll do it for you, for us." Brad threw out his arms and laughed. "I'll save the whole damned world for you, baby. Is that what it'll take? Then will you love me?"

Until that moment I hadn't been paying much attention to his ranting. "What the hell are you talking about?"

"Everything for you! I've worked so hard to prove myself. I transformed your chintzy small-time ethnic restaurant into an international Gothic sensation. I fed you my own blood, remade you, elevated you. I brought you back from the dead."

"First of all, not a turn-on. Second, you're the one who killed me in the first place. And third, Don Juan"— I gestured to the crowd—"it's not like you're all that picky about who you curse with your blood." Tightening my grip on the axe handle, I added, "Will I love you? Don't you realize what you've done? You murdered Vaggio. You framed Kieren. You poisoned his dog. Made Mitch undead. Used my mama's restaurant, which has *never* been in any way chintzy or small-time, to—"

"For you," Bradley said, pausing in place. "When I blessed you—"

"Blessed? You did not bless me. You stalked me. Lied to me. Slipped unholy blood into my wine. Drugged me, kidnapped me. Took my life.

"After all of your hypocritical talk about my own free will, you touched my body and mind when I couldn't say no. Made me think I wanted to touch you. And, worst of all, you turned me into this thing, knowing that I'd pay for it with my immortal soul."

"We're not puny humans," Brad replied. "Our ways of love are—"

"What you call love, I call evil, freakish, and deranged." I couldn't let him come back—not as Dracula, not as himself. God, what if I struck him—them—down, and the spell somehow managed to preserve *both* of their essences in the axe until they were freed again?

My gaze fell to Kieren. A full-blown Wolf who loved me. A young man who'd finally managed to conquer his inner beast. Who'd struggled with himself but never doubted me, even when I doubted myself. Nothing could hurt more than letting him go, even if we'd be like Zachary and Miranda and reunite in heaven someday. But it was time. I let the axe fall from my hand, prepared to obliterate Brad-Dracula forever.

No matter the price.

Forged in Heaven

Radiant—no other word could fully describe the holy weapon at my feet. Where the blade met the hilt, it flared into two gleaming gold wings. Wings like Zachary's.

Zachary, who'd warned me what would happen if I touched the sword. I'd have only a second, maybe three. And, after that, I'd be ash. But then again, how long did I really need? Just long enough to strike.

"What's all this fuss?" Bradley asked, ever the charmer. "I am your creator."

I hesitated at his words. My creator? *Brad?* I thought of Mama and Daddy, my grandparents Crimi and Morris, all the way back to my true Creator.

It was then that everything made sense, that my insecurities fell away, that I realized who I was and what was really happening on heaven and earth and inside of me.

I knew. No, better than that. Harder than that. I believed.

"I chose you," Bradley went on.

I could feel him, trying to push his will against mine. And failing.

As I reached for the blessed sword, Zachary, back on his feet, took Aimee's hand and Freddy's. Harrison, who'd joined them, reached for his brother's shoulder. They bowed their heads, but Kieren's gaze stayed fixed on the enemy.

"I made you a superior being," the monster added.

When I closed my hand around it, the hilt felt as cool and welcoming as the silver-and-turquoise crucifix against my chest. I rose, drawing the angel's weapon with one hand over my still-bleeding shoulder — grateful for the Grace.

"Baby, don't you see?" Brad finished. "I am your *god*."

With full faith that my aim was true, I let the sword fly. It flamed in midair and struck the Abomination, impaling the heart.

"Baby?" Brad staggered back, and his annoyed, self-important expression transformed to horror as he . . . they . . . went up like a torch. Flames leaped thirty feet into the air. Black and blue smoke billowed. Once again, Bradley had underestimated me.

I would never belong to him, to anyone, against my own free will.

WHOLLY SOULED

*W*e had no time to celebrate. The wolf-form sentries had been closing in, heads low, saliva dripping. They had us surrounded. And there were so freaking many of them!

"Zachary!" Harrison yelled. "The sentries are a lost cause. I'm ready. I am. Sabine said it—you can't save us all. Do it, man! I beg you!"

What was he shouting about?

A blinding light poured from Zachary's body. The word *supernova* crossed my mind, and I shielded my eyes from it. Against the sentries' screams and howls of pain.

I bent to draw Kieren close, at first to protect him and then, overjoyed, to more fully share the moment. Burying my fingers in his soft, damp fur, I felt surrounded by warmth and love, forgiveness and understanding. It came from the light. It was the light.

And I felt it with my whole and unbroken soul.

SAVED

*T*oo soon, the all-encompassing glow faded.

Blinking back black-and-blue spots, I whispered, "You okay?"

Kieren's wet nose nuzzled my cheek, and he woofed, soft and sure.

I squeezed my eyes closed as tightly as I could and then opened them again, at first seeing more spots, and then a moment or two later, the landscape came into focus.

The newly freed prisoners had fallen to their knees.

The fog had lifted. The sentries had vanished.

Heaven's light, emitted by the angel, had burned them all to dust.

Them, but not me. Not me, but Harrison.

I'd never trusted him, never saw in him what Zachary and Freddy did—not until the end. Maybe my fellow neophyte had lived in the service of evil—sought it, embraced it, sacrificed his humanity for it. But when Harrison had died, *truly* died, he'd done so at the side of his brother and an angel of the Lord, fighting for what was right. Harrison had died like my Uncle Quincey, so many generations earlier—as a gallant gentleman.

With Kieren at my heels, I jogged to fetch Zachary's holy sword, no longer flaming, from the burned grass. Now the only question was whether it had worked.

As Kieren and I neared, Freddy said, "Aimee, your collar!"

When she lowered it, the burn scar had disappeared from her neck. It was *gone*. And in its place the tattooed crosses were back again. Freddy let out a whoop, Kieren let out a *woof*. Aimee started laughing and crying, and Zachary gave her a hug.

Approaching, I ceremoniously held out the sword to him, one palm beneath the hilt and one beneath the blade. "I guess you'll want this back."

Zachary returned the weapon to its scabbard and then drew me into a celebratory embrace. "And I know," he whispered, "that you're not losing your soul."

We Interrupt Your Regularly Scheduled Programming . . .

"This is Maria Davis of Austin News Eleven, reporting live outside San Antonio, where tonight police, firefighters, and EMTs were summoned to a compound where they found over fifty people, some of whom had been reported missing. Several had suffered minor injuries, including bite marks.

"They've been telling tales of bloodsuckers, wolves, and werewolves, and—most remarkably—of a visitation from both an angel and what one called 'the literal and divine presence of the Lord.'

"I'm standing here with Dr. Kerly McNeal, a noted psychiatrist. Tell me, Doctor, what could trigger this sort of mass—hang on. I'm sorry, sir. We'll get back to you.

"This just in: the roof of a private home in the Fairview neighborhood has just exploded. Owners Meara and Roberto Morales were home at the time, along with their seventeen-year-old son, Kieren; Detective Konstantine Zaleski of the Austin Police Department; and sixteen-year-old Clyde Gilbert, a friend of the family.

"Miraculously, only Gilbert suffered serious injuries, though he reportedly was alert and responsive to EMTs at the scene."

EVER AFTER

*I*s this straight?" Kieren asked, holding the box-framed kukri and bowie knives against the wall in Sanguini's foyer.

We'd found them hanging over the fireplace in Bradley's Victorian mansion at the compound, along with an old book of hand-scribbled incantations (checked out of the New Schwarzwald Public Library by "Bugs" Moran in 1931).

We also came across a handful of pamphlets talking about the coming apocalypse and a new underworld order and calling for the overthrow of Sabine's Mantle of Dracul. Apparently, Brad had been some kind of revolutionary, and so were the established vamps at the compound who'd followed his lead.

That had been four nights ago, and since then, Kieren had referred to me out loud and in front of other people as his girlfriend—twice. It sounded kind of old-fashioned and clunky and ridiculously possessive, and of course, coming from him, I loved it.

He had also adjusted remarkably well to the idea of my having an earthbound guardian angel, almost as if he'd suspected all along.

"That'll do," Sergio said, picking up the hammer and nails from the hostess stand. "Where did y'all find these relics, anyway?"

"Family heirlooms," I said. The knives looked fierce alongside the photos of my parents, grandparents, and Vaggio. Maybe someday I'd add a photo of Uncle Davidson. For now, we'd scheduled his memorial service for next weekend and planned to scatter his ashes at Hippie Hollow.

"Quincie!" Zachary called from the empty dance floor. "A little help?"

"On my way!" I limped after him to the kitchen to carry platters of sausage lasagna to the private dining room.

I was still a vampire, and the blood would always call. But Kieren had been right. Despite my undead status, the Big Boss (AKA God) and I were on stellar terms. Or at least as good as we had been, back when I was a regular human person.

It was this huge deal. According to Zachary, no vampire before me had ever managed to resist taking a human life and, therefore, remain wholly souled.

Apparently, we'd had our wires crossed since day one. It had never occurred to me that the angel would assume that I'd killed, at least upon first rising, and it had never occurred to him that I hadn't.

My GA himself looked less beat-up today, though on Miz Morales's orders, he was supposed to be taking the rest of the week off. She'd stitched his cuts, and the bruises had begun to fade. It would be some time, though, before he flew again. In the meanwhile, he kept muttering and shaking his head, as if pleasantly stunned.

"Do you think it's big enough?" I asked.

Glancing up from a chafing dish, Zachary said, "It's miraculous. I'm still not sure where we go from here. You've rocked heaven itself, Quincie."

Talk about a one-track mind. "Um, thanks. But I was talking about the buffet table. It's too short. I'll grab another leaf."

The Morales family, Aimee and Clyde, Mr. Wu and Mrs. Levy, and Detectives Zaleski and Wertheimer arrived minutes later along with Sergio, Mercedes, Simone, Yani, Xio,

Jamal, Sebastian, and the rest of the veteran staffers.

Several came decked out to work that evening, but most of the guests—myself included—wore regular clothes, though I'd made a point of yanking on my blood-wine cowboy boots. This was, after all, still Sanguini's.

Every time I talked to Aimee, she hugged me and started dancing around.

"You have to stop doing that," I insisted. "You're freaking me out."

Aimee laughed. "Oh, I will. Next time you decide to go off and do something stupid, I'll be all over it. But for now . . ."

Freddy had told me that there had been a few dicey moments in the SUV when she had unwittingly responded to Brad's call. But then, when he'd tripped, charging up Brad's driveway, it had been Aimee—despite her sprained arm—who'd come to her senses and his rescue by taking out a wolf-form sentry with her holy-water gun.

I was proud of her. I could tell that she would never forget Travis, but Aimee had fully embraced her own second chance at life.

Before skipping off to grab some lasagna, she hugged me again. "My hero!"

"God!" I exclaimed. "That is so embarrassing!"

"Quincie," Zachary called from across the table, "watch your mouth."

Damn. My guardian angel's tone had been light, but I could tell from the look in his eyes that he didn't want to have to tell me twice.

"How're you feeling?" I asked Clyde, crouching beside his wheelchair.

He'd been brought out of his coma by the spell that had cost the Moraleses the roof of their house, but he still looked banged up.

"My whole body hurts." He gestured. "This, here, the crook of my elbow, it hurts. But I'm here and I'm hungry, and that's something."

Whatever tension there had been between the Opossum and the Wolf when Kieren had initially fled for the pack, it was gone now.

As Clyde pointed his wheels at the buffet, Nora and Miz Morales walked up, talking intently. Meara had refused to tell anyone the details of the healing spell, though I did know that Kieren had gotten home just moments before the place blew.

Nora offered me a gentle smile. "Quincie, hon, Meara and I have been talking, and, well, I'd like to personally invite you to move back into your own room."

"You're always welcome at our house," Miz Morales emphasized. "And we'll remain your legal guardians. But with the roof to replace and Kieren back for good—"

"It's okay," I said. "I love you guys, but I was starting to get homesick."

I could fess up later that I was probably failing Chem.

Dr. Morales made his way over with Meghan. "Quincie," he began, "I hate to bother you with this . . ."

"Oh, Roberto!" his wife exclaimed. "You can't possibly—"

Meghan pumped her plump, peach-fuzzy arm up at me, and I saw that she was holding a palm-size bottle labeled HOLY WATER. "Drink!"

"She won't let it go," Dr. Morales said.

"Now, Meghan," Miz Morales began, "how many times have we explained to you that Quincie is not what you think she is? You see . . ." Meara gestured to Kieren's crucifix, resting against my shirt. "But she has gone through a difficult time lately, and we have to understand that she's sensitive about the subject of—"

"It's no big deal," I replied, reaching for the bottle. "I'll drink it." If I could wield an angel's sword and bask in heaven's light, a little holy water couldn't hurt.

As I unscrewed the cap, Meghan's eyes went wide, and I realized that Zachary had come up behind me. Apparently, his famed appeal wasn't lost on the next generation.

Meghan was so transfixed by the angel that she hardly seemed to register that I threw back the whole bottle of holy water in one gulp. No harm done.

At almost midnight, Freddy headed out to change into his vampire-chef outfit. He seemed to be taking the loss of his twin as well as could be expected. All he'd say on the subject was "It's better this way."

Sabine was considerably less philosophical. Apparently losing Harrison, failing to find a competent event planner, and being almost displaced by Count Dracula had made it a rough month to be queen.

It had turned out, though, that according to eternal law, as Brad's only known heir, I had inherited the house in Old Enfield, the compound in San Antonio, and a still unfolding but enormous amount of money in various foreign accounts.

When Sabine told me on the phone, I was so flabbergasted that—much to Zachary's horror—I invited Her Majesty and Philippe to Sanguini's upcoming Halloween bash, and she said *oui*.

"How're you feeling?" I asked the angel, who'd taken a breather from the party to get some fresh air on Sanguini's roof.

I probably shouldn't have let him help set up today. Zachary hadn't broken any bones, but he'd taken a pretty brutal fall back at the compound. Miz Morales had done her best, but her healing power was based in magic, not miracles. I'd all but hid my own injuries but was still battle-sore myself.

"I miss her more at times like this," Zachary said, looking back at me. "When everything seems okay, at least for now, and I don't have anything to distract me."

Suddenly, we weren't talking about bruises on the outside.

"Still," he added, "I'll see Miranda again someday, if I just have faith."

"The way I see it," I replied, sitting beside him, "you've only traded places. You used to watch over her, and now she's watching over you."

Zachary brightened. "You know, I hadn't thought of it that way."

Finally, after much more chatter and laughter and Italian cuisine, it was time to say good night to family and friends, hand-in-hand with my tantalizing Wolf man.

On our way out, the GA winked at me, and Mrs. Levy gave Kieren a high five.

As we cut through the dining room, Sinatra was singing "Our Love Is Here to Stay." I felt so light and normal and happy in the midst of all the pseudosupernatural activity. The fan boys and fan girls, the urban cowboys and cowgirls, the button-down types out for a night with wild things.

The frolicking pretend fiends. I admired the hot blonde with the cat o' nine tails, the redhead in the monstrously huge pearl-and-diamond necklace, the pixie in a cool black felt cowboy hat. Mercedes's dads dancing, cheek-to-cheek, in matching tuxes . . . the buxom woman in flapper fringe . . . and the beauty with the heavily kohled eyes and a crescent-moon *bindi*. Deliciously wicked and wickedly delicious.

Sanguini's: A Very Rare Restaurant was my home.

"What's with Meghan?" I asked. "She went gaga over Zachary."

Kieren leaned in. "According to your angel, the pure of heart can recognize him for what he is. Little kids mostly. Mitch, before he was made undead."

I thought about it. "So, I may have a whole soul, but I'm not pure of heart?"

Kieren waggled his thick eyebrows. "Makes my life more interesting."

Wrapped around each other on a bench on the pedestrian bridge over Town Lake, Kieren and I stared at the heavens. It was hard to make out the stars, what with all the light pollution from the city. But we watched the black birds swoop and the black bats swirl. It almost looked as if they were dancing. If I someday reached Old Blood status, I'd be able to take bat form and join in their aerobatics. Just the idea of it was dizzying.

"I've been thinking . . .," Kieren began. "You'll always look like you, and Zachary will always look like him. Meanwhile, I'll grow old and mangy."

"Mangy?" I glanced at him sideways. "Don't say *mangy. Mangy* is harsh."

"Hmm." Kieren offered a Wolfish grin. "You don't suppose my guardian angel is impossibly good-looking?"

"Doubt it," I replied, and he growled playfully.

"By the way," I added, taking his hand. "I keep meaning to thank you."

He nuzzled my hair. "For . . . ?"

"Always believing in me."

As Kieren leaned in for a kiss, I noticed Mitch shuffling toward us on the bridge. In scratchy lettering, his cardboard sign read:

VAMPYRES
4
ANGELS

≈ contorno ≈

AUTHOR'S NOTE

Abraham "Bram" Stoker first introduced his title character Dracula, the king of all literary vampires, in a famed
1897 novel.

Blessed and my two novels that preceded it— *Tantalize*
and *Eternal*—are a conversation of sorts between me
and Stoker about several of his themes, including the
"other," the "dark" foreigner, invasion, plague, the role
of religion, and gender-power dynamics.

Throughout, I've made an affectionate effort to
honor his classic while still being willing to reinterpret
and extend its mythology. Nods to his work abound,
not the least of them being the integrated epistolary ele-
ments (correspondence, menus, obituary) and aspects of
the structure of this third novel. However, Stoker's world
doesn't, for example, appear to have more than one kind
of vampire, and so far as we know, his Count Dracula
didn't transform from one breed of undead to another.
Consequently, I enthusiastically recommend studying
Dracula yourself rather than relying on Quincie's rather
abbreviated summary and idiosyncratic interpretation

of the text. And keep in mind, as Nora mentions, in my fictional world, Stoker's story is only *loosely* based on truth.

Readers—both old-school and pop culture—may also spot passing references to the words and works of Forrest J Ackerman, Douglas Adams, Charles Addams, M. T. Anderson, Fred Astaire, Paul Barber (*Vampires, Burial, and Death*), L. Frank Baum, Jesse Belvin, Pat Benatar, William Peter Blatty, Blondie, Andy Breckman, the Brontë sisters, the Brothers Grimm, Dan Brown, Gottfried August Bürger ("Lenore"), Chris Carter (*The X-Files: I Want to Believe*), Stephen Chao, David Chase, Children's Television Workshop, Rosemary Clement-Moore, Montgomery Clift, Gene Colan, Davy Crockett, Don DaGradi, Sir Arthur Conan Doyle, Jean Evans, Bill Finger, Pink Floyd, Katie Ford, Clark Gable, Ward Greene, Doug Hajicek, Nathaniel Hawthorne, Gaynel Hodge, Shirley Jackson, Ed James, Billy Joel, Bob Kane, Erich Kästner, Jacqueline Kennedy, John F. Kennedy, Joseph Kesselring, Edward Khmara, Annette Curtis Klause, Noel Langley, Jesse Lasky, Jr., Marc Lawrence, Michael Linder, Jeph Loeb, Susan Lowell, Caryn Lucas, George Lucas, Robin Menken, Richard O'Brien, Ovid, Luciano Pavarotti, I. M. Pei, Erdman Penner, Edgar Allan Poe, Giacomo Puccini, Nicholas Ray, Anne Rice, Joe Rinaldi, Jerry Robinson, Gene Roddenberry,

J. K. Rowling, Joe Ruby, Jane Russell, Maurice Sendak, William Shakespeare, Mary Shelley, Fred Silverman, Frank Sinatra, John Sinclair, Ed Solomon, Ken Spears, Scott Spencer, Steven Spielberg, Henry Morton Stanley, David Swift, Algernon Sydney, Iwao Takamoto, J. R. R. Tolkien, Stevie Ray Vaughan, Matthew Weisman, Lawrence Welk, Joss Whedon, Curtis Williams, Marv Wolfman, Ralph Wright, and Vernon Zimmerman.

However, *The Blood-Drinker's Guide, A Taste of Transylvania, Demonic Digest, The Gothic Gourmet, Underworld Business Monthly, Eternal Elegance,* the Eternal News Network (ENN), and other media references are entirely fictional.

Likewise, I had fun playing with historical figures and events.

Thank you, President Buchanan. Sorry to ruin your inaugural ball like that.

When it comes to setting, Austinites will note that the official name of Town Lake has been changed to Lady Bird Lake, in honor of former first lady Lady Bird Johnson. However, old habits die harder than vampires, and many of us still call it Town Lake.

Furthermore, my novel incorporates a handful of fictional streets, private homes, businesses, and the nonprofit Bat Anti-Defamation League.

My own creations also include Whitby Estates on

Chicago's north shore; New Schwarzwald, Michigan; and—I'm saddened to admit—Sanguini's: A Very Rare Restaurant in south Austin. And yet I can assure you that the *essence* of the vampire-themed restaurant is quite real and eternally thirsty.

ACKNOWLEDGMENTS

Thanks to the choirs of angels in the Austin children's and YA book community, at Candlewick Press, and at Curtis Brown Ltd. Special thanks to Brian Anderson; another Brian (in admissions at the University of Texas); Elson Oshman Blunt; Gene Brenek; Shutta Crum; Ginger Knowlton of Curtis Brown; Shayne Leighton; Tracy Marchini and Anna Umansky; Elizabeth Miller (*A Dracula Handbook*); Greg Leitich Smith; everyone at Vermont College of Fine Arts; Jennifer Yoon; and especially Deborah Wayshak.

READ BETWEEN THE LINES

UNDERCOVER is the best
in young adult fiction from
Walker Books.

Scan this code to watch other
UNDERCOVER book trailers:

Get the mobile app
http://gettag.mobi

Turn the page to check out more
UNDERCOVER READS or visit
www.undercoverreads.com

*T*rouble brews when Quincie Morris and her uncle decide to remodel the family restaurant with a vampire theme. One month before the grand reopening the chef is mauled to death in the kitchen and the murder suspect is … a werewolf!

Quincie has to transform Henry, the new chef, into Sanguini's vampire extraordinaire – and fast. But strange things are happening to her boyfriend, Kieren, and a deadly love triangle forms.

"Readers will be tantalized by this dark, romantic, and disturbing fantasy … fans of Stephenie Meyer will eat it up." *School Library Journal*

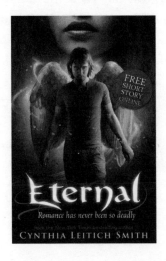

*A*t last, Miranda is the life of the party: all she had to do was die. In the afterlife, she goes from high-school stage wannabe to vixen vampire-princess overnight. Meanwhile, Zachary, her reckless guardian angel, goes undercover in a bid to save his girl's soul before all hell arrives – quite literally – on their doorstep.

Sink your teeth into a dangerous love story played out in a dark eternal world where vampires vie with angels.

"Stephenie Meyer, honey, watch out.
Twilight **fans, you are gonna LOVE** *Eternal.*"
Dallas Morning News

CYNTHIA LEITICH SMITH is the acclaimed and best-selling author of *Tantalize*, *Eternal*, and several other books for young readers. About *Blessed*, she says, "Who hasn't felt like their life is over? Like they're all alone, facing an infernal storm? That's when a little faith can save you, when you're fighting the hardest to believe in yourself." A member of the faculty at the Vermont College of Fine Arts MFA program in writing for children and young adults, she lives in Austin, Texas.